Nobilis: Seedling

by Stephen Coghlan

A THURSTON HOWL PUBLICATIONS BOOK

ISBN 978-1-945247-35-4

NOBILIS: SEEDLING

Copyright © 2016–2019 by Stephen Coghlan

First Edition, 2019. All rights reserved.

A Thurston Howl Publications Book
Published by Thurston Howl Publications
thurstonhowlpublications.com
Lansing, Michigan

jonathan.thurstonhowlpub@gmail.com

Edited by C.L. Methvin

Printed in the United States of America
10 9 8 7 6 5 4 3 2 1

Prologue

Thank you for your purchase of a subscription to Gorda Gionni's Ever Expanding Encyclopedia of our Galactic Sphere. For the last five generations we have strived to be the foremost database for humankind's understanding of the universe.

As a premium member, you are entitled to constant updates that help better represent the fluid nature of the galaxies. Unfortunately, due to the dynamic nature of the worlds around us, the information posted within may not always be 100% accurate. Please exercise due diligence.

Your comments are important to us because they help us provide the best service in the industry. So please, take a moment to fill out the attached survey in order to receive lifetime technical support and updates.

If you have any questions concerning our product, please contact our customer service department for free by using our app near any bright-star communication router.

Again, thank you for your purchase.

◆　◆　◆

THE CREW OF THE DREADNOUGHT did something that they had never done before, they panicked.

Las-beams, missiles, mass-kinetics, and charged particle cannons all fired at the white blur that sped towards them, but their efforts were futile.

The ivory machine crashed into the hull. Armor tore as if it was composed of gossamer thin fabric instead of thickly reinforced plating. Decking shredded into ribbons and crew members were pulverized into oblivion.

And then it was past. For a moment there was nothing, just stunned, ethereal silence. Then the vessel's breached reacto, failed.

The explosion ripped through the decks, vaporizing the damaged craft into absolute nothingness. The blast touched the nearby planet's atmosphere, and the flames traveled faster than sound with the intense heat of a small star. The giant trees of the ancient forests, the tall waving grass of the planes, the waters of the seas and oceans, the dry and arid sands of the desert, and the frozen, icy peaks of the poles were incinerated.

Millions of lives were snuffed from their mortal coil as several burgeoning civilizations were extinguished from existence.

Only three entities survived the apocalypse, and they had already turned their backs to the destruction as they fled from the extinction they had helped to cause.

Chapter 1

Standard and Basic:

The two common languages of the Galactic sphere, Standard and Basic were designed so that speech-capable races could communicate in a common tongue. The two languages share a mutual original language, but became divided as Standard, which is the official language of negotiations, and ship-to-ship communications, became too complex and technical.

Basic uses few adjectives or adverbs. For example, in English you might say "I want to sit on a comfortable chair by a roaring fire and enjoy my hot toddy in peace. In Basic, it translates to: "I want to sit on a soft chair by a fire and drink a toddy in quiet."

THE UNIVERSE WAS NEITHER a pristine utopia nor a dystopian hell, but it was far from perfect.

Corporations owned the lives of trillions.

Before humankind had reached the distant stars, they had complained about the mega-corps and the banks that controlled large portions of the Terran economy. It came as a shock to them, as a species, that their terrestrial corporations were nothing compared to the greed of intergalactic businesses.

Within a few weeks of joining the other, space-faring species, millions of humans found themselves turned into 'Debtees'. Debtees were peoples who were, literally, owned by the gigantic businesses and industries of the galactic sphere.

It wasn't a horrible and wretched life for the most part. Once one was considered property of a business, they were treated as such. Being owned meant that they got food and medical attention when it was both required and considered financially acceptable.

Although Debtees were compensated financially for their work, the corporations purposefully paid them too small an amount to survive on, so that the Debtees had to borrow money from their employers simply ty stay alive. Some Debtees decided to abuse the privileges of nicer owners, but the ever constant reality that they were property (and could be vivisected and sold for "scrap") kept most in line.

Once one was a Debtee, finding one's freedom, or becoming a "Freebie" was nigh impossible. There were several ways to become free. If one somehow earned enough, they could then buy their freedom. There were lotteries too, that offered liberty, and some companies rewarded hard working employees with the chance to become independent. A few militant companies recruited from the desperate, and awarded them their freedoms if they survived to the end of their contracts.

Kalle Aaron was a man who knew about the struggles for freedom all too well. He was often referred to as the 'old-hand' by his friends and acquaintances, partly because of his looks, and partly because he seemed to have experience on every topic of conversation.

As the head maintenance technician aboard one of the many jump-stations that littered the known sphere, Kalle was often tasked with troubles that ranged from mundane complaint, to critical system emergencies. He worked because he liked the challenge and even though a man of his skills could have found employment all over the galaxy, he had found a home among the miners and travelers.

Jump-stations, as important as they were, were rarely profitable on their own, and so, many jump-stations served alternate purposes. The one that the old-hand labored so diligently upon doubled as a mining colony.

The harvesting of minerals provided little interest to Kalle. He was more interested in finding an obstruction that had supposedly occurred in one of the main water lines that ran throughout the station's residential district.

With a mild curse, Kalle stretched out his arm and leaned sideways from his place upon a ladder. He looked to be either in his late-thirties by Earth Years or his mid-twenties in Standard Galactic Years. He was tall, but not overly so. Thin, but not rakish, dark haired, and light skinned, he wasn't starkly pale, but he wasn't heavily tanned either. His flesh looked like it received its weekly dose of ultraviolet treatment, but no more than what was recommended.

The sound of rapidly approaching footfalls distracted him. Looking down, Kalle spied four small bodies rushing towards him. They were not watching where they were going and it was too late for the old-hand to call out a warning before the little ones ran around, and beneath, his ladder.

The Drudges, as the children were called, were owned by the local corporation. They were tasked with cleaning the station, every day of their lives.

Kalle's scream of protest brought the Drudges' to a halt. The oldest boy, Joshua, caught the ladder, steadying it from its almost inevitable fall, which allowed Kalle to release the pipes he had been clutching in order to maintain his balance.

Joshua was from a race well-renowned for their technical advances. They were a peaceful race, but not smart with money. Aquatic by evolution, his peoples were covered in soft white fur that was regrettably, highly valued on the black market. Entire tribes had often been captured and executed before they had been skinned for their pelts alone. His native tongue had over a dozen words for his name, but he was referred to as Joshua, because that was what someone had once written upon his biological report.

The old-hand caught the eyes of the children before he spoke his mind. "Would you guys please be more careful? You almost got me killed!"

Shy, nervous, and definitely sorry, Adorinda looked down at her feet as she muttered out the words, "But we're in low gravity sir."

The youngest of her 'siblings', Adorinda was a four-earth-year-old human girl whose parents had overspent their finances. The father had been unable to pay the corporation after he had suffered an injury on some far away planet.

"Yes, its light, but it's not weightless. Look right there." Kalle pointed to his toolkit that rested at the foot of his ladder, "There are more than enough sharp things there to impale me if I fell."

"Sorry, sir." They all said at once, glancing down to their feet as per the method of apology that they had been taught.

"Are you going to punish us?" Sudhir asked as Kalle stepped off the ladder.

Sudhir had been purchased from Slavers about a galactic year ago. His species, which were recognized by their giant eyes and bald, round heads, were known for their limited telepathy.

Crouching down in front of Fallon, the old-hand asked the Drudges ringleader, "What time is it?"

Fallon, the oldest one of the Drudges, was only about six-earth-years old. She often had to be watched like a hawk because she was a bit of a thief. The rigid, reinforced bones of her skeleton showed under her flesh.

"Scheduled play time, Mister Aaron." The thief responded, still not meeting the gaze of the old-hand.

Kalle smiled gently. Punishment to the Drudges meant many things. If Kalle reported their reckless behavior, then the Drudges would either have had their two hours of playtime-per-day taken away or they would have been physically injured, and while it was sociably acceptable, it was not something that Kalle stood for.

The old-hand recalled an instant when a merchant's ship had docked at the station. Kalle had been asked to perform some maintenance aboard the craft while the Drudges had been ordered to clean the vessel as a gift of goodwill. While transporting some cleaning solvents, Fallon had tripped and had spilled the chemicals across one of the merchant's prized rugs. The merchant had started with a rather hard slap across Fallon's face, which had left her stunned and bleeding, and he had not stopped his revenge until Kalle had intervened vis-a-vis a heavy wrench to the back of the merchant's neck.

When he had recovered enough of his cognitive abilities, the merchant had sued the company for his 'treatment'. The company had wisely chosen to side with Kalle and had won the case by claiming that the old-hand had merely been protecting "company material".

Having calmed himself significantly, the old-hand answered the younger boy's question.

"No," he said lightly. "I'm not going to punish you. You just have to promise to be more careful, for everybody's sake."

"Thank you, Mister Aaron." Joshua said, relieved.

All four Drudges turned to leave but as they took their first steps Kalle found himself yelling after them once again. "I said, don't run in the halls!"

Instantly, the Drudges slowed down and disappeared behind the corner.

Smiling at the situation, Kalle made his way back up the ladder. As soon as his head was above the pipe the nearest apartment door opened and the occupant stuck her head out into the hallway.

Nozomi was also a human Freebie. Her dirty-dark hair was long, smooth and shiny. Her skin was tinged with a permanent brown glow that even her time aboard station had failed to decrease. Her eyes had the narrow look of those from the orient, but her nose was short and wide.

She had arrived at the station two galactic years past and had worked various jobs to afford the rent. She was well on her way to bondage to the company.

Nozomi greeted the old-hand with words that were familiar between the two of them. She had poked her bare shoulders and head from beyond the door. The old-hand guessed that if she showed any more of herself he would have seen more of her than ever before.

They had become fast friends, and Nozomi and Kalle had often shared dinners together, or had gone to events together as companions, when they occurred at the station. Their relationship was not romantic, just the comfortable bond of friendship.

"What can I do for you today?" He enquired.

"I paid for an extra water ration over a week ago and I don't think the order's gone through." She spoke.

Nozomi had been attempting to take a shower. She had often complained that the low pressure her apartment received meant that she had to take a long wash just to get wet.

"You know how long those reports can take." He said. Pulling out one of his fancy tools, Kalle inserted the probes into the pipe. "What's the pressure you're supposed to have?"

"I paid for a twenty-percent raise." Nozomi answered. There was a very strong hint of truth to her words but even if she had been lying, Kalle had already decided to help her. If she was being deceitful no harm would come to Kalle. He was too valuable to risk offending.

"That should do it." The old-hand proclaimed.

Still standing in the doorway, Nozomi smiled gratefully. "Are you free this evening?" She asked.

The old-hand had already busied himself with his original issue. He stopped and looked back, waiting for her to continue.

"I should probably take you out for coffee. As thanks." Nozomi finally spoke.

"Of course," Kalle laughed. "But aren't you busy?"

"Not since the flower shop closed down." She replied.

"Well, in that case I'm working for another hour, how about I see you in three." The old-hand offered.

"Great, I'll meet you there, we'll split." She said gratefully.

"I'd like that." He chuckled. "Just give me a chance to look after some things at home."

Smiling happily, Nozomi disappeared back inside her apartment.

Chapter 2

Jump-Stations:
    Jump-Stations are a necessity for both travel and trade in the galactic sphere. Jump-stations are capable of creating temporary folds between each other using massive gravity engines that compress space, allowing for faster-than-light travel from location to location. Use of a Jump-Station often requires a vessel to pay a tariff to both the sending, and the receiving, station. Jump-Stations once held a monopoly on interstellar travel, but have since been forced to offer competitive prices as Jump (aka. Fold) engines become more popular and easier to install in smaller and smaller craft.
    Since operating a Jump-Station is rarely profitable alone, most Jump-Stations are fitted for multiple duties. Some are installed near mining operations, and host the mining crew and their material, which also allows for quick unloading of gathered items. Others become tourist traps, pleasure centers, rec-spots, or hiring halls.

FOR WHAT FELT LIKE THE hundredth time, Nozomi wished that she had brought earplugs along with her to the bar. It wasn't loud music or the sounds of dozens of voices speaking all at once that annoyed her, it was one single alien that made her wish that the powers that be would have struck her deaf.

Her vexation was a Grondonian. They were great scientists of the universe, but as a species they lacked all social skills. For some reason, the boor of a creature had prattled ceaselessly to Nozomi about the proper uses of molybdenum, the benefits of xenon, and the various methods of handling selenium, despite the various hints of indifference that she had displayed. His lack of understanding was probably due to their vast physical differences. The Grondonian was tall and long limbed, with elbows that easily started at the creatures rounded torso.

She sighed inwardly. The desire to do something drastic, like jamming bottles into her ears in order to shut out the Grondonian's voice, was starting to become just a little too tempting.

"And then there's the property of Fold-Space." The Grondonian continued incessantly, waving its long limbs about. The forearms were just as long, and as a whole, looked rather ungainly, but the rounded shoulders must have been jointed oddly, because with a roll of the upper arms, his limbs compacted themselves rapidly against his green and mottled flesh, which was visible under the lightly armored research suit that he wore across his body. "Really, it's a remarkable feature that has simplified so much of our universe. What, my dear friend, is the best way to get the shortest distance between two objects?

"That woule normally be a straight line, would it not?" The Grondonian only paused long enough after his question to let himself grab a quick breath. The reflective materials had begun to give Nozomi a headache, but when she held her hands at her temples, the Grondonian snorted through its stubbed nose, which was almost flat to its face, blinked its faceted eyes, and continued waving its long, and plentiful fingered hands about. Unlike humans, Grondonians had six primary fingers, and a very powerful thumb that was exact opposite of the rest.

Nozomi considered jamming her empty glass down the

Grondonian's throat, not unlike sticking a vegetable in a pipe to block its exhaust.

"However, allow me to demonstrate what happens if I take this napkin here, and draw two points upon it." Dipping his finger into his own glass, the Grondonian dabbed two dots of liquid onto the serviette, one in each opposing corner. Lifting it up into the air, he happily folded it into half so that the two corners touched. "Regard, there is no physical space between these two points. Ergo, the fold is the shortest way to travel. This can be accomplished in the real world as well. It is for this reason that jump-stations, such as this one, exist. By using large amounts of gravity, just like using a black hole, one can warp space, essentially folding it."

His tall frame wiggled, but because of his long legs, and the double knees, he balanced effortlessly and maneuvered deftly to step out of the way of several patrons who passed too close.

"Although many private ships now use this method of travel, they themselves are not nearly as powerful as jump-stations. Jump-stations beam gravity between two stations, warping the space around them to near nothing in quantity, mere ripples really."

Taking his stained napkin, the Grondonian folded it accordion-style. "Imagine each of the plateaus here to be real space, and the more powerful your fold drive, the closer the napkin ripples in my cloth becomes. That's folded space. If you have a really strong gravity generator, you can even take some of the folds out of the napkin, like this." And so saying, the scientist relaxed his fingers and allowed a few of the accordioned folds fall away from the compact mess, allowing his hands to close together just the tiniest bit more. "This again shortens the distance that one travels.

"Of course, such a system does not come without its trials and tribulations." The Grondonian added with a threatening tone to his voice.

Wishing that the scientist would enter fold-space himself, without the assistance of a space-suit, Nozomi moaned out the words, "Of course."

"Yes, of course. If there is too strong a gravitational field, one might hazard sucking something foreign into the fold-space. And if that foreign object happens to be large enough it can damage one's vessel, or simply-" Using his many digited hand, the Grondonian shredded the napkin into confetti. "Disintegrate your vessel. Therefore, one should plot a rather, um, clean route."

Seeing that he was finished for the moment, Nozomi watched her lecturer enjoy the drink that he had ordered a long time ago.

Thank God! She thought to herself. *Maybe he'll finally shut up.*

No sooner did her companion drain his vessel, then he filled his rather ample lungs, and tipped his empty bottle over to grab it by the base.

A voice cut through the crowd as a familiar, and very welcome figure, interposed itself between the Grondonian and Nozomi.

"That's a very fine ship you have there, sir." Kalle spoke dryly. "One day it might even fly."

Wrapping his arm around Nozomi, Kalle made sure that his body blocked all of the Grondonian's sight from the human female. The old-hand was dressed in simple fashion: a light jacket, clean work pants, and space-boots.

oSo, hon, did you miss me?" Kalle asked, purposefully making his voice loud enough so that the Grondonian could hear it over the din of the bar.

"Oh you have no idea, mister." Nozomi spoke gratefully.

The scientist made a positively loud grunt of disapproval, but immediately turned to his neighbor on the other side toecarry on his teachings. The new victim was a brutish Kackle who paid the scientist no heed, and merely sipped aoits drink as the Grondonian continued on unabated.

Keeping his arm around her, Kalle moved Nozomi away from the bar.

"Sorry I wasn't here sooner." Kalle apologized. "I hope I'm not too late."

"N-no, it's okay, I was here early. I just thought I would start with something, but I didn't think I would start off with, *that.*" Nozomi hissed out the last word with as much vehemence as she could muster.

"Oh, don't worry, you know his race. They love mathematics and sciences more than they love breathing." Kalle said calmly.

"That's very apparent." She sighed. "Why are there even people like him aboard this station?"

"Well, the corporation will enslave all comers, it's not particularly, particular." Kalle answered. "Plus, being a jump-station, it is basically a rest stop, and meeting point, for anyone traveling. Naturally, there's going to be a lot of weird things that collect here."

"Yes, but why did that, thing, collect onto me?" Nozomi wondered. "His race, I don't know, they irritate me."

"They irritate anyone with even a measure of social grace. Don't worry about it." The old-hand attempted to smooth his friend's jagged nerves. "Who knows, sooner or later, you might even become calloused to it, just like me."

Kalle moved his friend over to his favorite table. They'd barely sat down before the previous owner of the restaurant shuffled over. Kong was from some eight-limbed species that seemed to be a combination of arachnid and cuttlefish. Despite an appearance that some found upsetting, Kong had many friends, which was helped by being reputed to have the best Forellian rock-crab dish in the entire known sphere.

Kong's was the social center of the station. His hovel was a place where the many races could come and relax, and forget about their problems for a few hours. No one wanted to be kicked out of Kong's, so they stuck to his rules.

"Can I get anything for my two friends today?" Their server spoke in his heavily accented Basic, which sounded like a combination of sick squelching noises mixed with sandpaper being dragged across a washboard, but it was not unintelligible.

Although Nozomi and Kalle spoke both Basic and Standard,

they had learned more than those two languages. Nozomi spoke Japanese and English. Kalle spoke a rough version of English, but he also spoke a real slathering of alien tongues including Kackle, Hurgad, Izmala, and several other languages that Nozomi could not remember, let alone pronounce.

"I'll just have the special today, Kong." Kalle said, not even glancing at the table where the menu appeared in digital letters, scrolling its way across the surface.

Nozomi read the list with a touch more caution. She wanted to pinch her pennies, but when she saw her favorite dish show up, she knew she just had to order it. "I'll have the spore and lichen stew, please." She requested.

"Those two things will be ready in no time." Kong said happily, before he turned and jerked his way back into the kitchen.

It was a small enough restaurant that it could normally be managed by itself, but Kong had not run it alone, even though it appeared that way. Inside the kitchen the real owners, Kong's family, were all busy at work. Kong's eight children were well supported by the family business, unlike Kong himself.

About four years ago, there had been a small recession at the station. Kong had struggled to keep his business going and finances had gotten so desperate that the station's owners had told Kong he had a simple choice, sell them the shop, or sell himself. He had made his eldest son sell him to the company.

Rumor had it that Kong was almost a Freebie again, since the restaurant had been doing so well in the past few months, but Kong did not mind being a Debtee; he had better health care than when he was independent, and with no desire to leave his establishment, he saw no reason not to take advantage.

With their host gone for the moment, the two humans looked at each other.

"Busy day?" Nozomi asked.

Kalle nodded slowly. When he answered, he did so in his English, which was far from perfect and heavily accented. He often had to stop and think about his next few words. <I had, more

than enough, work, to make me busy. How is your, search, for work going?>

The woman remained quiet. It was obvious that she was just a little uncomfortable with the topic. Nozomi had worked several odd jobs over her time on the station, but it had only been to complement the money that she had arrived with. Her finances had been slowly dwindling and she was only a few months away from achieving Debtee status.

There was something else that Kalle wanted to ask Nozomi about but he felt the topic was taboo: ever since she had arrived, the woman had zealously guarded a crate that she had rented space for in the loading dock. Rumor had it that she visited the storage case every day. To add to the mystique, no one except for Nozomi knew what was inside. The box was more than large enough to store a personal craft, but if that had been what was contained, she should have just stored it in the docking station.

<You are going to, have to get a, job, soon.> Kalle advised.

<I know.> Nozomi responded, playing nervously with her fork. <I don't really want to leave the station, but if my financial station gets just a little more desperate, I'm not going to have a chance. I'm already beginning to pack. Don't worry; I won't end up a Debtee. I'll Skag if I have to.>

What Nozomi was referring to, was a level of the socio-economic class of free-peoples.

Skags were almost universally hated. They were thieves or beggars who were thought to have no respect for themselves. Dregs, which were considered superior to Skags, but not by much, were the free who had no money or home, but who treated others and themselves with dignity.

Despite their differences, both Skags and Dregs had to look out for a threat that endangered them both: Slavers.

Slaving was a recognized practice. It kept the Skags and Dregs off the streets and away from those who could pay to be recognized as truly independent Freebies.

Real Freebies had passes that registered them as sovereign

and free, by law, from slavery. Freebies often worked for corporations at a decent cost because they generally had rare skills that were much in demand.

There were supposedly other levels above Freebie. They were rumored ranks that were whispered among the mouths of the Debtees, Slaves, and free, alike.

<I can lend you some, money.> Kalle offered. <I've got enough saved up. They've been paying me well.>

<It's your money Kalle. Besides, if I take your money I'll be in debt to you.> Nozomi explained.

<I understand.> The old-hand agreed before he made a very human sigh. <I wouldn't want to be a Debtee to anyone either.> Grinning his lopsided smile, he attempted to change the feeling of their dinner. <This is, a very depressing topic, no?>

<But it's a necessity these days.> His friend said, sadly. <I'll be fine, don't worry, Kalle.> Extending her hand, she brushed it across her companion's fingers. < I can look after myself.>

<You have gotten this far.> Kalle agreed.

At that moment, Kong returned to the table and slapped the plates upon the surface.

"So," The restaurant worker chuckled through his thick Basic. "Drinks?"

"House for me." Kalle said, lapsing naturally back into the more familiar tongue.

"Nozomi, your usual?" Their host asked.

"Ceylione Tea please Kong." Nozomi answered.

"And the bill?" Kong had served the two of them long enough to know that neither human would have preferred to have debts on them, even while eating. Nozomi opened her mouth, but Kalle beat her to the punch.

"It's on me tonight, Kong." And before Nozomi could object, Kalle touched his Datapad to the table and paid upfront.

"Right on." Kong said as he jerked back towards the kitchen.

Nozomi stared at her date with needles in her eyes. <I said we were going independent, didn't I?> She spoke acidly, instantly lapsing back to English.

"Well, we're not." Kalle answered, his language still Basic. "This is my thank you, for keeping me company. It helps me to relax."

Despite herself, Nozomi knew she could not argue that point. Still bitter, but not truly offended, she raised the first bite to her lips and instantly forgot all of her negative emotions as the delicacy touched her tongue.

The halls were dark and quiet. Several hours had passed since Nozomi and Kalle had gone their separate ways after dinner. Although there really was no night on the station, or in space, there was a best-calculated downtime that gave businesses and most of their employees a chance to rest. There were more than enough people who lived longer schedules, or preferred the quiet sanctuary of "night" shifts, that the station continued to function.

Kalle and Nozomi had stayed at Kong's well into the "evening." It had been a good chance for Nozomi to get some of the troubles that she had been carrying around off her chest. Kalle, who knew the station better than any of the resident gossipers, had provided Nozomi with many places where she would likely find employment.

They had parted ways eventually, with Kalle claiming to have a busy "morning" the next "day." Once he left, Nozomi had studied the list he had given her but had found it difficult to retain any of it to memory and after a while, she had given up and started wandering the abandoned halls.

When she reached the great steel door, Nozomi realized where her feet had taken her. She didn't smile about it as she reached out one hand and entered her private access code. A smaller door opened beside the behemoth portal and she used it to access one of the station's many cargo bays.

It was one place on the station that didn't ever sleep. Wraithloaders rushed back and forth, constantly loading and unloading materials. Workers yelled orders to each other, somehow avoiding disaster amid the chaos. Nozomi didn't mind the constant bustle. In a place that was so busy, she knew she would rarely be noticed.

Although one person was certain to notice her; Telfer Laughlin was busy guiding the corporate mining skiffs between the other, constant flows of traffic. He was a Debtee to the corporation, had been from birth, but that had not stopped him from rising to the position of one of the senior staff managers for the miners. He worked almost every day either directing traffic or out on the rocks. He toiled so, not out of acceptance of his role, or dedication to the company, but because he was trying to earn his freedom. He had married a Freebie, and one day he and his wife both hoped to afford his independence.

Spying Nozomi approaching, Telfer grinned and waved, but Nozomi detected a hint of sadness in the way that Telfer moved. Gravity was much lower in the hold, and with one push of her legs Nozomi floated several stories skyward until she grabbed at the scaffolding that Telfer was strapped to.

The two cordially greeted each other and made their usual small talk in Basic, the only language that Telfer truly understood, until Nozomi asked about her crate.

"Well," Telfer said, as one hand waved a clipboard in the apartment-sized box's general direction as his other hand stroked his square jaw. "It's doing its usual, sitting there, taking up room." Telfer's look became more serious. "Nozomi," He began. "The dock manager warned me that in a few more weeks your rent on the extra space around the crate is going to run out. I'm going to have to start boxing it in soon."

Now Nozomi knew why Telfer had been remorseful. The company creditors were already starting to forewarn, which was a classic sign that they did not think Nozomi would be able to afford life as a Freebie for much longer.

She grinned. "Don't worry about it. In another few weeks that old crate will probably disappear, and then you won't have to worry about me." Before Telfer could say anything Nozomi looked at the topic of their conversation. "I'm just going to head there and start getting my things organized for the move."

"So, it's definite then?" Telfer asked.

"Not yet, but it can't be that far behind. I don't want to end up ensnared." Nozomi sighed.

Telfer smiled sadly and extended his gloved hand. Nozomi took it and squeezed it in return.

"Well, traffic's clear for the moment, so it should be safe for you to head down there." The loader said. Without a word, Nozomi shoved her way towards her precious crate.

When she was certain that Telfer was too distracted to notice, Nozomi placed her hand upon her cargo container's touch-pad. With a hiss of released machinery a hatchway opened, which was just large enough for Nozomi to squeeze her slight frame inside. It closed behind her and Nozomi listened to the sounds of the locks sliding shut, before a second portal opened in front of her.

The container was originally designed to store things in inert gasses to prevent oxidization. It was not designed to hold a living creature. A huge, featureless humanoid figure lay upon the floor of the crate, curled into a fetal position. The smooth white skin was undisturbed, and the gargantuan thing rested there, not moving, not breathing—simply existing.

Even in its position it almost filled the crate. There was barely enough room left for Nozomi to squeeze herself around the figure, but she managed to worm around until she rested against the small of the thing's back.

Pressing herself against the humanoid's flesh, Nozomi whispered in her native tongue, <Brother, I'm here.>

The flesh opened on its own, exposing a small box of living walls. Nozomi pushed herself inside and the opening sealed itself, sealing her within the flesh. It was not dark. An eerie luminescence seemed to come from all around as if there were fireflies dancing within the walls.

A chair formed itself out of the floor. It was the same color and texture as the walls, but it was shaped comfortably and precisely for its intended user. It gave in to her, yielding to Nozomi's form as she sat gratefully. <Thank you Nobilis.> Nozomi said.

The giant and mysterious being answered, and the sounds of its language resounded from the walls of flesh. It sounded like thousands of crystals twinkling in a gentle breeze.

Nozomi did not fully comprehend the language of her friend, but that was not the only method that Nobilis had of communicating. Brilliantly colored letters scrawled themselves across the walls of flesh. It was an almost lost Japanese script, but one that Nozomi's family knew and had passed on from generation to generation.

Nozomi spoke in answer to the question. <I would like to see him please.>

The walls of flesh slowly became transparent. Nozomi watched with the same touch of mystery as the first time she had witnessed the spectacle. Arteries and veins became visible, and life fluids flowed visually within the flesh. The limited form of a skeletal structure soon became defined.

And there, where in a human the womb would have been located, rested the still form of Nozomi's brother. Lines and networked tubes fed him a continuous supply of life-giving fluids.

<Hi, I know I haven't visited in a few days, but I've been trying to find another job.> She sighed. <I missed you.>

The form of her brother did not respond.

<I don't know if you can hear me, but we're probably going to have to move soon. I hope you're strong enough to survive.>

The chimes sounded gently as Nobilis responded. The words seemed to form out of nowhere as they danced across Nozomi's field of vision. They were words of comfort and pride, boasts of the alien's strength.

<Thank you.> Nozomi responded. <It's probably better if we move soon anyways, who knows when they're going to finally find us?>

And allowing herself to settle gently into the chair, Nozomi listened to the steady beat of Nobilis's heart, the rhythm that was part of both the alien, and her brother's, life.

Chapter 3

The Confederates:

The largest and most popular of alf the militant companies, the Confederates have earned their employees' loyalty, because they free their indebted after one term of service. Debtees from all companies, species, and walks of life, are encouraged to enlist by recruiters, who negotiate with the enlistee's company. Very rarely are offers refused.

If the recruit is capable of militant service, then they are employed for two-and-a-half standard galactic years in one of the many *positions available. If not available for militant service, recruits are placed in the civil-service wing, where after a ten-year tenure they are released and granted the same advantages as their graduated militant counterparts: citizen status. Being a citizen for the Confederates is a privilege. Citizens may vote, are given both fiscal and healthcare security, and make up the upper-echelons of the Confederate ranks. Being born into the Confederacy gives one the automatic title of civilian, but it does not grant one the same privileges of their citizen counterparts.*

❖ ❖ ❖

A S FAR AS HER NATIVE SPECIES, and several others included, were concerned, Isa was very attractive.

The Selths were, as a whole, one of the smartest peoples ever to exist, and they were one of the oldest space-faring species in recorded galactic history. The majority of them had good grasps of technology, but unlike many of the species that they shared space with, the Selths had not lost their touch with the natural world.

They had climbed from their native oceans aeons ago, and had almost instantly taken to the trees. Their planet of origin, Selth Prime, had a notoriously high gravity, one that was over two and a half times that of Earth's.

They looked rather lizard like. Their scales were luminous and reflective, which caught the surrounding light and gave them an almost mythical glow. The scales served several purposes: they were one of the best barriers from the harsh sun. (The amount of ultraviolet light that their star threw out often varied, and sometimes the UV was powerful enough to burn human flesh in minutes.) While they also collected, or blocked, radiant heat, even though the Selths were warm blooded.

They were as tall as most humans, but all Selths had thicker legs, wide hips, digitigrade feet, and wide, bulbous shoulders. Their tails were skinny and flat enough to assist when swimming, but light enough to help steer their glides during leaps and bounds through heights of their forests.

Sometimes, the Selth people were called the grand-people of the galaxy. They were the wise council behind many corporations. It was their people that often ran the far-reaching outposts, and it was the station's only Selth who was the lead Space Traffic Controller.

Isa's consideration of her duty, and her love for good and honest work was a perfect example of her species' attitudes. It was not unheard of for this Selthian to pull many hours thanklessly working away to ensure that all traffic around the station moved perfectly and precisely. It was something that she did very, very well and it was the reason why Isa was a Freebie. Although,

Selthian society decreed that no Selth should ever lose their freedom, Isa had forsaken her people's respect for her when she had married a human Debtee.

The corporation had offered Isa the chance to reduce her husband's debt down by seventy-five percent, if she had matched his position in bondage. Isa had refused. She knew that if she ever slipped into Debtee status, the corporation would have tried their hardest to keep her there.

"X-ray-Lima-Niner, progress to jump point five." She ordered. In front of her, the Nav-globe, a three-dimensional rendering of station space, shifted as the delta-shaped representation of the vessel she had communicated with moved towards its requisite destination. With one final scan Isa assured herself that no other ships were close enough to offer a suitable threat to the craft.

"Wraith Zulu-Alpha, please continue holding pattern. Vessel two-two-eight, you are cleared to land on pad zero-see-van" As the ships responded to her commands the Selth took a moment to glance away from the Nav-globe.

It was peaceful, so the Selth leaned back in her chair and stretched. She bent so far backwards that her 'hairs' almost touched the tower's decking, which were not so much hair, but rather thick strands of fibrous materials that served as environmental sensory devices. They were short, not longer than her shoulders, but they helped her know everything that was going in the vicinity, such as how the door from the elevator had opened and revealed someone that Isa had been waiting to see.

"Hi Kalle." The Selth said happily, turning around to face the visitor. The old-hand pulled himself and his full tool belt onto the decking.

<Is the sun enjoyable?> Kalle asked, in the standard greeting and tongue of the Selth. Since the primary language of the Selths was a lot of rattles and fine whistles, most other races avoided it like the plague. Kalle however, had often complimented Isa's native tongue by calling it musical. Isa doubted that the human

understood just how much of an honor he did to the Selthian people every time he attempted their dialect. The Selth thought that any alien that learned their primary language was a great person, and worthy to be among their people.

<The sun is mild, but the crowds are annoying.> The Selth responded to the human's question. Instinctively, Isa switched back to Standard, so as not to confuse herself too much while controlling traffic. "I've had three ships already that haven't had a decent pilot."

"Maybe you should take a break." Kalle suggested, as he walked past her workstation.

"What, and let this station fall apart? The corporation would probably charge me for the downtime." Isa was only partly joking. "Anyways, what are you doing here?" She asked.

"I'm here to talk to the rep. My pay's been lost in cycle for almost two months now. I don't really miss the money, but it's the principle that counts." Kalle spoke easily. It was common knowledge that he was one of the highest paid people on board the station. If the corporation did not pay him in another week, Kalle could charge the company another interest. He didn't mind the extra cash; he just hated the paperwork that went with it.

"Well, he's up in the office but before you go, are you free tonight?" Isa asked calmly. Kalle shrugged his shoulders. He had nothing planned, and although Kalle had shared meals with Isa and her husband before, he could tell that Isa wanted something from him. He waited until Isa spilled the beans. "I need someone to install our new light fixtures. I'll cook dinner." She explained.

Kalle sighed, "Why can't you do it?"

"I don't know which lines are domestic on board this station, and I don't need the repair bill on my head." The Selth explained.

It was the honesty that kept Kalle smiling. Isa knew she had convinced Kalle anyways, she was one of the better cooks on the station, almost as good as Kong. The Selth was just about to make a little cheer of victory when the radio crackled and a thick, strange language came through the speakers. On the Nav-globe a new arrow appeared out of jump-gate nine.

"To new ship Charley-Romeo, I respectfully remind you that the recognized language for all air and space traffic communications is Standard." Isa said, polite in tone, frustrated in face.

There was a long and rather arrogant sounding babble. Kalle cocked his head to the side and stared with pity at the frustrated Selth. With an upset groan, Isa reached forward and touched one of her panels, forcing her computer to look for a translation.

The babble continued across the radio.

Leaning forward, Kalle shook his head sadly. "Damn Uruians, they're always so stubborn."

"Are you sure that's the language?" Isa asked irritably.

"Yeah, positive, have fun with them. They're already attempting an unauthorized landing." Kalle's words were cautious but light. Isa's remark was not, but it came from her native tongue, and was a word that Kalle was not familiar with. Grinning at the situation, the old-hand continued on his journey towards the person whose job it was to oversee everything that went on in the station.

The official title for the head of a jump-station was 'The Representative.' But the name given to the reps by the people who lived and worked on the stations was 'The Overseer.' No one knew who had originated that name, but it had stuck as lingo that was strictly reserved for those who inhabited the stations.

The current representative on board the station had earned the moniker of 'Pops' because he was kind and decent to everyone. It didn't help his Overseer title that Pops' race, the Oursinians, resembled giant teddy bears. His people were so physically large that they had no natural predators, and they had evolved into their arboreal world's largest herbivores.

Pops himself was so old that his fur had lost much of its natural greenish coloring, and had almost turned entirely grey. He was sitting at his desk where an unusually large number of Dataslates were piled high upon it. The representative was mumbling to himself as he shoved one plate aside, and then another.

Pausing for the briefest of moment, Pops shoved his rather gargantuan spectacles back up his nose.

With a great, rough grumble, Pops threw the latest Dataslate into his 'done' pile, which was much smaller than his 'to-do' pile. With his hands freed from their work, he reached over and grabbed a leafy green from a small plate. Chomping down on it, Pops chewed the vegetable as his brow furrowed in strong concentration.

Finally calmed, the representative acknowledged Kalle's presence with a hearty growl.

"And a good morning to you, as well." Kalle said in a deadpan voice. He knew enough of the Oursinian's mannerisms to understand that Pops was upset with the amount of paperwork that he had to complete.

Pops replied with a gutsy huff, which threatened to knock over his 'to-do' pile, before he shoved his spectacles as far up his rounded face as he could manage. Shoving more of the greenery into his mouth, he motioned for Kalle to take a seat.

When the representative finally swallowed, he looked farm-calmer and composed than he had upon Kalle's entry.

"Sorry for being so rough, but I don't enjoy this part of the job." Pops explained himself.

"I didn't think you enjoyed any part of this job." Kalle responded calmly. Pops did not argue. After a pause, Kalle decided that there was no reason to stall.

"My paychecks are overdue again." The old-hand spoke matter-of-factly. Pops did not take it well at all. His sigh threatened the pile's precarious balance once more.

"How long?" Pops asked aloud.

The last time the checks had been late Kalle had gone six months without a payment, and he had earned a small fortune on the interest. The company had been rather livid with the extensive payout, but it had been their fault. After that event, Pops had been cautioned that there were to be no encore performances.

"It's been almost two months." Kalle spoke easily about the

matter. He knew that such news would at least be good for Pops, because it was still within an acceptable time limit.

The Oursinian relaxed slightly, before he reached into his desk and produced yet another Dataslate. Lowering his glasses down to his eyes, Pops muttered as he wrote, "It must be good to be so free. You can complain if something doesn't go your way."

"It has its ups and downs." Kalle responded briefly. That caused the Oursinian to guffaw.

"Yeah, according to this it's all 'up' for you." The Overseer talked into the Dataslate. "You could probably retire with all the money you've made off this station. Out of curiosity, what are your retirement plans?"

The question shocked Kalle. Debtees did not talk about such taboo topics because Debtees never retired.

"Well, I, uh, that is . . ."

"Spit it out lad." Pops spoke easily. "I'm asking you to be sociable. Look, you know I've been saving up for retirement. I can almost afford my freedom. I just want to know what a Freebie would do. Or, if the rumors are true, what an Unbound would do."

The last comment caused Kalle to inhale sharply. Looking up from the Dataslate, Pops smiled happily. "So it is true then?" He said in amazement. Laughing, he slid the Dataslate back into his desk. "Don't worry Kalle, it doesn't change anything. So, what are your retirement plans, eh? Does it have to do with those rocks you purchased in the asteroid belt? Share them with an old Oursinian who's never known freedom."

"In all honesty, I have been working on a plan." Kalle spoke quietly. "I've been investing into limitless travel."

"That sounds nice." Pops admitted.

"What about you? Any plans yet?" Kalle asked.

The representative smiled softly as he leaned back in his chair. "I want to go home, buy a small orchard, and farm." The Oursinian admitted. "Not very exciting, but I'm too old to be gallivanting across the galaxy. At the moment though, they are dreams, and I won't achieve them by dilly-dallying. The sooner I get this paperwork done, the closer I will be to my freedom."

Pops picked up the next Dataslate. Kalle took the hint and stood to leave, but before he could exit the room the Overseer spoke once more.

"Kalle, if you retire before me, could you do me one favor?" Pops words stopped Kalle in his tracks. The old-hand looked back at the Oursinian.

"If you get your stuff in order before me, could you fly me home free of charge?"

Kalle laughed easily as he opened the door. "Sure Pops, that I will do."

It was not really break time at the loading docks, but there was no way that work could continue around the Ururian ship while it was being impounded by the station's small security force, since the vessel had forced its way onto a landing pad.

Two of the invaders were dragged past the room where Telfer and his crew waited for the disturbance to pass. One of the Ururians suddenly broke free from its escort and ran into the break room. It looked like a cross between a slug and an octopus, while its lower half resembled that of a giant and flightless bird. Various tentacles waved in excitement as it tried to avoid the grasping hands, claws, and talons of its captors. It found itself cornered and a moment later it was tackled and it disappeared under a pile of bodies.

Seeing that it was getting too crowded in the lunch-room, Telfer and his coworkers made a quick exit into the hall. As the human closed the door behind his team, a Friedlon jumped into the air and raised two of its four arms in preparation for an 'elbow smash'.

Looking at the captive ship, and the officers swarming all over it, Telfer made a very simple comment about his dislike for the Ururian species.

"What kind of idea did those cast-offs have, landing here?"

He wondered aloud. The Ururian race was recognized as being one of the most arrogant peoples because although they were relatively young to space, the Ururians thought that everybody should learn their language rather than they learn either Standard or Basic.

One of the Kackles that worked with the human made his own comment. "Maybe they were attacked by Pirates?"

There was a general hush among the dock-workers. All of them looked at each other with general concern.

Although there were those who survived off of theft, extortion, kidnapping and pillaging, they were called Raiders. The word Pirate belonged to a specific species. A few years ago, a race had begun to terrorize the galactic rim. No one knew where they came from but when Pirates attacked, they generally left nothing of value in their wake. Very few had ever survived battles with them. Every ship in their fleet was more maneuverable and packed more firepower than any other vessel known. Even the Confederates, the largest militant company in the galaxy, could not hold a candle to them in battle.

The team's somberness was shattered a moment later when the Kackle suddenly grunted something in his native tongue, before he attempted to disappear, and the rest of the team found ways to be busy, stranding Telfer as he looked for something to occupy himself with. There was nothing he could do, and the next moment he found himself the center of attention from the same Grondonian who had, only a night before, harassed the Kackle at Kong's bar.

"You must be the dockhand on station!" The Grondonian called out from across the hall before he shoved himself off a wall. He barreled past several of Telfer's workers, almost knocking three of them over. It was only with the greatest effort that the Grondonian managed to stop his flight before he collided with the hapless human. At least, that was how it appeared to the uneducated, but Telfer saw how the *thing* folded its multi jointed legs, how it settled its center, how it eased its final descent with subtle wavings of its long arms.

"I need to talk to you." The Grondonian spoke with arrogant authority. "I need a skiff prepared, and I'm told that you are the one who can do it for me."

"What gives you the reason to assume I can even do such a thing to begin with?" The human asked. Without verbal reply, the Grondonian shoved his hands into one of his many pockets before he produced the required Dataslate. Telfer took it from the Grondonian's long fingers.

The information was scrawled in Standard, but with a touch of his fingers Telfer changed the language to Basic, and even then Telfer used his finger to scroll beneath the words.

"The hegemony of blah blah blah . . . respectfully informs you of yada yada yada . . .to be our current mineral geologist for la la la . . . to assist him in means towards this end, signed, someone."

It was official. If it wasn't the signature that clued Telfer in, then it was the fact that the Grondonian had handed him a high quality, sealed, company-only memo-Dataslate.

The Grondonian produced another Dataslate. "I need a mining wraith, two spare life tanks and this assortment of tools." The new 'slate was much lengthier than the last. Telfer only took a cursory glance at it before he sighed out of aggravation.

"I'd love to help you," Telfer lied as he handed the Dataslates back. "But right now I can't really do anything for you."

"And why not?" The scientist asked with a tone that was more than indignant.

"Because I have yet to slap the restraining devices upon the Ururian vessel." A new voice joined into the conversation. Telfer's relief was evident as it crossed his face and the Grondonian seemed disturbed by the invader.

Kalle walked over and took Telfer's hand in his. The two clutched palms in the human sign of friendship.

"You made it here quickly." Telfer said happily.

"Yeah well, I saw the Ururians come out of jump. I figured I'd get here before I got the work order." Kalle explained. A moment later he looked at his left wrist. His soft-core Datapad was attached to his maintenance uniform's jacket.

"Well, it appears the work order just came in." Kalle spoke lightly. "I'll have the ship restrained in under the hour. Oh Telfer, your wife wants me to remind you to get home on time tonight."

Telfer nodded, and was about to reply when a nearby cargo cratepopened. Nozomi's head popped out of the hatch at the side, and she stopped when she noticed that everyone around her was staring. Almost everyone hurried back to doing nothing at all, except the Grondonian who excused himself.

As soon as he was out of his ear-shot, Nozomi pushed herself completely out of the crate and sealed the door behind her. "Hello." Nozomi said to the two men. They greeted her with equal remarks.

"What were you doing with the crate today?" Telfer enquired.

"Preparing it for voyage." Nozomi answered flatly as she floated through the air. She landed with skill and competence in the lower gravity, naturally finding her feet beneath her. "I was just going to see about getting a cargo shipment for next week."

The news seemed to sadden Kalle. "So, I take it then that you are leaving soon?" He asked.

"Yeah, I'm going to go look for a job off-station." At Nozomi's explanation Kalle's face clouded a little further, but instead of saying anything the old-hand reached out and took Nozomi into his arms. She did not object to the hug, and instead seemed to welcome it. The two closed their eyes as they held each other.

<I'm going to miss you.> Kalle spoke out in English. <Take care of yourself.>

<Thanks,> Nozomi responded. <You too, okay?>

Telfer watched the exchange with his usual frustration when conversations around him were impossible to follow. A moment later though, he found himself receiving a hug from Nozomi as they exchanged well wishes in his own tongue.

Chapter 4

Data-device:

Both a status symbol and a necessity for the discerning Freebie. Data-devices are micro-computers that range from the miniscule 2-inch pocket screen, to the 14-inch flexible variety that can be adhered to clothing.

Datapads and Datacards are Data-devices that are open-source and open-operational. They are the modern personal electronic device of the era, and are generally outfitted with apps that make life easier for the wielder. Most transactions are performed through said devices. Debtees, since they are paid mostly in owner credits, rarely find themselves able to afford Data-devices of their own.

Dataslates are the closed-source variety of Data-devices. They are most commonly used as business cards or for displaying company commands and/or orders. Dataslates are legally binding once one has been 'sealed' by its author.

ISA STOOD FROM HER CONSOLE and stretched. Since the Ururian ship's arrival there had been a backlog of ships that she had been forced to deal with, but she was more than skilled enough to have everything rectified by the time her replacement had arrived.

The new traffic controller slid into Isa's seat and plugged his head into the control panel. Her coworker was a tireless Haraway, which was one of the races that believed the best way to evolve their species was through cybernetic enhancements.

With a smile across her face, the Selth pulled on her jacket. It was warm by her seat but Isa always found herself momentarily chilled once she moved from her workstation.

Pops exited from his office and folded his spectacles. He had spent many long hours at his desk just catching up on the never-shrinking pile of corporate Dataslates.

Isa liked Pops, and had often ended her shift by walking with him. He was a wealth of knowledge and experience, even if he had always been bonded to the company.

"So, I heard you have company coming over." Pops remarked as they walked towards the lift that traveled between the main deck and the station's command tower.

"Yes, Kalle promised to help install the new lights I just purchased." Isa explained.

Pops chuckled. "Well, hopefully those Ururians didn't throw him too much of a loop." He remarked. "It would be horrible if he missed his bribery dinner."

"I wouldn't worry. Kalle had that ship impounded in under an hour." Isa remarked. The two stepped into the lift together, and Pops closed the safety cage with his usual flair for the dramatic.

As the elevator began its descent the Oursinian continued the conversation. "Those Ururians were more pushy than normal. Just what was the big idea?" He asked.

"I'm not quite sure, some of the Ururians refused to talk, but the ones that did have been repeating 'Pirates' over and over again." Isa explained, tiredly. It was an old ploy played by the guilty, to claim that Pirates had been responsible for their actions.

"You don't suppose they were attacked, do you?" Pops fancied.

"No, I think they might have witnessed an attack. Anyways, they're refusing to talk right now until they have an Ururian official to talk to." Isa sighed. "I didn't place an order for one yet, I'm going to wait and see what being in a cell overnight will do for them."

The lift stopped its descent and Pops opened the door, stepping into a very crowded throughway.

"Well, let's see if they talk tomorrow then. Good night Isa, have fun." Pops called out.

"See you then." Isa responded, as she tried to figure out the best way to walk out into the busy pedestrian traffic.

"Honey, I'm home." Telfer called out as he stepped into the apartment, but he was greeted with silence.

Kicking off his work boots, Telfer made his way to the washroom. His, and his wife's, place wasn't luxurious or extravagant, but it was a far cry better than where he had lived as a child. His mother, father, two sisters and he had shared an apartment that was one room and it was barely large enough for the five of them to sleep in. Isa's suite resembled luxury to him.

Selecting the setting on the shower, Telfer stripped down to his lean body and stepped into the box. Until he had met his wife, Telfer has been rakish and undernourished, even though the company relied of him for heavy labor, but Isa was a good cook, and since she made real food for him, he had finally been able to develop actual mass.

Sensors read his body temperature and stress levels, and a hot sudsy foam sprayed out from the various nozzles and plastered the human. He took it well, only whooping slightly as his body adjusted to the heat that worked its way into tired muscles.

The front door opened and he was brought out of his hypnotic state by the familiar sing-song voice of his wife as she called out his name.

"I'm in the shower, Isa." Telfer replied, still reluctant to move. The door to the bathroom opened and Telfer's Selthian bride walked into the room. There was no masking the smells of freshly boiled Oolod Leaks, and the sweat smell of Miattan flour that emanated from her clothes.

Opening the shower door, Isa Laughlin kissed her husband on the lips. Unlike the regular superstition about Selthian kisses, one did not carry an aftertaste, nor was it cold and uninviting, Isa's lips were soft and warm. Selths had a higher body temperature than humans.

"I'm glad to see you're getting ready for dinner." Isa said when she leaned back out of the shower. "But please try to hurry. I want to clean up too, before Kalle gets here." Isa explained.

Telfer sighed as he closed the door to the shower again. As much as he loved his wife, and appreciated what she did for him, he always found it frustrating when she updated the apartment without asking his opinion. Telfer knew it was little more than a formality if she ever bothered, but it was something that he would have appreciated.

"Rinse." Telfer snapped and a blast of water scraped away the foam that had collected onto him. It was refreshing, just what he needed to wake up. It was immediately replaced with a blast of lukewarm air that blew the liquids off his flesh.

Stepping from the tub, Telfer wrapped a towel around himself for dignity's sake. Isa had already stripped down to her undergarments and was just reaching behind herself to undo her single-piece compression suit. It was a Selthian staple that maintained her temperature and humidity in emergency situations, could compress a wound, and came with a convenient plug so that she did not have to expose herself to the common toilets to go to the washroom.

She was very happy to be rid of it when home, but it did save time when outside of the apartment.

"I'll just be a minute, hon, but could you get the pots warmed up for me?" Isa asked. Telfer nodded as he left the warmth of his wife's side.

◆ ◆ ◆

Kalle studied himself in the reflective sheen of the door. The stress of the day was finally dissipating from his body. The Ururians had caused him another headache. One of the aliens had escaped from its cell and had attempted to wipe-out all of the evidence of their forced landing. The Ururian had been apprehended, minutes later, but not by Kalle.

Raising one hand, he knocked, rather than rang the doorcall, and heard the echo as it rattled down the relatively empty hall. The door opened and Telfer welcomed the guest of the evening inside.

"I hope I'm not too late." Kalle apologized in Basic.

Before Telfer could respond, Isa's voice came from the kitchen. "Not really, no. I'm still finishing with the soup."

The entire apartment smelled of a wonderful concoction that warmed the heart and sent the stomach growling in instant anticipation.

Telfer shrugged. "We had to go get some ingredients when we realized that we had none of the proper meats in the fridge."

The old-hand chuckled. "And here I was fearing that I would make all of us wait. Well, this is a relief. So, since it's going to take a few minutes yet, why don't you show me where Isa wishes me to put the lights?"

"I'll show you in a moment, the stew has to rest." Isa stepped from the kitchen. Her flowing dress was opaque in places where it was required, but almost transparent over the rest where the see-through materials allowed her skin to shine through as the fabric caught the light and danced spectacularly. It was the traditional garb of a noble Selth, one that Isa was entitled to wear by birth.

Walking along the length of the room, Isa pointed upwards. Kalle reached into his tool kit and removed a flat box. Setting the tool upon the floor, Kalle squeezed the handle and pulled, and the box seemed to unwind, until it ended its transformation as a pyramid-shaped ladder. Climbing to the ceiling, Kalle opened a service hatch and pushed himself into the small space, his Datapad's glow was all the light he needed.

"Isa," He called out. "Why didn't you just tie into the other lights?"

"There's already too much on the reduced breaker. I didn't want to have to upgrade again." She replied, her voice muffled by the ceiling between them

Kalle nodded his head as he investigated the area around him. "That sounds fair." Squeezing himself back down the ladder Kalle continued his explanation. "Well, I have two different ways to do the job. I can either run a line from your primary control, but that would take me a few minutes and I might have to upgrade your breaker system, or I cheat, and I use the station line and give your lights free power."

He needn't have asked. He caught the look shared between the couple before he chuckled. "So, it's option two then. Alright."

Climbing back up the ladder, Kalle pulled a small box from his pocket. His fingers began to open the carton when suddenly his right arm began to burn. Grunting, the old-hand dropped the box and clutched fitfully at his limb. It twitched of its own accord and only with the greatest of concentration did he manage to shove the rogue appendage under his left arm and restrain it. His pain did not go unnoticed, and Isa called with concern evident in her voice.

"I'm okay, it'll pass." Kalle assured his friends. Moments later the limb did indeed stop its twitching and, satisfied that it was back to normal, he continued without further incident, brushing aside any and all concerns and worries that his companions piled upon him. They stopped asking soon enough.

Kalle set his spoon upon his plate. If he ate anymore he doubted that he would be able to walk back to his apartment. The company, and the nourishment, of the evening had done wonders for everyone. Isa was still eating with the delicateness of royalty, while Telfer had consumed his helpings with wondrous glee. Not having his mouth full for the moment, Kalle looked at his hosts as he asked, "Kids?"

The couple looked at each other. Children were a topic that had recently found its way into their general conversations, and neither of them had come to a conclusion about it.

"Well, we have discussed adoption." Telfer admitted.

"What about splicing?" Kalle asked. Splicing was a technique where two incompatible beings could form a child. Some species frowned on it because it required scientific intervention in order to work. Companies may even pay for it, but to offset the cost they would charge the debtees incredible fees, an especially useful tactic for keeping down those who they wanted. Isa and Telfer refused to extend their debt.

"We're not ready to have kids yet, Kalle." Isa answered. "Not until Telfer is free."

"That can't be too far, now." The old-hand responded.

"Two years, give or take a couple of months." Telfer smiled. He could taste the freedom.

Congratulations were in order, and as a sign of respect Kalle raised his glass. The Brandian firewater had gone straight to his head, and he was feeling more than clumsy enough so he required concentration to not spill his glass.

"And what of you? When did you become free, because I know you weren't always a Freebie?" Telfer asked a moment later.

"No," Kalle said, suddenly becoming serious. "I earned my freedom through sweat and blood." Pausing, he stared at the limb that had gone into spasms earlier. Without realizing it, his other hand traced its way up his limb. The path followed two faint, silver lines that ran up his arm. They were barely visible against his skin.

There was silence as the couple noticed that their guest had become lost in his own thoughts. Trying to break the seriousness, Telfer then asked another question. "What about retirement? Rumor has it that you've bought some rocks in the field."

"That's true." Kalle admitted, once more leaving his arm alone. "The company's not going to get to them for a few years,

but I figure one of them is bound to have a nice deposit somewhere on it. They were willing to sell them to me because they
figured that I'll move on before they get there. You know, they're
probably right."

"Is that where you've been going?" Telfer continued. During
his 'weekends' Kalle had often rented a skiff from the company
and vanished into the belt.

Grinning, Kalle touched his nose. "I've just been checking
on them, placing sensors and whatnot. I figure, why bother giving the company a chance to do some sneaky mining behind my
back."

"Would they do that?" Isa asked, mocking horror in her tone.

Both Telfer and Kalle shot Isa a glance that was so bitter, she
broke out laughing and almost spilled her drink.

Chapter 5

General Atmosphere:

Since multiple races require different vapors at varying pressures to breathe, a solution has been implemented on most Galactic Standard vessels and stations. General Atmosphere is a blend of the important gasses that most species require to survive. Each crewmember is then outfitted with an implant, either in the lungs or the throat, which filters the gassed that their physiques require, from the blend.

Implants themselves range from mechanical cybernetic implants, to bred parasitic organisms, to genetic engineering. The alternative is to wear an SCBA or exterior filter mask whenever entering a space that uses General Atmosphere.

Since only some of the gasses are reactive, there is generally little to no increased risk of combustion or damage from fire.

FALLON WIPED THE SCREEN with a final flourish, before she motioned that it was okay for Isa to return to her seat. Done with their cleaning of the tower, the four children made their way to the lift and hurried off to their next designated working zone.

Plugging her headset back in, Isa sank into her seat and scanned her Nav-globe for new ships. There was nothing that was impending on theeshort-range scan, and no ships were due for another few minutes. Relaxed, she leaned back and looked out the window. It had been a few days since Kalle had joined her and her husband for supper. The Ururians of earlier had been sent to the company's home planet to face charges from the company court for trespassing while their ship had remained impounded, but it had been moved to another part of the station so that no one was impeded by it.

Something outside the window caught her attention. Without moving from her reclined position, Isa lazily tapped on her controls as she focused one of the long-range sensors onto what had caught her attention. There was something out there, but whatever it was, it did not match the readings of any known ship.

With nothing else to worry about, Isa let her curiosity guide her. The Selth stood and grabbed a very powerful telescope. Pulling it to the full length, she stared out into the blackness of space.

Her single question grew into a multitude of enquiries as she watched another glint appear beside the first.

"You called?" Kalle asked as the lift reached its apogee. The tension on the tower was so palpable that he felt he could have cleaved through it with his micro-torch. Isa was against the observation bubble, ignorant of all the calls that clamored for her attention. Upon hearing Kalle's voice, she lowered the telescope and turned to face her friend.

"We have three ships that have folded." She said nervously. "They appeared only minutes apart, and are sitting out of regular visual scanner range."

"That's an odd thing to do." Kalle agreed. "You think they're prospectors?"

"I doubt it. Prospector ships usually show up under laser ID. These guys just, exist." Isa admitted warily.

The old-hand chewed at his bottom lip as he pondered the situation. "Then why call me?" He asked.

"I was wondering if you could somehow boost our visual signal." Isa requested. "Or maybe outfit one of our security drones with a better sensor package?"

"Outfitting a probe would at least take twenty minutes." Kalle said to himself, but then his grin grew across his face. "But I do have an idea." Raising his left arm, the human fiddled with his Datapad. Isa watched him work until another glint caught her eye, and she looked back outside with the lens, once more, glued to her eye.

"That makes four." She said, swallowing.

"Whatever." Her friend's voice had become horribly calm as he pointed his Datapad at a bank of monitors that lined a wall. Several different views and readouts became visible across the bank of screens and all of it was filled with the terribly eclectic scrawl of the Ururian race. Kalle explained himself as he continued to type away. "I was paid to put a slave circuit on the Ururian ship so when the company's legal team came, they could escort it out safely. They have yet to arrive."

Isa looked back at the Nav-globe and saw the Ururian ship's representation move away from the station.

"Now, I'll just give it a quick order to fly within full visual range of those mystery ships out there, and we should be good." Punching the last command into his Datapad, Kalle waited. The ship moved slowly, and as it took its time the old-hand made one final comment. "Of course, there is one flaw to this: That ship's unscheduled launch and flight path is impossible to hide." Kalle shrugged, unworried—the station wouldn't risk losing one of their dedicated Freebies by arguing over a flight path.

The two in the tower watched in silence. Before Ururians sensors would have been useful, the impounded ship vanished in a hail of weapon fire that, for an instant, became almost brighter than the nearby stars . . . and then it was no more. It vanished into silent oblivion.

Klaxons began screaming into the air, one signifying that there was an emergency, the other alarm was a reminder to alert the company's scavenger crew.

Recovering his composure, the old-hand warned his friend. "Isa, if anyone was watching that, we're going to have a mass panic on our hands."

The lift suddenly began an emergency descent. A moment later it reappeared, and Pops stormed his way onto the tower.

"Just what is going on?" The Oursinian yelled. "I just saw six crews running for their crafts, and somebody yelled that the Ururian ship exploded. I thought it was-"

"That's because it did." Kalle interrupted. "Look Pops, we've got a bad situation that's just waiting to explode and like the Ururians, it is not going to be pleasant."

The Oursinian sighed and cradled his head in his hands. He looked frustrated. After he composed himself, Pops once more regarded the other two people aboard the tower. "Explain." He spoke, curtly.

"We're probably going to endure an attack." Kalle responded, as calmly as he could.

Pops sigh dissolved into an impressive string of obscenities as the Oursinian took hold of the telescope that Isa offered to him. There was no mistaking the organization of the unannounced ships. They were lined abreast, and the ships themselves ranged from the smooth, sleek look of trans-atmospheric vessels, to the bulky, warped and asymmetrical forms of deep space warships. As Pops continued to examine them, he could not help but notice the small pieces of debris that had once been the Ururian vessel drift across his vision.

Another ship appeared out of fold and immediately began disgorging dozens of smaller fighter craft.

Letting the gravity of the situation sink in, Pops lowered the telescope. "How many people know of this?" He asked.

"Anybody who has been paying attention to our communications has probably figured it out by now." Isa responded.

The Selth stiffened as her headset crackled. Looking back towards the Nav-globe, Isa cursed with the same comment she had used against the Ururians only days ago. Ignoring the curious looks of Kalle and Pops, the Selth slid into her seat and began to speak in rapid fire Standard. "Charley-Queen-Uniform, you have broken holding pattern."

Reaching across the console, Kalle switched on the speakers so the exchange was broadcast throughout the tower.

//This is Charley-Queen-Uniform, we are experiencing some troubles with our navigation system and have been forced to break pattern to avoid collisions.// The voice of the rogue vessel was loud and clear. Isa covered the pickup on her headset as she turned to face her companions.

"Bet you fifty that he's just scared." Isa said snidely before she attempted to continue communications. "Charley-Queen-Uniform, I must remind you that to break holding without a request is a chargeable offence."

//The problem was immediate Tower. We could not hold position without endangering the lives of all other vessels.//

Kalle hissed aloud. "Like hell, he's positioning himself for a fold."

Sure enough the vessel was pointed in the exact opposite direction of the attackers. Still attempting to stop the vessel, Isa gave one more warning. "Your identification has been noticed, if you attempt an unauthorized jump in station space, you will be fined and your ship will be confiscated the next time it appears in compa-"

Without a care in the galaxy, the rogue vessel seemed to elongate for a moment, and then it disappeared only to appear several kilometers away, a feat which it repeated more and more rapidly, eventually disappearing from sight. As soon as it was gone, two more vessels broke their patterns.

"Well, we'd best try and restrain a few ships." Pops ordered. "Isa, I want you to start banning empty ships from leaving. We're going to have a panic on our hands any moment now and I want every available ship to fill its capacity." Pops voice had grown firm with conviction. The real reason why he had been chosen as the representative showed its colors as he continued without faltering. "Mr. Aaron, I want you to start tagging ships with restraining clamps. Once they are full, you can send them off. I'll put the bonus pay for this endeavor straight to your accounts."

Kalle was already running towards the lift pad.

"Isa, kill all incoming flights. Drop them out of jump and get them to depart from the jump-ways." Pops ordered. "Then send out an emergency clearance, code Delta-Delta-One-Zero. That'll stop all other jump-stations and put them directly into emergency receive mode."

Isa hurried to comply with Pop's orders as Kalle vaulted into the lift and hit the button for an emergency descent.

The halls were complete pandemonium. Panic had already taken hold, and those that had not prepared themselves for such scenarios mulled about in uncertainty. Kalle ran through the crowds, shoving those aside that he thought could pick themselves up, but those that looked fragile the human dragged to the outer fringes of the brewing mob.

He had no illusions about how desperate the situation was. Anybody who was on a ship with its own fold-drive would try to leave the station, if they hadn't already.

The old-hand did not hurry to any vessel. His path took him towards the center of the station. As he got closer to the bowels of steel and metal, he felt the pressure of heavier gravity close over him.

When he reached the main control for the hydraulic docking clamps, Kalle removed two wires from his Datapad and plugged them into a set of jacks at a very complicated device's base. A handful of others knew where the hydraulic controller was, but only Kalle knew the programming.

A great whine became audible as the unit built its pressure. The only way now, for the ships to break free, was if the old-hand freed them personally.

If the hallways had been chaotic, than there was no possible classification for the tower itself. Isa had not moved from her position, and two of her screens were cracked from the force of her finger's impacts. Pops had continued issuing orders to various staff members, and had requested aid from the company's small ad-hoc military force. It was just a symbolic gesture though, as there were no ships close enough to help.

"Situation on the departure, Isa?" Pops asked, shoving a Dataslate so hard that it slid all the way across the floor and disappeared under his office door.

"Kalle's busy working on making sure that the ships are loaded, and our favorite little Haraway has also joined him. I've sent security to monitor and load vessels. I don't really see a point launching any of our skiffs. They might just cause whoever's out there to attack." Isa spoke plainly as she continued to work at her console.

Pops agreed with a nod before he raised his audio pickup back to his lips. "*This is the company representative speaking.*" His voice seemed to vibrate the Standard from the very walls themselves. "*As of this moment I am hereby issuing the following order: All hands are to immediately vacate the station. This is an 'Abandon-All-Quarters.' Everyone is to head to their assigned positions, and those who do not have a set duty are to find themselves safe transit off this station. This is not a drill.*"

Several calls began to appear on the monitors of the tower. Pops handled the first two straight away, but it was Isa who found herself answering the third.

"Tower here, go ahead." Isa said in Standard.

A moment later Telfer's voice cut through the noise and spoke in his touched tone of Basic. //*Isa, the guys and I just heard the AAQ. Is everything alright?*//

"Did you not hear Pops?" Isa asked of her husband.

There was only a slight pause before he answered. //*He spoke in Standard. We're already on our way back in. I just wanted to double check.//*

Pushing her claws against the thick skin of her temples, Isa sighed into the microphone, certain that her husband would hear the sound. "It's the real deal, boot it back here, pronto. And what the hell are you doing out there anyways?"

//Mining with the boys. Cargo was slow so I figured that I'd pull some time in the field for the day and pull a stronger commission.// Telfer answered. *//But obviously I chose the wrong job for the day, didn't I?//*

Isa allowed herself a moment to smile. "You always do make bad decisions if you don't consult me first." Even though she was smiling, the concern Isa felt for her husband's safety was very real. Looking over at the Nav-globe the Selth swallowed nervously. It was something she had learned from her husband's species. He was too far from the station for her liking. She would have preferred her husband to have been standing directly beside her.

Another call caught her attention and Isa found herself having to ignore her husband for the moment. *//This is security unit three. The ships out there are moving.//*

The comment stopped both Isa and Pops in the middle of conversations. Raising the telescope, Isa focused on the vessels. They were reorganizing themselves. The Selth squinted, trying to be certain of their goals, and cursed rather strongly, not even caring anymore that her comments were audible. Something was incoming, and fast. She had seen the flash of light that signaled the firing of a kinetic weapon.

Reaching behind herself, Isa grabbed something from the back of her Selthian body-suit. She pulled the soft, flexible bag over her head even as she jumped out of her seat and threw her considerable mass on top of Pops. A massive hole appeared in the top of the primary window, and there was a whooshing sound as the atmosphere of the tower began to vanish into the vacuum of space. A second later, a large slab of durasheet slid over the window, blurring the view from outside but sealing the leak. Isa could only think about how thankful she was that the security sensors had not been compromised in the blast.

The station shook beneath his feet, and Kalle was thrown against the wall. His body cushioned a rather elderly Wazand who had lost its footing too. The little alien burbled its thanks, even as it collided with the old-hand and crushed itself against his diaphragm. Without replying, Kalle waved the alien into the cargo ship, filling it to capacity. Raising himself from the floor, The old-hand struggled to suck air back into his lungs, but his hands worked automatically and punched in the release code.

The ship closed its doors and powered its engines.

With a raspinghbreath, the old-hand managed to inhale, and he gratefully sucked his lungs full of air. He took two more tentative gasps until he dared to pull himself to his feet again. As he stood, the ship pulled away from the station.

Kalle looked at the other airlocks beside him. They were still feeding a steady crowd into their respective ships, but everyone had become more frantic, and the lone security guard who was trying to maintain the line's formations was stressed as the crowds surged, lost morale and spiraled towards mob panic.

Some of the cooler heads were pulling people out of the pressed horde in order to prevent them from being trampled, but more than one inhabitant limped or cradled their injuries.

Kalle knew what an attack-impact felt like. His concern was for the most potential target. Raising his Datapad to his face, he pushed the send button.

//Isa, Pops, are you two okay?//

The Selth lifted herself effortlessly, relieving the crushing weight that she had imposed upon the Oursinian. Pops was lying on his back, his arms and legs were splayed out, and his glasses were bent oddly, and blood ran rather heavily from his nose.

Groaning, the representative reached up and cradled his head as he said something in his natural tongue. Isa offered a helping hand to the overseer, and he let himself be pulled to his feet, albeit shakily.

"Well, it can't be that bad if you're standing." Isa said with relief more than palatable in her voice. Pops only comment was to sneeze, and spray stuff from his nose across the console that he had been working on.

//I'll take it that everybody's alright?// The old-hand's voice sounded from the speakers.

"We're fine Kalle." Isa responded. "Just a little shaken. That round hit the tower."

//That was more than one collision.// The mechanic pointed out. *//From where I was, the shaking took me to the floor. That shouldn't have happened for* just *a tower hit.//*

Isa used her sleeve to wipe a screen clean of the saliva Pops had sprayed across her console. The outline of the station was visible, and there were more than a few red blinking lights on its structure. "You're right Kalle, but the only hull breach where there's life was the tower. Everything else that was hit was just . . ."

//Just what?// The old-hand's voice sounded rather annoyed.

"Just several vital power nodes Kalle. I think you're going to be very busy." Isa said slowly.

"I don't think we have the time to worry about those impacts Isa." Pops said. The Oursinian was staring out of the fuzzy, newly armored window. Where Isa looked there was debris everywhere. More than one ship had been hit. The station had not been the main target.

"How many ships just died?" Isa asked in horror, but she was already looking at the Nav-globe, and her hands flew along her controls. It played back the destruction for her in slow motion. Each ship's avatar that was hit winked out and vanished. None of the ships that died had civilian populations on them.

"That's odd." Isa commented, and her remark caused Pops to shoot her a quizzical look. "Why did they spare the civilian transports?

"Maybe they're not after a kill count." Pops suggested.

"Maybe they're trying to stop our resources. Cut the supply line, leaving the overwhelmed populations at their mercy. Standard occupational tactic."

Pops moved back to his console. The Oursinian looked up to the Selth once, and spoke briefly.

"Isa, let's hurry thesevacuations, shall we?"

Telfer leapt off of the skiff as he cut the transport's power, and used the momentum to fling himself deeper into the station. His crew followed his example, and everyone landed in the main airlock. The outer door slammed closed and as soon as the pressure between the station and the lock was equalized, he opened the inner door.

Kalle was standing there, waiting for him. "I've got new orders for you, Telfer. Do you think you can handle them?" Kalle shouted in the loudest Basic he could manage.

The sounds of Kalle's voice were muted by Telfer's helmet, so he disengaged the locks across his suit, and removed both the outer shell, and the inner layer which was filled with sensors and delicate communication gear. "Maybe Kalle, depending on what your new orders are." Telfer answered, but even as he spoke his entire team mimicked him

"Your crew is to help with the loading of civilians. Get them into the ships, and when the ship's full take a free ride out of here. Here's the code to unlock the hydraulic clamps." Kalle ordered. The next moment he repeated the order in Standard, but he spoke it too fast for Telfer to follow.

"Do you think that's okay?" Kalle asked when he was done. Telfer's crew were all agreeing with their various motions, indicating complacency. Raising one hand, Telfer whirled it around his head. It was the sign to 'get going.' His gang dispersed, hurrying to either their tasks or their families.

It was only Telfer and Kalle left after a moment. The oldhand was listening to his Datapad.

//New problem, Kalle.// Isa's voice sang. *//Two of the gravity*

drives are overheating.//

"How close until their high-limits trip out?" Kllle replied, his brow furrowed in concern.

//They already have. We need them all if we're going to get everyone out of here in the next few minutes and most of the others are already running hot. That hit we took surged a lot of power through our systems.//

"I can cool those two units Isa, but in order to do that I'm going to have to break the coolant system and flood the rooms. You'll have maybe five jumps per unit once I do." The old-hand explained.

Back in the tower Isa shook her head.

"We need at least another eight or more jumps, per." She said in aggravation.

Pops, who had been trying to do the math, sighed. "We have no choice Isa. We're going to have to stack-jump."

Stack-jumping was the technique of sending multiple ships through the jump-stream at the same time. It was dangerous, risky, and normally illegal.

"Do you think you can handle it?' Pops asked. He knew full well what the ratios of success versus failures were. There was so much that could go wrong, but Isa was a Selth, and was not afraid to try her skills as a controller. Swinging her head back, she flared her 'hair' in dramatic fashion.

Her voice was loud and authoritative. "Ships Bravo-Echo-One-Zero, Two-Two-Niner-Uniform, Delta-Mike-Romeo and Alpha-Zulu-Lima-Juliet, converge on jump-gate Niner."

//Uh, Roger, will proceed in fashion.// One of the pilot's voices answered.

"Negative, you will proceed simultaneously." Isa snapped back. Her command was crisp and unmistakable. "Position yourselves as far apart as you can within the jump-stream. You will be jumping in seven-five seconds."

//Tower, do I read correctly?// Another pilot asked.

"Seven-zero seconds." Isa answered.

On the Nav-globe the four ships began to madly scramble to follow Isa's commands.

Kalle burst into his apartment. There was not much in his room other than a simple cot and a few tool pouches that lay around the floor. He stopped his momentum when he put out one foot and shoved against his bedroom door. Hanging in the closet was upper-half of a soft-suit. He was already wearing the pants and boots of the suit—the strength and durability of the materials' resistance to both vacuum and sharp objects proved invaluable when working.

The old-hand completed dressing himself, and as the jacket sealed he felt the familiar tingle of the suit pressurizing around him. The armored vest that followed contained two emergency air bladders that gave him twenty minutes of reserve atmosphere. Ignoring the more cumbersome oxygen belt, he grabbed the thick gloves and his smart-helmet. Content that he had all the gear he needed, the old-hand slid on his helmet. Sensors read the atmosphere and determined that it was still within human conditions, and so his suit's air-vents remained open.

Without anything else to collect, Kalle ran back into the hall. His arms and legs moved comfortably in the lower gravity and his body naturally adjusted to the stride of a long distance runner. He knew where he had to go, and he knew just how far away it was.

The siren sang loudly across the tower as another gravity drive fell into thermal lock-down. Although the cooling system was more than sufficient for the average load of day-to-day activities, the sheer number of jumps taking place in such a short amount of time had already strained the equipment far past its normal levels. The stack-jumping had helped to delay the inevitable breakdown, but not for long.

With the fourth engine down, Isa automatically altered

traffic. Pops was beginning to show very species-specific signs of stress. He was blinking madly, as if his eyes had lost all hydration.

Touching his microphone, Pops triggered the old-hand's frequency. "Kalle, are you almost there?"

//*I'm just opening the engine room now.*// The human's voice shot back.

Down by the engine room, the old-hand pushed two final buttons and the entire door-assembly opened. The blast of heat was severe, and it physically pushed itself against him. The soft-suit did its job and the air filter kicked in, cooling its vents enough to make the air breathable. The room's noise was tremendous. Four loud klaxons were singing, and four large red lights were blinking.

//*We've just lost our fourth engine.*// Pops updated Kalle on the status of the situation.

"Yeah, I kind of got that hint." The old-hand spoke back. His Datapad picked the words from his helmet and relayed them through the station's communication system.

Stepping through the doors, the old-hand stared at the glowing engines. The station had six gravity drives, and the remaining two were already sounding rough.

The coolant was shunted to an exterior radiator, where the cold vacuum of space was normally sufficient enough to absorb the drive's heat. The main coolant pipe had a termination that extended into the engine room. It was capped by a large, bolted end. The bolts were easily the size of Kalle's wrists, and the time it would have taken to remove even one manually would have been too long for the life of the remaining engines. Besides, none of the wrenches Kalle wore were strong enough to move a single bolt, and his micro-torch did not have near enough power to cut a hole in the large end-cap.

There had to be a quicker way.

Fortunately, the room also doubled as a storage for company tools. Grabbing the first tool-chest he saw, Kalle cut the lock with his torch. The gear inside wasn't great, but it was more than adequate for the job. He was thankful for the gloves he'd grabbed from his apartment, as they protected him from the otherwise searing metal surfaces

Isa's strings of Selthian curses were loud in Kalle's helmet. The old-hand took a moment to lower his headset's volume, and it was a good thing too because the next moment another klaxon joined the quartet.

//Kalle, we—//

"I know, Isa." The old-hand said, interrupting the Selthian controller. "I'm right here."

Grabbing a grinding wheel, Kalle ran for the end-cap. The tool was loaded with a diamond and Urite cutting grit. It was more than strong enough to handle a few bolt-heads. He pulled the trigger and the old-hand felt the wheel begin to spin.

"I'm fixing your problem right now." The human spoke sharply, and then touched the wheel to the first bolt he could reach.

"I've got one jump left, and still a dozen ships to launch." Isa yelled in frustration, but she had enough sense to cover her mouthpiece so as not to panic anyone listening in.

"I'm aware of the situation." Pops replied, still attempting to maneuver more people on board the few remaining vessels. "Kalle's on it. He will fix it."

"I wish I had your certainty, Pops, but things are looking a little drastic from where I'm sitting." Isa replied acidly. Releasing the microphone, she snarled into it with complete and total vehemence. "Cargo ship one-zero-six, why are you launching? You are carrying no civilians."

//We are carrying all-important data-files that belong to the company. Our ship does not have sufficient life support for civilians.//

Isa was about to reply but Pops caught her attention. "He's right, Isa. I used to run a small fleet of those and they barely carry enough atmosphere for one person, let alone any passengers."

The Selth replied with her own comment. "It seems like a waste. Isn't there something we can do?"

Pop's suggestion was instant. "Don't jump him, until all the civvies are gone."

Isa's reply was cut short when she saw a flash from the viewing window. Reaching over, the Selth dragged Pops around the desk and shoved him to the ground. There was the sound of hundreds of pin-headed impacts against the shield of the tower. The two senior staff looked firstly at each other, then, as one, the peered over the counter and out the dura-shield.

The cargo-ship was gone, blown into thousands upon thousands of tiny particles. No other ships had disappeared, but there was little time for relief. The remaining civilian population was beginning to riot.

The sudden pain caught Telfer by surprise. The rock had almost taken out his eye. It had been thrown from the crowd and had probably been stolen from one of the rare horticultural displays in the market. Putting his helmet back on, Telfer still felt small within the armor of his suit. He had no way to tame the sea of frightened people that were trying to squeeze their way into the ships.

"Pops, Isa, could you two please hurry up?" He called out into his helmet. A large alien that Telfer was unfamiliar with appeared out of nowhere and demanded a place on board the ship. "NOW."

"Wait your turn like everyone else. Skipping the line will get you nowhere. The ships will fit every single one of you, but you are slowing down the process for everyone." Telfer tried to explain in hurried Basic, but the brute was having none of it. The beast bodily picked Telfer up by his shoulders and seemed about to throw the tiny human, but then the alien crumbled to the ground and Telfer fell with a little less eloquence than he desired.

It was Telfer's Kackle coworker who had subdued the brute, with a very heavy pipe. Turning to face the crowd, the giant warrior-alien roared as loud as he could for peace and quiet. It worked, and the crowds seemed to straighten magically.

"Thanks." Telfer said, happily taking the offered arm.

"Don't mention it." The Kackle said calmly. "I just thought you might have needed some help."

"Yeah, I do, but we're all going to need lots of help real soon." The human admitted.

Help was on its way. Kalle cut through the sixth bolt, leaving another half a dozen still in place. Coolant already leaked through the seals, but it wasn't leaking fast enough to cool the engines.

Stepping out of the way of the cap, Kalle tried to figure out how to cut the next bolt. The old-hand was certain that when the pressure cap let go, it would do so on a grand scale. He had already felt the end-cap tremble as it held back the pressurized coolant.

The entire station shuddered as another jump took place and the station's overtaxed system began to shut down.

"Oh well, I'm going to die sooner or later." Kalle sighed, as he climbed atop the pipe and leaned forward. He touched the blade to the bolt. Disk and metal wore away, eroding each other at an incredible rate. Kalle watched, hoping to stop cutting before the bolt failed. He dug the blade deeper, delicately feeling for that fine line before-

The end cap snapped off and traveled the length of the room. Coolant flooded the engine chamber, freezing everything it contacted and sucking the heat from the over-strained engines.

The sudden silencing of the alarms was a welcome relief. "To all ships, please head to your closest jump-point. Be prepared as I will maneuver each ship as I see fit." The Selth controller cried victoriously.

Happily cupping her pickup, Isa cheered gratefully. On the Nav-globe, ships hurried to their closest jump-points. Sparing a moment, the Selth caught Pop's glance. The Oursinian was smiling.

"Well, Isa," Pops chuckled. "Can I say, I-told-you-so?"

"Bite me, you old badger." Isa responded as she stuck out her tongue playfully. Switching communication frequencies, she once more spoke into her microphone.

"Kalle, you did it. We're back in business."

The Selth paused, expecting one of the human's witty retorts, but when one was not forthcoming Isa leaned closer to her console.

"Kalle?"

Reaching out with her hands, the Selth began typing out a text message. The simple words 'Are you alright?' were sent a moment later, but they never got to their intended destination. Instead, Isa's computer flashed out with the words . . .

USER UNAVAILABLE.

Chapter 6

Galactic Standard Time:

GST is the time system recognized as standard by the Galactic Sphere. Since time is both affected by gravity and velocity, GST is calibrated by the Time Stations located around the neutral star Vsg1961951. There, multiple chronological devices calculate an exact time, which is then transmitted throughout the galaxy along Network nodes. Any ship that travels past a GST emitting node is synchronized. This allows for a much more standard dating system.

Although seconds are relatively unchanged, and minutes and hours have their own equivalents, which can be seen on this table here, the measurements of days, months, weeks and years are different.

A day in GST time is about 32 GST Long Units, or 32.012 Earth Standard hours. One day is broken up into four Quarters, and Quarters are halved into Eighths (4 hours equivalent).

One week in GST time is 10 GST days long, and it takes 4 Weeks to make a month, and 10 months to a year. This makes 1 GST year 400 GST days long or almost one-and-a-half Earth Years, for comparison.

I**F THE STINGING PAIN FROM** the rock's collision under his eye wasn't enough, his ears felt like they were about to explode as his wife's desperate voice sent them to ringing, almost causing him to stumble.

"Isa, I heard you." He grunted through the pain. "What's going on to make you scream so loud?"

//*It's Kalle.*// Isa's voice responded in urgent terror. //*I just lost him. I can't talk to him. Oh Gods, I, I might have killed him! You have to go find him!*//

"Slow down, Isa. I have a hard enough time understanding anything when the person who's talking to me is not panicking." Telfer snapped. His harsh comment worked, and Isa seemed to quiet. "Now, please speak to me in calm and relaxed Basic, and let's see if I can help you."

//*Something's wrong with Kalle.*// The Selth answered, attempting to relax. //*I sent him to the engine room to crash-cool the jump engines, but I've lost communication with him. He might be seriously hurt.*//

"So you want me to check on him?" Telfer asked calmly.

//*Pretty please, honey?*// Though her tone did not change, Telfer recognized the pleading in her words.

"I'm on my way." Her husband responded, and he began to jog the length of the station. It was a good thing that the artificial gravity was already low, because the hard-suit that Telfer wore was exhausting to move in.

The Kackle that Telfer had stood beside, began to run with him as well, but Telfer yelled through his com system. "Get the rest of the people loaded, and once they're on, get yourself out of here."

The Kackle snorted as he replied. //*But what about you? You won't make it back in time.*//

"I'll find another way!" Telfer answered as he disappeared around a corner. "Don't worry about me, I'm resilient."

And then, the human mumbled for his own ears alone, "I'm also going to be lost, very soon."

Although Isa's husband had worked on the station for years, he had never once had the need to work on the internal area. Sheepishly, Telfer cued up his communication device again. There was only a moment of static, and then his wife's voice came back into his helmet.

//Where are you?// The Selth spoke impatiently. *//Every second is crucial.//*

"You don't have to remind me." Telfer snapped back, "But you do have to guide me."

//I'm busy, but I'll try my best.// She sighed.

"Good, now where do I turn first?"

//Your other left!// Isa screamed in frustration.

Pushing out his hands, Telfer stopped his forward momentum as he attempted to realign himself, but he still smashed into the wall with force that would have bruised his ribs were it not for his hardsuit.

"Thanks, honey." He gasped, taking a moment to catch his breath. He was sweating inside of his suit and he would have removed it ages ago if he wasn't worried about explosive decompression if the station was breached.

"Is this the right corridor?" Telfer panted.

//Hold on. Keep moving. I need to track your movements.//

"I love you and all, Isa, but you're going to kill me." Telfer complained, but dutifully started to run.

//I love you too, but shut up and save your breath, dear.// Isa said, and from the tone of her voice, Telfer imagined that his wife was smiling. *//That's correct. Now keep your eyes to the left, and you should see a large set of heavy doors.//*

Following his wife's directions, Telfer finally found himself looking what his wife had explained to him. Panting like a Grazzead mountbeast, the human threw himself against the thick portal and struggled to catch his breath.

//Did you find it?// Isa asked.

"I'm leaning up against it. Give me a moment to breathe."

//Okay, I have to guide another ship, but keep me posted, please.//

"Yeah, sure." Telfer cried out, and then he fell to his knees. The suit's environmental dampers were working overtime just to keep the visor from fogging. He grumbled to himself between billowing breaths. He had just run half the station. He was exhausted, and he hadn't told Isa the bad news: the engine room doors were sealed behind an even thicker set of blast doors.

With an exaggerated exhale, the human thumped his helmet against the doors. His visor crackled, and the outside section of his view froze solid. The environmental gear kicked in and defogged the hardsuit, but the results had been noticed. The doors were thick with frost, and were so cold that the floor around it was freezing solid.

"Oh great." Telfer spoke to no one in particular. "If Kalle is in there, than he's as stiff as a board by now."

He needed some way to open the door. Slowly pulling himself to his feet, Telfer searched around him for anything that could help. There was nothing he recognized except for a number-pad mounted beside the portal. It was the same kind of number-pad used on the doors at the cargo-bay. The human had once been briefed on a series of codes that would open station access in event of an emergency.

"I hope the numbers are the same for all the doors." Telfer whispered to himself. He was so nervous that it took three tries to get the combination correct, but he succeeded and the moment the doors were slightly apart the atmosphere of the hallway collided with the sub-zero temperatures of the engine room and a heavy, icy mist was formed. It was so thick that it became impossible to see and it was only the fact that Telfer had been facing the doors when they opened that allowed him to find his way inside.

"Kalle!" Telfer screamed, but he quickly remembered there

was no way for the old-hand to hear Telfer through the hardsuit. Mentally slapping himself upside the head, the Debtee walked through the doors with his arms stretched out in front of him. He made several unsteady steps and suddenly there was nothing beneath his leading foot. The weight of his suit overbalanced him and Telfer fell onto the descending steps. The final impact hurt the worst, and Telfer lay there, not really stunned, more embarrassed.

Summoning up his resolution Telfer pulled himself to his feet and continued to wander deeper into the thick, icy fog. He was lost, but his suit had more than enough air for him to wait out the mists. However, he did not know how bad Kalle's situation was.

"Would you please just show me a clue?" Telfer sighed into the clouds.

A hand reached from the mists and closed itself about Telfer's neck as the cracked and splintered visor of Kalle Aaron clunked against Telfer's helmet. There was a brief moment of mumbling, and then Telfer's hardsuit realized what was going on and adjusted itself for contact communication.

". . . *Ignorant, stupid, selfless conceited IDIOT!*" Kalle's voice was loud and Telfer thanked his stars that he had already lowered his hardsuit's volume. "*What were you thinking?*" The old-hand continued to scream, obviously no worse for wear.

"I'm here to rescue you." Telfer stumbled over the words, realizing that it was Kalle who had found him in the thickly congealed mists. "Isa lost contact with you."

"*Of course she lost contact with me.*" The old-hand shouted, and then he held up his left arm. The Datapad that he wore was smashed, and its cracked and frozen surface was lifeless. "*The end cap blew off and took me for a ride across the engine room. I flung myself clear at the last second.*"

"Not without some apparent injuries though." Telfer added, and tapped one finger against Kalle's helmet.

"Hazards of the occupation." His friend snapped and swatted

Telfer's finger aside. "*C'mon, your hardsuit is freezing up. The joints are going to lock soon.*" And before Telfer could comment,Tthe old-hand dragged the dock-worker over to one of the jump engines. It was cherry red, and all the coolant did as it touched the hot metal was vaporize.

Continuing his hold on Telfer's neck, Kalle continued speaking. "*You shouldn't be here. We have maybe two jumps left, and then all the engines are going to trip out on thermal overload. I doubt that any ships are going to wait for us.*" His voice was cross. "*You should have been on a vessel long ago.*"

Stepping closer to the hot engine Telfer felt the joints of his suit begin to loosen. "I came looking for you. Isa thought you might have been seriously hurt. Besides, I'm not leaving this station without my wife."

"*Bah, married people and your damned sentimentalities.*" Kalle snorted.

//*Telfer, did you find him?*// Isa had tapped back into her husband's channel. Her unexpected voice caused Telfer to jump.

"He's fine Isa," The husband answered. "Just a little cantankerous from a near brush with death. Otherwise, he's no worse for wear."

//*That's a relief. Does he think he can milk one more jump for us?*//

Kalle moved Telfer's head so that he was looking at the jump engine. It sparked, sizzled, and the next moment there was a loud clunk that shook the decking of the engineering section.

The old-hand shook his head. "*Isa, this is Kalle.*" The old-hand spoke, knowing that Isa would have heard his comments through her husband's suit. "*Three engines are dead, and the other three will maybe let you jump once more each.*"

There was no response. When they realized that Isa was silent Kalle began to pull upon Telfer's arm.

"*We'd better get going, if we want to get out of here in one piece.*" Kalle explained, as he dragged his companion along with him. "*We don't have a hope of getting to any of the other ships on time.*"

"Well, I did have a plan." Telfer added, almost as an afterthought.

"*Like what, grab a skiff, fill it with spare oxygen, and hide in the asteroids?*" Kalle snapped back bitterly, somehow locating the stairs that had tripped his companion.

The hard-suited one gawked for a moment as he tried to find a witty retort, yet none came and the human simply shrugged his shoulders as he uttered out the word, "Maybe."

Kalle snorted loudly into his helmet before he pulled Telfer through the doors and out into the hall. Once the two of them were free from the mists, the old-hand spun back to face his companion. "*Continue with your plan then, but Telfer, make sure you have four skiffs ready to go. I'm certain that neither your wife nor Pops have even considered any route of escape. I'll see you at the docks shortly. Do you understand?*"

"Perfectly." Telfer agreed, and then he paused. "Which way to the docks?"

"*Down that hall, for a good five to ten minutes at a full-out run.*" Kalle thumbed the direction. "*I've got a few things I have to do first.*"

The humans split, each heading to their own destinations.

The door slammed open and Kalle once more ran into his room. He had already removed his cracked helmet and ripped the remains of his Datapad from his arm. Flinging the refuse as far from him as he could, Kalle dug into his closet and removed spares of both, along with the oxygen belt that he had previously abandoned. The two air bladders inside his vest had recharged their tanks and Kalle felt just a little safer with the extra time that the belt afforded. He had come close to expending the vest's supply already back in the engine room. Telfer had probably saved his life after all. Feeling a moment of guilt, the old-hand sighed regretfully and made a mental note to thank him.

"One jump left, Isa." Pops said, as he checked the distance from the station to the attacking fleet. "And they still just wait."

"I don't like it." The controller agreed. "I wonder, what're they're waiting for?"

Even as the Selth asked that question, another two ships appeared out of fold-space and joined the mysterious fleet. There were dozens of enemy ships already lined up outside and they had demonstrated their firepower enough times to make the two on the bridge twitchy.

"I'm not quite sure." Pops admitted. "Are the jump lines clear yet?"

"They should be, in about one more minute." Isa spoke as she took another glance out the window to the ships beyond.

"I just hope our visitors wait that long." Pops said. His nose wrinkled in very Oursinian fashion.

Although he had spent the better part of an hour running about the station, Kalle was not tired. The sirens echoed along the empty hall and it added adrenaline to the old-hand's movements. The old-hand turned a corner, and had to avoid a collision with the little girl who was crying on the middle of the floor. Stepping aside rapidly, Kalle felt himself collide with the wall of the corridor, and he used the impact to throw himself back to the center of the hallway. With his momentum spent, the old-hand turned to look at who he had almost run over.

"Adorinda?" He asked, before he bent down to examine if he had hurt her.

"DIE PIRATE, DIE, YAAAAH!" A broom swatted the old-hand across his helmet. Kalle took the blow with more grace than he felt before he grabbed the handle and ripped it from Fallon's grasp. Without caring about its flight path, he threw the broom down the hall and immediately stood to his full height.

"STAY AWAY FROM MY SISTERS!" It was Joshua who ran forward, which surprised Kalle because he had never expected the young tech to be brave, or foolish enough, to attack him. Joshua had found an old frying pan, and was waving it madly back and forth as he charged.

Stepping out of the way, Kalle reached out with one hand and snatched the pan from Joshua's fingers. Again, the old-hand tossed the improvised weapon down the hall.

Unwilling to admit defeat, both Fallon and Joshua leapt at him and without any effort Kalle shoved the two fighting children to the floor. "That's ENOUGH!" He shouted, his voice easily bellowing out from the breathing vents of his helmet. Adorinda stopped crying, Fallon froze, and Joshua continued to struggle until Sudhir finally spoke from the doorway he had been hiding in.

"That's not a Pirate. That's Mister Aaron."

The two pinned children froze. Adorinda, pulled herself to her feet and immediately latched on to the old-hand. She was crying out of fear, and the sudden gift of any familiar figure was a welcome relief for the little girl. Sheepishly, the two attackers pulled themselves to their feet. "Are we going to be punished?" Fallon asked, casting her eyes to the floor.

"I don't care about that, right now." Kalle snapped crossly. "I want to know why you guys aren't on a ship or already through a jump-gate?"

"We were never assigned one, sir." Fallon spokel keeping her gaze downcast. The comment that Kalle was about to make died in his throat. Taking one steadying breath, the old-hand hugged the little girl who was still clinging to him, before he set her down beside her companions and raised his Datapad to his mouth.

Isa heard a familiar chime through her headset. "Go ahead, Kalle." Isa spoke with her voice remarkably level.

Back with the Drudges, Kalle glanced at the kids before he spoke.

"Isa, how many jump-worthy ships are left aboard the station?"

//One, but it's at the opposite end of the station from where you are. You want to get aboard it?//

"Maybe, how soon until you make the last jump?" The old-hand enquired.

//As soon as the jump lanes are clean. Maybe a minute?// Isa answered.

It was too late to get the Drudges aboard that ship nor was there a way he could get them to the jump point either, short of a miracle. Kalle grunted one final word into his Datapad before he released the communications.

"Thanks."

Crouching down so that he was looking all four of the Drudges in the eyes, Kalle spoke to them.

"I want you guys to head to the cargo bay where Mr. Laughlin works, and when you get there, tell Mr. Laughlin to find you guys some suits to wear." Kalle paused, and watched as hope and realization slowly spread across the Drudges' faces. "I've got a few things I have to do first, but I'll be there soon, and I want you guys to be ready to leave. Do you understand?"

The four children paused, and then all of them started nodding at once. It was all Kalle could do not to suddenly break out in laughter. The children looked ridiculously cute.

"Good, go, I'll see you soon." He ordered.

Telfer was a little frustrated. He had fueled three wraiths and had thrown as many emergency supplies as he could onto them. He was sweating and he wished that he could wipe the perspiration from his brow, but the hardsuit prevented such movements. Placing his hands upon his hips, the human surveyed his work.

It was time for the hardest task of all: waiting.

"All ships, stand by for jump." Isa advised. She took a deep breath and held it for a moment.

"It's about time. That last ship took forever." Pops said, nervously glancing between the Nav-globe and the looming fleet.

Exhaling, the Selth let her hand cover the microphone. "Well, if that last ship had told us about its engine problems beforehand, we wouldn't have had to wait. Anyways . . ."

Freeing her hand from the audio pickup, the Selth began the countdown. Pops listened, eagerly wringing his hands. Unnoticed by either of the two, the lift began to move.

As Isa threw the switch, Kalle stepped his foot onto the tower's decking. He watched from across the room as the last ships winked out of existence from the Nav-globe. A sixth and final light appeared on the error screen and with it came a lessening of pressure as the dampener system tried to compensate for the lack of gravity generators.

"Well, there we go." Pops said as he sighed in a mixture of relief and defeat. Only once his lungs were empty did the Oursinian become aware of the figure that stood in the doorway.

Without further ado, the old-hand strode across the bridge, his heavy space-boots clanked along the planking, until he stood where both Isa and Pops could see him. "Get your gear and let's get out of here." The old-hand ordered

"Where to?" Isa asked, slowly removing her headset. "I just sent the final ships into jump-space." Once more the Selth let her eyes journey out to the window.

"Your husband has a plan, and let's just speculate something for a moment." The human took his own deep breath. "Let's just say that my retirement policy is not just a hunk of stones, floating in space. Now, let's also assume that it's deep enough in a field of rocks so that we could get lost in there. Does that interest you any?"

"Sounds pretty static." Isa spoke out hesitantly, Pops however, seemed to be on the edge of his seat.

"When something in those hunk of stones, if you would let me continue my idea here, has a fold engine?" Kalle continued, unfazed.

Isa was not, and she jumped to her feet, grabbed the old-hand's helmet in both of her strong hands, and planted a kiss onto his visor. "Kalle Aaron, that's the best news I've heard all day." Spinning away, the Selth started for the lift, but paused when she realized that neither of her friends were moving. The human's visor was pointed at the Oursinian representative, who sat there, chewing his lips.

"Pops?" Kalle asked, hesitantly.

"Go on ahead. I'll catch up if the chance arises. I would be with you right now, but what happens if those ships out there decide to move? Someone has to buy you guys a window of opportunity. If you guys make it to the cargo bay, and our friends out there haven't attacked, I'll join you then." Pops slowly stood up, and made his way to a closet where he opened the door and began removing an old, ancient hardsuit. Looking back at the two Freebies that he had shared the last few years with, the old Oursinian smiled.

"Now get going, you two. The faster you get out of here, the faster I can join you."

Without another word, Kalle and Isa ran for the lift.

Telfer looked up from his welding job. He admired his rushed, but suitable work. He had realized that if several wraiths were joined together, then they would be faster and more powerful than just one sled alone.

It looked like something that had been chewed on, and then spat out by, a Tarronian Dargo Beast.

"I just hope it holds." The human admitted to himself.

"Can I ride in that one?"

The voice caused Telfer to jump, but his movements were so minimal that the hardsuit did not respond and launch him off the decking. The four Drudges were eyeing Telfer's contraption.

"What are you kids doing here?!" Telfer shouted out in surprise.

"Mister Aaron sent us here." Adorinda spoke quietly.

"And he said you could fit us in some space suits." Fallon finished.

"He did? Well," Telfer eyed the children, and inwardly cursed his friend for sticking him with this latest task. "Let's go see what

I can find. C'mon, over here."

The children practically squealed in delight and relief.

The only stop that Isa and Kalle had made was at her quarters. Kalle had waited outside before the Selth returned, already buckling herself into a space suit that Kalle had rarely seen. It was a Selthian dancer suit.

Kalle was glad that he was wearing his helmet. It stopped Isa from noticing just how badly he was gawking, but he recovered almost instantly from the shock and hurried to keep pace with her. It was obvious that the Selth was running at less than her full speed, and the grace she had in the suit revealed the warrior training that she must have had growing up.

Isa suddenly stopped and held out an arm. Both human and Selth instinctively became silent. Something happened between the two of them. It was a blending of thoughts rarely seen outside of militant units. Remaining silent, the two peaked at the reflections in the hallway. There was someone approaching.

Together the two stepped into the intersection, and the sight of the suited figures caught Nozomi by surprise. She screamed and leapt back in horror.

"Nozomi?" Kalle asked in shock at seeing his friend still on the station.

"Nozomi?" Isa asked a moment later, as she tried to process the same thoughts.

"Who are you, and how do you know my name?" She demanded.

Reaching up to his helmet, Kalle removed it and at the sight of a familiar face Nozomi relaxed before her face clouded with rage. "What are you two still doing on the station?" Nozomi yelled angrily. "Didn't you two hear the sirens?"

If the look of frustration on Kalle's face could have been captured and sold, it would have been used in place of most refrigeration units.

"That's what I was going to ask you." He shot back. "Isa and

I have been helping the others to escape. What's your excuse?"

Nozomi seemed taken aback and she stumbled on her tongue for a moment. Finally, she looked away slightly, as a crimson flush began to tinge her skin. "I was waiting for everyone else to leave." She finally answered.

"What, why?" Kalle shot back.

"Because I have my own escape plan."

"So do we." Isa responded. "We're on our way to the loading docks."

"So am I." Nozomi snapped.

"Well, what are we waiting for?" The Selth said acidly. "When the going gets tough, the tough get going."

"What about the rest of us?" Nozomi asked, but she had already stepped forward. Isa and Kalle looked at each other, shrugged, and followed.

"Somehow, I don't think that's going to work." Telfer sighed. He had searched through every closet that he had found and had been forced to admit defeat. Even if two children squeezed themselves together into one suit, the waste disposal system might have accidently sucked the air from one of the Drudge's lungs, or captured a toe, or the suit would respond wrongly to the motions of the children and potentially fling them off into space.

The best option, although the human didn't want to inform the children, was to stick each of the kids into live-animal transport boxes. It wasn't glamorous, but it would do in a pinch. Rapidly growing frustrated, Telfer took his eyes off of the empty stack of transport crates. He hoped to find another way around the situation.

"Why don't we go another bay down? Maybe we'll find something there." Telfer suggested as he guided the children along.

The three were almost at the loading dock's doors when Kalle signaled a halt. Nozomi pushed herself against a wall and tried to remain silent while the two suited figures waited, unsure of what they were about to face, until the old-hand cursed in some alien tongue that Nozomi had never heard.

"What are you doing here? Haven't you heard the sirens?" He screamed out in frustration.

The Grondonian practically leapt out of its skin as it turned to face the trio. His arms flailed in panic but he managed to hold onto a small package in his long and deceptively maneuverable arms.

Kalle strode forward and practically bowled the geologist over. "Don't tell me you had an alternate escape route planned." The human demanded. The Grondonian seemed to chuckle as it rapidly blinked its multi-faceted eyes. Nozomi did not know the species as well as either of her companions did, so she missed out on the obvious tells that indicated the Grondonian was ashamed.

"I was, in the powder room." He spoke out.

"For that many units? What were you doing in there?" Kalle roared through his helmet.

The Grondonian pulled himself to his full height, which was surprisingly tall, dwarfing even Isa, before responding. "Some of my people's natural functions should not be rushed for fear of-"

Cutting the Grondonian short, the old-hand stormed past the scientist and slapped his hands against the loading dock's doors. Spinning back to face the geologist, Kalle posed one more question.

"Do you have an escape plan?"

"Not really. I was just going to get into one of the wraiths that I was issued and-gagh!" The Grondonian's words were cut short again as Kalle used one arm to grab the geologist, and the other to brace himself as he shoved the Grondonian through the doors. The geologist stumbled and almost tripped over a bastardized merging of several wraith-loaders.

The other three followed behind the geologist. Telfer was knelt beside his hastily welded contraption, praying that the Grondonian had not broken it.

Raising his hands, Kalle yelled loudly into the air.

"Does everybody have a suit?"

Only Telfer and Isa raised their hands.

Groaning in frustration, Kalle grabbed the Grondonian's overly reflective clothing, exposing the green and brown mottled flesh beneath as he pulled the hapless geologist along with him. Pointing his free hand at the live-cargo-containers, Kalle began to issue orders.

"Kids, see if you guys can squeeze into those things. Telfer, find this Grondonian a suit. Isa, let's go get some more wraiths ready. There's bound to be enough here to work with."

Ignored in the hubbub, Nozomi quietly slipped away to her cargo container.

The squealing and yelling in the cargo bay only continued to grow in intensity as Isa and Kalle attempted to wrestle a damaged wraith out from amongst a pile of scraps, the Grondonian complained that not one suit was suitable for him, and Fallon struggled with her until-then-unrealized claustrophobia.

They all stopped when Nozomi's cargo box split apart with a tremendous bang. The sides fell open, and the naked, giant mass pulled itself to its feet. The thing was almost as tall as the whole bay and there was no mistaking the awesome grace with which it rose.

There, standing before the small crowd of onlookers, did the Nobilis reveal itself.

Chapter 7

Burrow Bombs:

Originally created by the Lertista Mining Corp, Burrow Bombs are essentially explosive charges with drill bits mounted on one end. They had originally been designed and programmed to drill into rock, close to precious minerals, and then detonate to assist the miners in extracting the ore.

In a short time though, it was found that Burrow Bombs were more expensive to produce and operate than the minerals they helped to mine.

Militant companies however, were more than willing to purchase the design as Burrow Bombs are very useful in destroying installations and fortifications.

POPS WAS SURPRISED THAT it had taken the threatening ships so long to advance, but when they finally did, there was no hesitation about their intent. The Overseer slapped the last piece of his hardsuit closed before he took a seat by Isa's panel. Reaching for the communications table, Pops plugged his suit into the console.

◆ ◆ ◆

The Oursinian's voice crackled over Isa's helmet, Telfer's headdress, and Kalle's Datapad. //*Our uninvited guests are inbound, and they're not taking it slow.*//

Almost everyone reacted to the warning. The only one who had not moved was the Grondonian. He had not stopped staring at the beast in front of him.

The Nobilis was almost a dozen times high as Kalle was tall. It was smooth, white and obviously organic. Its two center toes were cloven, and a smaller clawed toe rested on each side of each foot. The heel was lifted off of the ground, even though there was an opposing toe where the ankle was bent. The arms were standard in proportion to a human, but they ended at hands which had three fingers and two thumbs each, one on each side of the palm.

The body was curved, and wide "hips" jutted out at the waist. The legs—although different than a human's—were nonetheless fine and elegant, like a ballerina. The chest was femininely rounded; the abdomen was slight, smooth, but when the creature moved, muscles could be seen shifting beneath the flesh, revealing the great strength held within. Mounted on the wide shoulders were two large cylinders, pointing back to front, and out of the front of each cylinder were tiny cones, recessed far enough inside the cylinders that Doc could not tell how they attached to the rest of the beast. Sequestered between the two cylinders was the head. It was gaunt and featureless, save for two opaque, blank eyes that stared into nothingness, a spike that emerged from the chin, and a sail, that started at the spike, divided the face in half, and rose almost as tall again as the head was high.

It towered above them with its back open as the Drudges were loaded within. Telfer threw Adorinda up to Nozomi, who hurriedly stuffed the youngest child into a corner of the cockpit before Joshua could be lifted next.

Isa and Kalle tried to figure out if Telfer's bashed together inventions would work. "How fast is fast, Pops?" Kalle asked, before he freed his hands to flip one of the cargo sleds over.

//*Very, as in I'm watching them get steadily bigger, right now.*//

"Get out of there. Get to an escape pod!" Isa yelled as she frantically heaved a busted booster across the loading dock.

//*I'm afraid there's very little time for even that, my dear.*//

Pops voice sounded frighteningly calm.

The Oursinian continued to stare at the approaching vessels. He held himself erect and his hands maintained a death grip upon the communication wire that joined him to his friends.

"Might I suggest that you put your energy towards flight from this station, and I do mean immediately." Taking a steadying breath, Pops blinked to clear his eyes.

There was a flash from the mass of approaching vessels, and a moment later the station shuddered and alarms began to sing across the tower. Without worry Pops prepared himself to meet his fate. Sinking into his chair, the Oursinian took one more moment to reflect on the friendships he had made with all who he was trying to protect. His death, he decided, would be a noble end, and while it was not the death that Pops truly desired, it would be fittingly heroic all the same.

"Make your escape soon though, because I do not want my sacrifice to be a waste."

With a touch of his fingers, he released all of the security drones that had been kept waiting. Guiding them into a swarm, Pops built a mobile shield between his friends and the attackers.

"Good luck, and may you find yourselves blessed with speed."

Fallon clutched desperately to Nozomi's neck before she was dragged within the confines of the living giant. Having thrown all of the children into the waiting arms of Nobilis' pilot, Telfer yelled up to the woman who towered above him. "How much room is left in there?"

Ducking her head inside for only an instant, Nozomi poked back out to face the miner.

"We can probably fit two more adults inside."

Pausing for a moment, Isa looked over to her husband, and then aimed her sights at the Grondonian, who just continued to stare in awe at the living giant.

"Well, help us find some more boosters, Telfer, and we can all leave together." Isa commanded.

The white giant bent down and offered its hands.

"That's not necessary." Nozomi explained, still leaning out from her, thing. "We can't afford to waste time. Nobilis can carry whoever doesn't fit inside."

There was a chiming, musical sound that erupted from within the hole that Nozomi and the kids occupied. Nozomi continued with a slight, embarrassed grin on her face "Just one thing. Um, the ones riding in the hands have to have a strong constitution, and a suit that can handle vacuum." She added the last part of her sentence almost as if it was an afterthought.

Stepping forward, Kalle was about to volunteer when both Telfer and Isa put their hands against the old-hand's softsuit. Leaning close, the Selth spoke so that only the two human males could hear her.

"It has to be Telfer and me, Kalle." Isa said hurriedly. "You know where your rocks are. Besides, my suit has gravity compensators."

"And my suit has a G-Ballast." Telfer added casually. "Plus, my hardsuit's twice the size of anyone else's. I'll ride, you steer."

Stepping away from the old-hand, the couple turned and faced Nozomi and her mecha. For a fleeting moment, they both reached out, and touched their gloved hands together, before they climbed into the waiting palms.

//*Get going.*// Isa advised.

Listening to the good advice, Kalle grabbed the Grondonian and then leapt for the opening that Nozomi occupied.

It was surprisingly roomy. Nozomi was seated in a chair that was formed out of the very same organic-like substance that formed the rest of the room, and so were the four children. The adult female rested her hands against two small domes that protruded from her seats', 'hand rests'. Her concentration was solely focused on the opposite wall from the entry point while the children had their eyes glued to Kalle and the geologist.

No sooner had the old-hand and the Grondonian set foot within the room then the chamber closed behind them. The white organic substance flowed shut. It moved as if the flesh was almost liquid in substance.

"Grab on to something." Nozomi spoke out. The chamber walls became invisible. The entire loading dock seemed to spin as the mecha spun to face the massive cargo doors.

"LAUNCH!" Nozomi yelled, and the walls of the cargo bay seemed to blur as the mecha leaned forward and, through some strange method of propulsion, flung itself into the heavy material of the portals. The metal buckled and tore with almost no resistance as they flew out into the blackness of the vacuum.

He had been among the stars for far too long to have made it as a farmer. Space owned him, it ruled him, and it would hold the corpse that he was about to leave behind. At least, he would no longer be in bondage to the company. Pops had always felt, deep down in his heart, that he would never have escaped the chains of the corporation that held him while he breathed.

The camera that was focused on the loading dock displayed the quick, rather abrupt visual of something as it fled into space. The time for the final act had arrived. Reaching forward, the Oursinian gently touched one finger against his console and the station shuddered with the departure of every remaining device, pod and raft that it had.

There was very little indication that the advancing ships had fired again. The station did not shift as invisible light burned the metals of the hull beyond their melting points. One laser blast traveled right through the center of the station and destroyed the gravity dampeners. Released from his hold to the decking, Pops floated free from the chair.

Opening his mouth, Pops spoke his final words, his requiem.

"Kalle, I'm sorry that I will be unable to join you, but I have come to the conclusion that I shall stay here for the rest of my life, however brief it is.

"Isa, dear, may you one day find your blood welcoming you back with open arms. I understand you miss your family, and no woman should ever be apart from the ones that she loves.

"Telfer, may you earn the freedom that I have found to be fleeting, and may you cherish it with all the preciousness that you have in your heart, left over after caring for your lovely wife, of course.

"And to all those who flee with my friends, take care, and do not squander your lives. This is my epitaph, the request of a dying Oursinian."

Pops pulled the com line free from the console. The old representative cast his gaze back upon the glowing weapon ports of the advancing fleet. Spreading his arms wide, the stocky, powerful, yet gentle beast welcomed the rays of death and tubes of destruction that shot towards him. Filling his lungs one final time, the Oursinian sang out across the empty station that had been his final prison.

"I am Pops, the Freebie. Hear me roar!"

//POPS!//

Isa's voice echoed from the living walls but Kalle and the Grondonian did not notice. They had not found the time to settle into the flesh that surrounded them and with the mecha's launch the old-hand and the geologist had been flung against the recently closed wall at their backs. It had given slightly which had helped Kalle's body absorb the impact of the Grondonian colliding with him, but his ribs still bruised and he had no doubt that he was going to feel the new pain for a while.

Nozomi's machine was surprisingly agile. It had accelerated faster than almost any known vessel in existence, and it had done so with a far superior smoothness and control.

Swinging itself around, the living machine faced the station at the very moment that the refugee's former home expelled itself. Sleds and ships zoomed by as the attacking ships fired upon the jump-station and at the fleeing giant. The various vessels that Pops had controlled formed a protective umbrella over the refugees, shielding them from the destruction that rained down towards them.

The station vanished under the hail of fire, disintegrated, and disappeared. There was a momentary flash of light and only the tiniest of debris seemed to remain in place of the former steel behemoth.

Adorinda would have choked out a sob, but the sudden movement of the living machine forced the young girl to exhale sharply as it spun and evaded a sharp piece of the former station that flew by them.

Another glint of light caught the attention of the old-hand and it took alf his effort, even with the assistance of his suit, for Kalle to grunt out his singular warning.

"Incoming."

For some reason, Nozomi seemed to have full control of her consciousness as she spun her head and managed to maintain her mecha on its course for the floating rocks. She saw the very things that Kalle had warned her about.

"Pirate space fighters" Nozomi hissed, as she identified the threats, and in the process, named the ones who had destroyed the station.

Kalle wanted to ask her how she knew what they were up against, but he was still under too much pressure to make more than a grunt.

"Where do we go?" The pilot asked, desperate for some guidance.

"In." Kalle forced the word from his mouth.

With reckless abandon, Nozomi's mecha flew pell-mell into the asteroid field. The belt was relatively young, and it had not perfectly stabilized. There were still dangerous clusters of rocks

where collisions were imminent, while in other places the asteroids had spaced themselves out at safe and consistent distances.

Dropping several body-lengths, Nozomi's machine spiraled
past a gigantic rock as she attempted to put the stone between
them and their pursuers. No sooner were their pursuers out of
sight than the mecha seemed to come to a virtual standstill. The
sudden stop would have flung everyone from their seats, except
that Nozomi's mecha spun once and sealed everyone into their
place.

Finally able to breathe again, Kalle drew precious air into his
lungs. With a cough and gasp, Joshua regained consciousness.
Released from inertia's hold, the Grondonian clunked down to
the floor and the living flesh molded itself about the geologist.
Twisting herself around, Nozomi rested with her knees against
the back of her 'chair', and impatiently waited for Kalle to find
his voice.

"That's . . . eight times faster . . . than the sled I normally
rent . . . could possibly maneuver." Kalle panted.

From his place upon the floor the Grondonian seemed none-
the-worse-for-wear. "The movements that your mecha exhumes
seem to defy the normal laws of physics."

Ignoring the geologist, Nozomi looked with concern at the
old-hand.

"Are you alright, Kalle?" she asked.

"Not really, but I don't think I have a choice right now."
Kalle blurted out, and immediately followed his comment with
another deep breath. "I want you to head to the coordinates on
my Datapad."

Grabbing the device, Kalle ripped it off his suit and handed
it to his friend. Nozomi turned the device so that the screen was
upside down before she slapped the pad against the floor, where
it stuck fast.

<Can you find it?> Nozomi asked in her native tongue. The
Nobilis answered in its crystal clear, melodious sounds before it
blasted forward, deeper into the rocks as the asteroid that it had

hid behind exploded.

"They've found us! Hang on; it's going to get rough." Nozomi warned.

The brief moment of consciousness that he had suffered, vanished as Telfer once more felt the painful g-forces crush his body. Even with the high G-ballasts in his suit, Telfer felt every acceleration as a physical blow.

It was obvious that Nozomi's machine was trying to compensate for the incredible strain being put upon the couple it carried in its hands. Every time the mecha slowed down it pushed its hands out, which lessened the impact slightly, and it was vice-versa with the accelerations, but it was not enough to shield the couple from the pain of the great forces that they suffered through.

Naturally stronger than her husband and assisted by her reinforced, higher tech suit, Isa managed to maintain her consciousness, but it was no blessing. Since she was cupped within the hands of the mecha the Selth had not seen much of what had occurred, but every move, dip and turn left the Selth with numb feelings in her extremities, and she was beginning to see spots behind her eyes.

There was another sudden acceleration, and Isa felt her mind beginning to fade. She gritted her teeth so strongly that she feared she would crack several of her molars.

"There's . . . at least . . . a dozen . . . of them."

And with that warning Kalle passed into blessed blackness.

Craning her neck around Nozomi began to feel sick from the forces upon her. Nobilis was able to protect those who sat upon the floor far easier than the mecha was able to protect Kalle, Telfer, or Isa.

Even so, the Drudges did not have the physical endurance of their adult counterparts, and Adorinda and Joshua had already fallen unconscious due to the sheer power that the Nobilis's movements forced onto them.

Despite their speed, their aggressors were following without falter. Nozomi groaned. It didn't make sense to lead the Pirates to Kalle's hideout.

<Nobilis, deal with them.> The 'pilot' ordered in her native tongue. The chimes that were its voice sang out curtly. Straining her eyes, Nozomi could just make out the words that wrote themselves upon the fleshy wall.

<That's fine. Do what you have to.> Nozomi answered the question.

There were some very vibrant colors coming through from between the giant fingers . . . far more than what Isa wanted to view of the outside world. A feeling of horror suddenly eclipsed her, as the hand that held her had opened.

Unable to grab hold of the smooth flesh, Isa flew out at a tangent to the mecha's spin. Beside her, Telfer floated along. At least, that was what it felt like, but it was not the case. They had been released when Nozomi's machine had been traveling at high velocity, and since space offered little friction the couple was flying at the same speed, which was very fast indeed. To make matters worse, the path of their journey led directly towards an asteroid that was probably a quarter of the size of the station. At such a speed of impact there was no way that the couple would have survived.

Telfer was concentrating on their pursuers. Their ships were conical with two thruster jets that seemed to pivot, allowing the ships to move and twist in patterns that Telfer had never seen done in the vacuum of space. He swore that he could imitate the shape of the craft with his hand as he stuck his three central fingers together and wiggled his thumb and pinky. It was an amazing resemblance. It was only then that Telfer understood that he was no longer held in the Nobilis' massive hands.

Not that the hands were a good place to be. The white mecha spun, glowed, and seemed to leave a trail of light behind itself. One of the arms stretched outwards and the fingers straightened, and the hand traveled as if it was trying to slap one of the enemy ships from existence. Adjusting its thrusters, the Pirate's ship danced just out of reach of the swinging palm, and yet, as the hand passed close to the enemy vessel, the fingers glowed brighter and the enemy vessel passed from existence and vanished into oblivion.

Isa had not taken her eyes away from the approaching stone, which had amplified frighteningly in size. There was no way for the Selth to slow either her or her husband's velocity in time to save them from becoming smears upon the rock's surface. Closing her eyes, Isa prepared for the worst before she felt the soft feeling of Nozomi's mecha cushion her. It slowed the couple down and acted as a bolster between them and the rock, as the beast rolled along the surface with its body until it had put the boulder between itself and those that were chasing it.

Kalle came to. He felt like he wanted to be sick, but he couldn't, as everything in his body seemed to be knotted up at once. Swallowing, the human tried to understand where he was and what was going on.

There was a huge rock in front of him. A big pair of hands opened up, releasing Isa and Telfer from their grasps before they were caught again as only one of the hands closed over them. The other formed a fist, pulled itself all the way back, and then hammered against the giant asteroid. The rock flew away and there came from behind it three winks of light, as if something had exploded. It was silent though, and completely ethereal, but such was the nature of vacuum.

Whatever Kalle was inside turned then, and accelerated so rapidly that he once more passed into darkness.

The Grondonian, on the other hand, was awake and alert enough to speak.

"There's still at least eight left, miss." He spoke.

"I'm aware of that. I'm not blind." Nozomi's patience was obviously little for the geologist, but instead of raging against the thing that sat behind her, Nozomi focused her anger on their pursuers. The almost-instant destruction of four of their comrades had hardly slowed the remaining attackers down at all. There was a brilliant streak of light, and an arcing ball of energy flew past Nozomi's mecha.

Another asteroid was blown to smithereens as the weapon's blast vented its powers against the stone. As the rock disintegrated, Nozomi's mecha shot to the side and instantly changed directions. A large hunk of debris flew past the refugees and one more ship vanished under the impact it had with the stone.

Unable to maintain his silence, the Grondonian spoke out again. "Careful ma'am, the gravitational balance of the asteroid field is being disturbed with all of this destruction."

"Is that a serious problem in the short term?" Nozomi snapped back.

"In the immediate vicinity, yes!" The geologist screamed.

<Can you use that to your advantage?> Nozomi asked her mecha. There was a loud boom inside the cockpit before the Nobilis rocketed in the direction of its legs. The closest asteroids were sucked into a maelstrom that the machine's departure had left behind. Four of the enemy ships also became entangled, and they all succumbed to the bashing of multiple rocks against their hulls.

Without pause, the white giant shot back towards the three remaining vessels. Using its open hand, Nobilis crushed one of the ships against another asteroid. Spinning into a lovely pirouette, the mecha kicked out one cloven foot and removed the piloting booster from the side of another Pirate's vessel. Unable to control itself, the ship careened into its partner and the two of them exploded silently, their bright colors the only indication of their passing.

Taking a breath of relief, Nozomi sagged into her seat. The Drudges were recovering, through tears and moans of agony.

Falling to his hands and knees, the old-hand shook his head from side to side in an attempt to clear the cobwebs from his mind. As he was gyrating his skull, Kalle attempted to gasp out a cognitive sentence without vomiting into his helmet.""Continue ahead." Kalle coughed the words out of his mouth. "It usually takes me . . . at least three . . . long units to get to my hideout." Kalle spoke in amazement. It hadn't even been a sixth of the time, but they were almost there. Pulling himself off of the wall, the old-hand flattened himself against the floor and reached for the Datapad. As soon as he was prostrate, Kalle felt the living floor mold to him. It was suddenly easier to breath, and Kalle felt a little more cohesive as he realized that the surface he lay against was helping to absorb the movements of the machine.

"Do you see that asteroid up to the left? Head straight for it." Kalle spoke, already typing something into his Datapad. As the old-hand's fingers flew, he took the occasional glance upwards to re-coordinate Nozomi's mech.

"Now, head up ten degrees." Kalle directed as he risked a glance backwards. He could not see any pursuers. Casting his eyes forward once more, Kalle directed Nozomi to head straight for the largest of his three rocks.

From inside the hand, Isa and her husband watched in amazement as the Nobilis traveled towards a crater that occupied one of the poles of a spinning asteroid. The closer they got, the easier it was to see that the rock was opening, until it had made a hole in itself, large enough for the Nobilis to fit through.

Chapter 8

Dampeners:

*When humankind first began travelling in space, As-
tronauts, as they were called then, lived and worked in
micro-gravity environments. Not only did it take time to
adapt to the different lifestyle, but health of the early ex-
plorers suffered as their bone densities and muscle masses
were easily affected.*

*As they reached further into space, humankind at-
tempted to use centrifuges, heavy-mass generators or constantly accelerating vessels in order to create gravitational
environments. It wasn't until they made contact with the
Galactic Sphere that humans became party to elemental
gravitrons, which make both folding space, and artificially
induced gravity, possible.*

*Dampeners are systems that create small pockets of
gravity, normally by exciting gravitrons. As gravitrons
move, they attract together and become incredibly dense,
creating a small area of strong gravity. Placed both horizontally and vertically around the exterior of the vessel,
Dampeners are used to provide both comfortable levels of*

gravity for day to day operations, as well as dampening the effects of accelerations, from which they get their name.

L ADIES AND GENTLEMEN," Kalle's voice rang out clear and proud for all to hear. "Welcome to my retirement policy."

None of his friends had an easy time believing what was before their eyes; there was a small freighter hidden within the asteroid. The vessel was long and almost rectangular. The bridge stuck out in a pronounced distention at the bow. Above that a lifted area ran from the front to the center part of the ship, where the hull lost its rectangular shape and instead bulged out in almost a cylinder. The bow of the vessel was again rectangular, but at the top and bottom of a massive set of cargo-doors, were the primary thrusters arranged in two recessed crescents.

Happy that they had made it, Kalle directed Nozomi to the rear of his ship. The aperture opened for them, and the white alien folded itself into the fetal position, shaping its mass into a near sphere as it glided inside. The doors sealed themselves behind them, and the cargo-bay's darkness was countered as the exterior of Nozomi's machine began to glow.

"I have never seen a ship of this design before." The Grondonian spoke matter-of-factly.

"I don't doubt that." Kalle responded, before he looked up from his Datapad which he had once more affixed to his arm. Above their heads a select few lights began to burn, bringing slightly more illumination to the interior of the rather empty bay. The only change from the flat walls were two stairways that led from a single door at ground level, only to climb above their heads and turn into a cat-walk that circled the room.

"There's quite some history behind her, but it's nothing that would ever have made galactic news." Pulling himself to his feet, the old-hand turned back to the wall that had 'cushioned' him for most of the journey. "Atmosphere is light in here. Only the bridge and engine room have enough air for us to survive unassisted. I'm going to fetch a few atmo-masks, so hold your breath."

The flesh-walls opened, and the old-hand stepped through.

Gravity was much lighter than on the station. It took Kalle almost thirty seconds to fall the distance to the floor of the bay. As the old-hand made his descent, the white mecha opened its hands and released the couple that it had held within. Without much grace, Telfer and his hardsuit almost crashed to the floor, but he managed to retain his footing. His wife put the two humans to shame as she flipped from the palms that had held her and arched gracefully in the lessened gravity as it traveled across the empty bay, almost making it to the doors that led deeper into the bowels of the vessel. She grabbed the masks that Kalle would have undoubtedly taken much longer to get to. In the reduced gravity, her throw sent the masks flying straight and true to the two humans.

//*Catch.*// Isa yelled, and her husband fought with his suit to comply with his better-half's wishes. He managed to catch two of the objects, but that still left Kalle to grab the other four. Collecting alf the gear, the old-hand lifted one foot, which Telfer grabbed before Kalle straightened his back. Telfer stood as fast as he could, launching Kalle back towards the ceiling. One of the giant's hands grabbed the old-hand, and almost squished him against its smooth back, but at the last second the fleshy walls opened, and as he stumbled within, Kalle deposited the masks upon the floor, save one, which he offered to the Grondonian.

"You're coming with me." Kalle ordered as his voice leaked out from his helmet. "I need you on the bridge. Nozomi, stay here with the Drudges. If we can't get out of here in time, it's up to you to save them."

Before she could comment, the geologist snapped his mask into place with the motions of somebody who'd done it many times before.

"Kalle," Nozomi called out, causing the old-hand to pause. "Be careful." She advised. Even though she couldn't see his reaction through the visor of his helmet, Kalle smiled and threw a salute.

Once more the old-hand began to fall, but this time he had more to concern himself with as he tried to avoid landing on the geologist. The two touched down without incident and began the hopping, bouncing journey across the bay to the doors that took them deeper into the vessel.

By the time the two joined her, Isa was showing signs of impatience, but Telfer, who had already worked a full shift before the events of the day had started, just looked exhausted. Seeing that the team was more or less assembled, Isa opened the door and stepped through into the dimly lit hallway.

The ship was on emergency power, and the only lighting available was a dim, reddish hue that came from recessed panels in the walls and floor.

Reaching over, Kalle grabbed the wall, hung his body horizontally, and shoved off. Isa was next, and her movements belied the grace that was naturally hers. Telfer attempted to imitate the other two's actions, but his timing was off, and he only made several feet. Meanwhile the Grondonian easily passed the lingering human.

"Where's my skiff when I need it?" Telfer sighed, and instead of trying to imitate the others and their motions, he simply began to bounce his way along the floor.

Leading the motley gang, Kalle continued his rhythmic flight as he explained a few things to his remaining companions. //*This ship is a unique design. Originally a Terran-owned luxury cruiser; I got her at an auction a few years ago. I've been working on her ever since to make her space worthy.*//

Kalle did not miss the physical grimace that Isa's body betrayed. //*Is it?*// She asked.

//*I hope so.*// Kalle answered, but it wasn't a comforting sentence. Casting a glance behind him, he looked at Isa's husband, who was several lengths back from the others. //*Telfer, stay there, I'm coming back for you in a moment.*// The old-hand ordered.

Telfer paused, and then thankfully settled to his knees. Gasping for air, bruised, pained, and understanding that he was going to be hurting tomorrow if he lived that long, the husband stretched out on the floor and fell into a fitful slumber.

The secondary airlock doors opened and Kalle, Isa, and the Grondonian floated onto the bridge.

The primary viewport spread almost the entire length of the bridge's bow, port, and starboard walls. Monitor screens hung almost everywhere that there was free space and their dead screens reflected the dim light, bathing everything in an ominous crimson. In the center of the bridge sat a special cockpit that was recessed into the floor and was surrounded by its own bank of monitors and touch-screens. Behind that, there was a bank of acceleration couches and chairs across the rear wall. The port of the bridge composed several stations, including a massive communication unit. The starboard of the bridge though, was solely occupied by the navigation station.

Removing his helmet, Kalle let himself take his first breath of ship air. "Remind me to turn on the scrubbers, when I get the chance." He said, gagging as his lungs adjusted to the moldy, sharp taste.

Ripping off his own mask, the Grondonian inhaled the atmosphere and smiled. It smelled closely of his home world.

Isa's helmet had already compensated for the local air and killed anything that it deemed harmful to the user

Recovered, the old-hand set about delegating tasks to the two others aboard the bridge.

"Isa, see what you can do to get this hunk flying." Kalle ordered. Turning to the Grondonian, the old-hand furrowed his brow as he tried to remember if he had ever learned of the Grondonian's specialty.

"Doc, what's your primary study?" And with those words, the Grondonian's moniker was born. Despite his relaxed action, he lifted his face to the air and snorted sharply. It was a tell that he was both okay with being given such a nickname, though offended all the same that no one had bothered to ask his real one instead.

"Jump sciences and fold tech-" Doc began, but Kalle shut him up as he grabbed one of the Grondonian's extraordinarily long limbs and dragged him over to the navigator's station.

"That's great, Doc. See what you can do to program a fold out of here. The navigation system on this thing is archaic, and it could use a good scientist's touch." Kalle's words made the Grondonian physically swell with pride, but the old-hand missed it because he was already jumping back towards the primary airlocks and slapping his helmet back into place.

"I'm going to go get the, umph, engines started up. Once we have established life on this ship we can figure out where we need to go. See you later." Kalle disappeared back into the door they had arrived from.

Casting her visored gaze back over at the Grondonian, Isa spoke one word. "Doc?"

"Eh, it fits, doesn't it?" The aptly named geologist said without care, before he bent over the first nav-panel in study.

Something had nudged him in the ribs and whatever had done it was far more aggressive than his wife usually was. With a moan of complaint, Telfer rolled his thicker-than-normal body over before he opened his eyes. He was so tired that he fought to bring his gaze into focus. Raising one hand, he tried to rub his eyes but only succeeded in scaring himself when he heard his glove make contact with the clear visor of his helmet.

"Wake up and get moving, sweetie." Kalle chuckled as Telfer finally realized who had awoken him. "We've got lots of work to do, and very little time to do it in."

The old-hand helped his friend to his feet before he dragged the still-groggy husband down a sub-corridor and through another airlock.

They entered the primary mechanical room of the ship. Although it was a large room that spanned from the top of the hull to the edge of the keep, it was crammed full of equipment. No sooner had the doors closed behind them then Kalle began to shed the bulkier pieces of his suit. Following the old-hand's example, the husband cracked open his hardsuit, and stepped from it gratefully.

Stripped down to his pants, boots and undershirt, Kalle ripped open one of the many cabinet doors that littered the room before he selected a very nice tool belt that was loaded with high quality gear.

"Telfer, head over to that wall there." Kalle ordered as he buckled the gear to his body. He indicated the location by moving his head. "You'll find a very large switch. Flip it."

Telfer hurried to comply. He bounced along in the low gravity, until he saw what he thought Kalle had pointed out to him. Putting his weight beneath the large lever Telfer heaved upwards and suddenly the switch snapped aloft, taking him by surprise.

Within the cargo-bay the lights came to life, starkly illuminating the entire area and finally demonstrating the sheer size of the bay itself. It was almost empty, save a few boxes and crates in the corners.

Although the Drudges were able to glance about the area through the clear walls of the Nobilis, they were too miserable to be amazed.

Nozomi though, took notice of the situation. Kanji script had begun to flow in front of her eyes. Even if the Asteroid had electronic scramblers inside of it, there was almost a guarantee that the Pirates would have sensed the vessel coming to life, just like they had sensed it when Nobilis had risen.

Back upon the bridge, Doc turned on the first of his screens and a very primitive Nav-globe came into focus. It was all red and glitchy and it continued to phase in and out of existence. It was merely for show, so the Grondonian ignored it as he focused on more useful displays.

Isa was upside down, having removed her helmet, and was

buried in a panel which held a myriad of electronics. She had heard something pop. It wasn't a good sound when she needed the piloting equipment to work.

Grabbing a special tool, Kalle inspected a narrow space between two large pieces of equipment.

"Once the generator is fireh," The old-hand began a lecture. "The reactor should kick in. I've got enough fuel in here to let her fly, but I don't hearneither the engine starting up,nor the fuel pumps."

Kalle peered into the catacombs of pipes and wires that composed the claustrophobic space between the two machines. Wite movements that belied his confidence, Kalle pulled himself over one piece of gear, and disappeared into the hole he had inspected. Telfer watched Kalle vanish and he dreaded that he would hear a loud sizzle as electricity met flesh, but that was not the case. From within the hole a gloved hand emerged, and Kalle's voice yelled out from the depths: "Micro-driver."

"What?" Telfer asked, confused.

"I said hand me a micro-driver." Kalle responded.

"What's a micro-driver?" The husband repeated himself.

Grabbing the ledge with both hands, Kalle popped his head back above the machinery. "And you call yourself a man? You work in a loading bay and you do maintenance on skiffs. You know what a micro-driver is!" He practically screamed.

"I only know things by the company's names for them." Telfer shot back.

The old-hand cursed in one of the other languages that the husband was not familiar with as he sank back down into the labyrinth. Telfer could hear the murmurs of Kalle's voice as he mumbled to himself. "And I pick the most useless help aboard this ship. Alright Telfer, it's the little, gun-like device with a smooth shaft that fits in the hand, and has a variable adjusted grip on the end."

Telfer finally located what he thought his friend had meant.

It was hanging on the wall, and it was a device that the husband recognized as an 'electro-mini-bit-accelerator'. Micro-driver instantly sounded far catchier.

"Is this what you're looking for?" Telfer asked as he leaned over the bulky equipment. Kalle looked up, the bright light from his Datapad illuminated the old-hand's face. Seeing the micro-driver, Kalle raised a hand and Telfer slapped the device into the waiting palm. Without another word, the old-hand bent back down to a panel and began to work it free.

It wasn't the best job that she had ever done, but it wasn't that bad either. When she connected the wires together, the console powered up, and the Selth gratefully pulled herself back to her feet.

Doc meanwhile, appeared to be having a conversation with himself in his native tongue as he moved energetically about the navigation station.

Brushing her 'hair' out of her face, Isa triggered the translator program that her suit had built into it.

<<*And just how did he expect us to go anywhere with ancient maps like these?*>> Doc said acidly. <<*No, this simply won't do. I'll have to redraw these by hand until we can get an updated download. Honestly, humans and their expectations . . .*>>

Despite herself, Isa grinned. The complaints were universal from species to species. Ignoring her companion once more, the Selth began to check the readouts to see how archaic the system was with her own eyes. The monitoring systems and exterior scanners showed Isa exactly what she expected to find; the ship was surrounded by rock. A quick diagnostic program was run: thrusters functioned, barely, and there were four separately crashed programs in the basic piloting computers and the combat computer was down, and what was such a ship even doing with a combat computer?

Another panel displayed views from the stern, starboard, port, bottom, and top of the vessel while another screen was filled with readouts, including heading, velocity, acceleration, and an old 3 D imitation of a Nav-globe. The craft was far different from what the Selth had learned to use, but it wasn't something that she doubted that she could handle.

At least the controls were familiar to her; it was almost as if they had been taken from a fighter craft. Luxury ships usually had far bulkier, more glamorous controls. There was no present way to test them, unfortunately, as the thrusters still had no power being fed to them and the fuel readouts were all still dead.

"Oh for crying out loud Telfer, it's called an adjustable wrench! It's a wrench that can be adjusted. This is a pipe wrench, used on pipes!" Kalle waved the offending tool back and forth in front of his companion. "And pipe wrenches are always used in pairs."

"You're the one wearing a tool-belt. Shouldn't you have the tools already with you?" Telfer yelled angrily.

"This is an electronic tool-belt." The old-hand fired back. "It has a multi-meter, a scanner, a proximity detector, insulated electrical tools and spare wire, not mechanical tools." Frustrated, Kalle pointed with the pipe wrench that he still held in his hand. "Over there. Yes, *that*, that is an *adjustable* wrench."

"Sheesh, alright, I get that my education is different from yours. You don't have to yell." The embarrassed Telfer exclaimed to the old-hand.

"I know I don't have to yell." Kalle said as he slipped back into the hole, leaving the pipe wrench balanced precariously on the machinery. "I just like to."

Removing herself from the barely functioning cockpit, Isa made her way over to the communications panel. There were a select few readouts there that interested her: One screen displayed information on the ship's status: what had power, what needed repairs, hull breachesd etcetera. The other screen that Isa was interested in displayed information from sensors that Kalle had installed all across the trio os rocks that he owned. The sensors weren't cheap, they were high class, practically militant grade. They were so advanced that Isa was able to see some of the compositions of the asteroids around her, like the high-iron rock that was a few rock-lengths away, or the tungsten infused boulder nearby, or, the rock that had just exploded.

That wasn't normal.

Reaching over the console, Isa set one of the monitors to show what was going on around their asteroid. There was a flash, and something burrowed into another rock. Isa waited, counting the seconds, and when she reached thirty, the rock exploded into tiny fragments.

Raising her communication gear, the Selth spoke into the device with as much aplomb as she could muster:

//*I don't mean to rush you guys, but I think the Pirates are on to us. I just saw a burrow-bomb in use.*//

Isa's voice caused the two men to stiffen in anxiety before Kalle dove back into the hole that he had been about to climb from. "Telfer, turn off the electrical shunt, not the main, I need the reactor to continue on warm-up!" He screamed as he braced his hands around a large pipe. Hearing the orders, Telfer ran to a large wall that was filled with panels, but there was not one thing there that he recognized the writing of.

"Which is it?" Telfer screamed out.

"I told you it's the one labeled electrical."

"Which is it?" The frustrated human repeated himself. "I can't read this language."

"It's English, of course you can't." Kalle's voice was exasperated as he poked his head back above the floor. "It's the main panel with the lightning bolt above it."

"This one?"

"Yes!"

Grabbing the lever with both hands, Telfer yanked downwards and threw the ship back into almost darkness.

"Miss Nozomi?" Joshua said quietly of the sole remaining adult.

Nozomi had been so engrossed on reading the messages that had flashed in front of her eyes that she had not noticed that the lights had died. The four children had observed for her, and they clung together, instinctively seeking comfort.

"Don't worry." Nozomi said, faking a smile. "I'm sure we'll be okay." The other three children relaxed, but Sudhir met Nozomi's eyes, and a moment of understanding crossed between them.

The junction box slammed shut with incredible violence. Raising his hand, the old-hand motioned for the husband's attention. "Telfer, hand me an RTR."

"And that is?"

"It's a box, labeled in Basic. You'll find it on the roller counter, over beside the job-box." Kalle described it as best as he could. Telfer ran over to where he thought Kalle meant but there were several dera-boxes, and more than one was clearly labeled RTR. Grabbing one of the boxes, the husband opened it.

"Is this it?"

"That's it, Telfer. Hand it over here." Kalle snapped as he bent back down to work. Eager to help, Telfer took a step, and then the flooring seemed to go out from beneath him. Luckily, the gravity was still low enough that he was able to keep his footing, but the precariously balanced pipe wrench shifted. Surprised by the commotion, Kalle stood, and conked the top of his skull on the thick metal tool.

"What was that?" Telfer wondered as he ignored the many ignoble words that streamed from his companion's mouth.

"That was a little too close." Doc observed as he pulled himself back to his feet. Isa, having known about the debris ahead of the collision, had maintained her footing. Wreckage from another shattered rock had collided with their asteroid and had caused significant damage to their hiding place.

The Selth dove back into the cockpit and began to strap herself in. Taking a hint from Isa, Doc hurried to do the same using two pads that were connected to the leaning bar behind him. He clamped his legs into place.

Isa spoke worriedly into her microphone.

//Guys?//

"Dammit, I know we're in trouble. Just give me five more minutes." Kalle screamed angrily, as he strapped another wire into place. "I just got the dampening system online, I think."

"You think?" Telfer asked worriedly. "How confident are you?"

"Not very." The old-hand admitted as he pulled another wire. "But it's not like I have the time to-"

Even Kalle became quiet as the sounds penetrated the mechanical room. They were coming through the communications gear located in the old-hand's Datapad.

//I know you guys hear that.// Isa's panicked voice was clear. She had allowed real fear to creep into her voice. *//We have approximately twenty seconds and then we're space dust!//*

Cursing, Kalle dropped everything that he had held in his hands. His fingers flew along the Datapad as he spoke, "Telfer, flip the switch."

"Which one?" Telfer asked.

Frustration and anger caused Kalle to scream at the top of his lungs, "The only switch that you turned off!"

In front of Isa the main doors to the asteroid began to crack open. Bracing herself, the Selth put her hands upon the controls and waited for the systems to come online.

Throwing the Datapad up to Telfer, Kalle bent back down and grabbed a trio of very thick wires as he continued to direct his apprentice. "When the green light flashes, hit it!"

Looking at the caught pad, Telfer watched a red button flash once.

Kalle pulled his arm back and turned his eyes away.

Flash twice.

The old-hand swallowed.

The light went green and Telfer punched his finger onto the screen, even as Kalle leaned forward and attempted to jam the suddenly sparking wires into a large set of terminal blocks.

The ship lurched forward and Kalle felt his shoulder crack against a panel as his gloved hand landed micro-meters above the metal that he was trying to secure.

Telfer was flung the length of the mechanical room, or would have been if the dampeners hadn't kicked in.

Back on the bridge Isa read the words *'Catapult Engaged'* flash by on her screens. The next instant the ship shot forward out of the rock as power returned to her consoles.

The burrow-bomb appeared behind them, right where the ship had been, and detonated. The resulting blast tore the asteroid into tiny shards, but because the hanger doors had been open no debris came directly their way.

The familiar weight of a dampener system kicking in. Strong gravity returned as Isa's readouts screamed at her. Pushing forward on the controls, the Selth felt the ship respond as it rocketed out into the field of floating rocks.

Chapter 9

Charged Particle Cannon (CPC):

Consisting of a nucleus, an ablative coating, and a dangerously charged outer coating, CPC's are, for the most part, theoretical weapons. A CPC round, when fired, is charged as it travels down the barrel of the firing mechanism. Upon exiting the barrel, the outer coating begins rapidly discharging its energies. The ablative interior often becomes fuel for the process, allowing the round to continue to discharge as required.

Upon impact, the central round forces its way inside the target, all the while carrying the charged outer layer with it, which, in theory, delivers the remaining charge into the target at dangerously lethal levels.

So far, no militant company has successfully used such a weapon in conflict.

THE ACCELERATION'S FORCE was muted by both the dampeners, and by the white giant. The Drudges had yelled in shock at the sudden movement.

Nozomi bit her bottom lip. She needed to protect her friends, and it was unfair for her to have put them under such a burden. She turned to face the children. "Kids, I want you to step out of Nobilis please." Nozomi asked politely. Fallon began to ensure that her siblings had their masks on.

"Are you sure this is smart, Miss Nozomi?" Sudhir asked quietly, having read the adult's mind.

Deciding that it wasn't time to try and beat around the bush, Nozomi said her next words confidently. "Probably not, but do you see any other way to save us?"

The little child shrugged, but then the ship shook again and it was all that the Nobilis could do to prevent the Drudges from flying all over its cockpit.

Isa cranked the heading yolk counter-clockwise and threw the power yolk all the way to port. Her feet backed off from the main thruster pedals as the ship side-slipped, barely avoiding the path of a spinning asteroid. The only thing that saved the observation deck from being crushed was a canyon that gave enough room for the deck to squeeze through.

Another charge flew past the bridge's observational portal and the Selth cursed. It was so impolite that not one of her pursuers crashed after she had made such a complicated maneuver.

Doc was more than willing to comment as the ship's dampeners were either not at full power, or not powerful enough to put up with the high-powered thrust that the ship seemed to have. "Force equals mass times acceleration." The Grondonian screamed. "We are victims of our large size. Watch out!"

Cautioned by Doc's end-of-lesson cry, Isa thumbed the left yolk's lever and the ship shot upwards relative to itself. The Pirate fighter that had just attempted a suicide run passed 'beneath' them.

Trying not to lose his cool, the Grondonian continued with his lecture. "Their ships are much lighter in mass, and so they can maneuver much faster without as much force."

"So, what would happen if the two of us collided?" Isa

grinned wolfishly, although she already knew the answer.

"The denser one would do more damage, but I do think the enemy ship would probably suffer severely, why?" The Grondonian answered.

Without pause, Isa swung the ship around and clipped the vent off another Pirate vessel that had gotten too close. The fighter careened out of control.

"I'm just trying to apply some physics to everyday life." Isa cackled as she flipped their ship. It was still travelling in the same direction, but was now flying backwards, limiting Doc's view of their progress. His anxiety climbed as he watched their pursuers—and their weapon-fire—in full glory through the viewport.

The decking disappeared beneath his feet again before it rushed back up with such force that Telfer's knees buckled and his neck rammed against a rack of immovable trays. The delicate equipment's humming was almost soothing amidst the chaos.

Kalle had a softer landing than the husband. He had recently escaped from his hole when the change in gravity had flung him against a tangle of wires. "What is your wife doing up there?" the old-hand asked irritably, before he too crashed to the floor.

The husband tried to answer, but suddenly the two of them were flung across the floor. The decking scraped at Telfer's jumpsuit, but it did far worse to the stripped down old-hand.

Something skittered by the two men. It was Kalle's Datapad. Grabbing it, the old-hand slapped it to his leg, where it held fast.

//*Can't you hold this thing straight?*// Kalle's irritated voice sang over the com.

"Not really, Kalle." Isa answered, as she changed the ship's vector again. "Not unless you want us to be shot or crushed; of course, if you want I can easily remedy that."

"There are more than three choices." A third voice entered the conversation. Nozomi had somehow spun the Nobilis to face the grand doors of the cargo-bay.

"I can take them." She continued her sentence. "Let me go and fight them."

"No dice Nozomi." Kalle shouted back as he somehow scrambled to his knees, opened a panel in the floor and began to worm his way inside. "Because if you leave this ship you probably won't survive."

//We won't survive unless I get the Pirates off of our backs. You've seen my giant in action and you know what it can do.// Nozomi protested.

"Yes and no, sister." The old-hand stated between grunts as he continued to fight his way past a maze of pipes and conduits. A sudden acceleration caused the mechanic to crack his elbow on an exposed pipe, and it barked more skin from his flesh. Barely restraining a yell, Kalle continued his lecture.

"I just need a few minutes to fix some problems and we can all get out of here in one piece. If you leave, I don't think you're going to get out alive. Pops sacrificed himself for all of us."

Finally, having wormed his way into the hole, he braced his feet at the top to keep himself from rocking back and forth too much. Sparing one hand, the old-hand yelled out loudly, "Linesman!"

"What?" Telfer asked back.

"Big, flat . . ."

//Teethed pliers, that's what!// Kalle's voice continued to berate Telfer for his lack of knowledge. Isa shoved the words to the back of her mind and focused on squeezing the ship through a gap between two larger asteroids.

"I don't think we're going to make it!" Doc screamed, and he put his hands in front of his eyes. The ship seemed to stand on its bow as it flew along. Rocks closed in on either side but the ship was on its course and there was no way to turn back.

"We're doomed!" Doc yelled, certain of their ultimate

demise.

Isa opened her eyes and released her breath. They had passed that obstacle, but they were rapidly approaching the end of the unstable patch of rocks and once they were free from there, they would be exposed and incredibly vulnerable.

Ripping his hand back and away, Kalle exposed the fused metal that had once been the power converter for the fold drive's engines. He swore at it before he requested help. "Telfer, check the cabinet fourth from your left. It holds spare parts. See if there's something grey and cylindrical, about as big as your boot."

Grabbing the decking, Telfer managed to pull himself along to the cabinet. He opened the door and saw things that resembled the old-hand's comments.

"Do you see them yet?" Kalle asked from the floor.

"I see two types." Telfer replied.

"Grab me the one with ten wires, now!"

The husband yanked it free, and turned back to head for the hole, but another maneuver caught Telfer by surprise and the human fell. He watched as the device he had been asked to retrieve headed straight for the hole and fell directly between the old-hand's feet.

Kalle's scream of pain was heard throughout the ship.

Gasping for breath, he tried to grab the converter that had nailed him in his most tender area, and even with his thick trousers the old-hand had felt the impact. It took both hands to grab the exchanger and while Kalle's hands were in use, Isa threw the ship into a tight, erratic spiral.

Unable to brace himself, Kalle felt a pipe smash him in the eye, and a piece of decking stabbed him in the side, breaking skin before something knocked the Datapad from its position on his leg. It fell onto the old-hand's face before it slid off, and vanished further into the bowels of the ship.

Shoving the pain away from his mind, the old-hand tried to concentrate on replacing the converter.

◆ ◆ ◆

Isa's apprehension grew to alarming levels as her equipment confirmed her fears. Inemere moments they were going to be without any cover from their pursuers.

As she tried to fight back the feelings of dread that boiled away in her stomach, Doc said something that added to her concern. "You may be interested to know, that our pursuers are backing off."

"What?" The Selth asked, but she knew, she had seen the reason why.

The Pirate fleet had relocated themselves in a perfect ambush position. As soon as Isa and the ship exited the smorgasbord of stones, they would fly directly into a killing field.

"Doc, please tell me you have jump-coordinates ready." Isa said as she toyed with the idea of staying in their little clump of sanctuary, but at that moment a dumbfire missile slid by beneath them. They were pinned, with very few options left to them.

"Coordinates yes, but we don't have any power to the fold engines." The Grondonian explained.

Hissing, Isa once more attempted to out-maneuver another blast of weapons. "Come on Kalle, let's see another miracle."

"I'm trying Isa." Kalle moaned as he pushed the last wire into place. He listened as he expected to hear the hum of the converter warming up, but instead there was nothing.

"Oh, for crying out loud!" He snapped as he pulled back one hand and smashed his fist against the freshly replaced part, but all that did was scrape more skin from his knuckles. "What did I do to deserve this? Telfer, proximity detector!"

"What?" Telfer asked.

Kalle's blood pressure soared so high his entire body seemed to flush with crimson rage. "The pen-like thing in my electronics tool belt!" The old-hand screamed. "Do I have to do everything around here?"

◆ ◆ ◆

Isa was about to shut off the com system when they emerged into clear and empty space, excluding one final rock that blocked them from the largest body of the ambush. Their barrier though, was directly in front of them.

Filling her lungs, Isa cursed before she spoke directly into her headset.

//Guys?//

"I heard you, Dammit!" Kalle snapped as he tried to figure out why the converter wasn't being fed the power it needed. Ripping open another junction box, he jammed the proximity detector within and again felt nothing.

Another voice came from the bowels of the ship where the Datapad was stored.

//I can distract them!// Nozomi offered.

"No one is leaving this ship. We're going to get out of here. I just need a few more minutes." Kalle yelled out angrily.

//Seconds Kalle, you have seconds!// Isa yelled back.

Telfer was more or less oblivious to the exchange going on between everyone else as he studied the breaker panel. All of the switches were either on or off, except for one that seemed to be stuck halfway. Grabbing it, the husband tried to turn it to one edge.

"Doc?" Isa screamed, but the Grondonian shook his head.

"We have to move, we'll collide with that last asteroid in ten, nine, eight,"

//Seven,//

Nozomi leaned forward. The Drudges stayed silent, but held each other tighter.

//Six,//

Realizing that turning it to 'on' wasn't working, Telfer jammed the switch to 'off' and then he heard a click as the switch stayed. It was promising.

//*Five,*//

Then he shoved it to 'on' and it finally travelled all the way.

Back in the hole Kalle yelled victoriously as he heard the converter begin to hum.

"Power!" Doc yelled.

The jump-solution reticule appeared on Isa's screen. With a warrior's cry, the Selth twisted her controls, bringing the ship to the proper bearings.

Doc did not have to be told what to do next as he smashed his hand against the console.

The ship seemed to stop in place and began to stretch. For a brief instant it was visible in two places at once. One where it had stopped, another, several kilometers to its bow.

Then it vanished. And the only indication that it had ever been there, was the sudden acceleration of the asteroid that they had almost hit, as it jerked towards where the ship had been only a moment ago.

Chapter 10

Recyclers:

As the distances that vessels were supposed to travel increased, so did the materials required to maintain life. Eventually, it became impossible for ships to bring enough resources and cargo with them to last for the entire journey. Although crude oxygen and water recyclers had been present even in early human space ships, they were nothing compared to what is used in modern vessels these days.

Modern recyclers are the first step towards disposal of materials. A recycler is a piece of equipment or chemical bath that extracts raw elements from the garbage thrown into them. Most of the time, only important gasses and water are generally extracted, but there are some military and scientific grade extractors that work with just about everything.

Generally, what is left over after the extraction process, is converted into fuel for the engines.

THE DRUDGES AND THEIR guardian marched along the narrow halls. Nozomi tried to breathe slowly but her intense dislike for the oxygen mask she wore made her breathing fast and shallow. She preferred the safe and comfortable feel of the interior of the Nobilis, but there was no way that her beloved mecha would have fit inside the corridors of the ship.

They had walked through an alleyway, climbed a gangway, and crossed through the primary corridor before they had finally reached the end of the hall where airlock doors waited on either side. The outer shield opened, and Nozomi and the children entered.

Pressure built upon them and when Nozomi's ears popped she removed her mask. The air was rather like an arboreal forest during a muddy autumn day, but since it wasn't coming from something that was directly strapped to her face she allowed herself to breathe of it deeply. One by one the others removed their masks and waited for the inner door to open. Seeking comfort, the Drudges formed a ring about her.

The first site that greeted them was the Grondonian, who leaned over a table that shone its light into his face. His suit was open, exposing his earthy flesh. He was murmuring something to himself through his squashed nose, and occasionally stabbed or scribbled on the surface with a soft-pen, blinking his odd eyes every time he did so. He broke his concentration long enough to wave the new arrivalshin, showing all six of his fingers and his decidedly clawed thumb, before he once more concentrated on whatever he was doing.

Although the Drudges had not been born on the station, not one of them had been old enough to recall their first real spaceflight. Pains and agonies were forgotten as the children allowed themselves a moment of fantastic wonder at the single bright glow that eclipsed the viewport. It was the indication that the ship was travelling faster than light. Unable to help themselves, Sudhir and Joshua ran to the bow. Fallon though, waited with her younger sister and comforted Adorinda as best as she could.

Isa waved to the two boys as they passed her, but the Selth seemed more interested in programming the piloting computer than anything else as she continually padded away at the keyboard, paused, and then scanned one of the screens with her own Datapad.

Guiding the two little girls along with her, Nozomi sat in one of the observational chairs. Adorinda climbed into her lap and clung to her. Fallon took a seat beside the pair, and sat quietly.

"Where are we heading?" Nozomi asked after time had passed.

"Away." Isa answered. The Grondonian for his part, shrugged.

Understanding that she was not going to get any more of a response, Nozomi decided to remain mute.

The other airlock opened. Stumbling from around the great doors, Telfer and Kalle, both badly beaten and bruising, limped onto the bridge. Kalle's elbows were both bloodied, his arms were raw, his side was bleeding, one eye was turning an angry red and swelling, and his undershirt was torn, exposing raw flesh beneath. Telfer wasn't as bad, but he still limped, and he favored one shoulder with special care.

Seeing the state of the two men, Isa removed herself from the piloting seat, but before she could approach them Kalle struggled to make some sounds through his split lips.

Nozomi meanwhile, had handed Adorinda to Fallon before she ran to Kalle's side and put herself under his good arm.

"It's over there." Kalle finally managed to speak as his head jerked to indicate the room that was attached to the bridge, closest to the com station. Since Isa was helping her husband and Nozomi was busy supporting Kalle, the Selth called for the attention of the two boys. Sudhir ran over to the old hand. The young drudge used his telepathic abilities, and figured out what Kalle was looking fod.

The two male Drudges disappeared into the adjoining room.

Sinking into the captain's seat, the old-hand chuckled before his injuries caused him too much agony.

When the two Drudges returned, they were wheeling a full med-kit with them. They had barely gotten back onto the bridge before Isa bound over to them, ripped open a compartment, and selected two syringes. The Selth jabbed one of the needles directly into the muscles of Kalle's neck and the other needle into her husband's shoulder. The syringes automatically fed out the injection, and both men relaxed slightly.

The nanite brew were composed of tiny machines that worked themselves to death before dissolving as vitamins in the blood stream. They stopped bleeding holes, repaired minor torn ligaments, and helped to reduce swelling all at once.

Telfer smiled in relief. The inflammation had stopped but it had not receded.

Kalle found it easier to talk although the first words out of his mouth were not anything profound.

"Could someone kindly hand me a chill pack?"

Joshua complied and broke the interior contents of the medical bag by stomping on it. The bag's contents mixed and became very, very cold as the old-hand took it and shoved it into the front of his space-pants.

Finally more comfortable, Kalle took notice of an off and funky smell that came from Adorinda. He spoke in a gentle voice to Nozomi. "That room there," He indicated a door that was behind the navigation station. "That's my quarters. Why don't you and the girls go clean up? One of us will take the boys in once you're done."

Smiling thankfully, Nozomi stood and guided Fallon and Adorinda. The three ladies had to pass through yet another airlock. They were assaulted with a surprise when the door opened. It was a known fact that Kalle kept his room on the station rather Spartan, but his quarters aboard ship was the complete opposite. A gentle carpet lined the floor, and the walls were painted in soothing colors. There was a large couch, a dining area, a full washroom, and a private sleeping chamber.

After a moment of silence Fallon said, in awe, "This is not like Mr. Aaron at all."

"Hush dear." Nozomi spoke softly before she moved into the

private quarters.

"Just where are we going, Doc?" Kalle asked.

Doc looked up from the screen as his moniker was called. He had taken notice of the others in the room but had been too busy to say anything. The system's archaic systes was a curse that the Grondonian had to fight through, and it didn't help that alf the technical data was in some old and inept language.

Fluffing himself up, the Grondonian unclasped his legs and wormed his way to the front of the table before he tilted it on a set of hinges, so that the rest of the refugees could see the diagram that the Grondonian had drawn.

"Well," the alien huffed. "As far as I can tell, from this thing's computer, the middle of nowhere. However, do not fret my peons, for I, the greatest mathematical mind here, have calculated our direct and current trajectory. The map on this vessel is horribly outdated, however, using my boundless knowledge of the cosmos I have concluded that we are headed between the Ceta system and the Aor system. Therefore, if my calculations are correct, and I'm certain that they are, having double checked them for you, we are approximately here right now."

While he had spoken, the Grondonian had drawn across the table with his light-pen. He waited for approval, but what he got as an answer was far from what he wished for.

"Great Doc. Plot us a new course." Kalle demanded.

"Whatever for? I just figured out where we are." The Grondonian protested, but Kalle raised one hand in a call for silence.

"Yes, Doc, you figured out where we are, which means our pursuers can too. Why don't you use some of that boundless knowledge and find us a safe place to hide for a while, or at least change our direction enough so that we won't be noticeable." The old-hand's words were orders. There was no denying them.

Grumbling angrily, but with understanding, the Grondonian bent the table back and attempted to rework a new course.

While their navigator was busy, the remaining crew members

sat in silence except for Isa, who attempted to do her best with the medical supplies as she worked on patching up the guys' injuries.

Eventually, the lack of something to do combined with the adrenaline leaving their systems, left the two remaining Drudges tired. Joshua had just stretched out on a chair when Nozomi reentered the bridge, alone. She had changed into a long t-shirt that went down to her bare knees, and she walked upon the cold decking barefoot, without complaint. Upon the sight of her, Kalle began to laugh again, but unlike before he was not stopped by the pain.

"You must be feeling better." Isa observed. "You aren't wincing anymore."

The old-hand found his voice after he had recovered somewhat. "I see that you found the old captain's clothes."

"I didn't think these were yours." Nozomi responded, pointing to the shirt. She turned around to display a rather gaudy picture of a space suited figure, giving the thumbs up. "It looked a little too relaxed for you."

"It's about two sizes too big, too." Kalle admitted.

The arch in Nozomi's eyebrow caught the old-hand again and he had to refuse the laugh that struggled to escape from his chest.

Looking for a distraction, Isa poked her husband in a spot of flesh that wasn't beaten. "Honey." The Selth said. "Why don't you get Joshua and Sudhir cleaned up?"

Not having to be told twice, the human stood, but before he could take a step Kalle spoke to him. "If you take a shower, Telfer, there are clothes that would probably fit you in the dresser."

Telfer nodded as he guided the two boys into Kalle's quarters.

After they had disappeared Nozomi leaned closer to the old-hand. "Just what kind of ship is this, Kalle?"

"This is my retirement policy." Kalle said the words again, and realized that they had become rather stale. "Welcome aboard my ship, the *Chrysanthemum*."

Kalle waited through a dramatic pause before he began a

fuller explanation of the vessel's history. "The *Chrysanthemum* was designed by a Terran company that was trying to provide luxurious spaceflight for humans, while also attempting to branch into trade between galaxies. It failed. A ship this size can either be a luxury vessel or a trading vessel, not both.

"They moth-balled her after her second voyage and attempted to slave-jump her back to earth in an unmanned convoy, but the ships failed to materialize. This baby ended up orbiting a distant moon. Someone had miscalculated the fold coordinates by only a few units and had managed to lose almost everything. It was a real pity too, because this baby was fully loaded with trade goods that were supposed to make it back to earth.

"She flew that circle until her engines ran dry, and then she stayed there, slowly degrading that orbit for over an earth century.

"The vessel was found by a salvage company and tagged for auction. I was looking for a ship and the company that had built the Chrysanthemum had gone bankrupt thanks to the navigator's mistake. For a handyman like me, it was like manna, and I got her at a practical steal. I've been working on her ever since."

Finished with his explanation for the moment, Kalle leaned into his chair and rested his head against the back.

"Really, I'm very glad I picked her up. I've had her ever since I bought the rocks and she seemed such a better investment than a hunk of boulders, although I was lucky with the asteroids as well. One of the rocks had enough raw minerals to redo must of her hull."

"And that's probably the only thing you've upgraded, isn't it." Doc said sarcastically from his place by the nav-table.

"I don't think the original helm controls were based on combat vessels." Isa said.

"Nor do I think that was the original shower." Nozomi added.

"No, you're both right." Kalle answered. "I upgraded the piloting controls to something that I'm more familiar with, ditched the old slave system, built some algae tanks, installed the first recycler I could get my hands on, and bought myself the same shower unit that Isa and Telfer had in their apartment."

At that moment, the doors to Kalle's quarters opened and Telfer emerged, wearing a pair of deck-pants and a sweater. Unlike Nozomi, his feet were stuffed into soft-shoes that prevented the cold of the decking from irritating his feet.

"I see why you've been disappearing here every few weeks." Telfer commented. "You live like a king."

Kalle shrugged, and everyone waited for Telfer to take a seat beside his wife. As he sat the Selth asked about the boys. Telfer smiled lightly.

"I found some clothes that fit them and they crawled right into the bed and fell asleep. The previous captain must have had quite a few people share his quarters."

Kalle commented gently. "I moved the family photos to the other room over there." He pointed to the room that Sudhir and Joshua had gotten the medical kit from. "It was the old executive meeting room."

A small smile had creased the old-hand's face. He looked more relaxed than he ever had back on the station. He was home. "Since my room is the only quarters available until we can refuel, we're going to have to share."

"Speaking of landing, Doc," Kalle continued, oblivious to Nozomi, Isa or Telfer as they physically expressed discomfort. "Have you figured out how much fuel we have left, where we can go?"

Since he was involved in the conversation the Grondonian became animated, and once more tilted his table upwards for all to view.

"Since we are currently here on the map, as far as my calculations have demonstrated." The Grondonian spoke rapidly. "And since I estimate we only have enough fuel for a few minor course changes, and assuming the Pirates don't know this, we can make it to several inhabited worlds and stations."

"List 'em." Kalle ordered.

If Doc was disturbed at being cut short, he had the decency

not to show it. "Well, we have the Aorian belt, as well as the Aor-oc home world, then there's the Belescian trading posts, the Ce-treti, and finally, we should be able to reach the Malore Lagrange point where-"

Kalle spoke instantly at the name of the final location. He did not give anyone else a chance to argue. "But," The old-hand added, "Get us there in the most roundabout way possible. Do you think you can swing that?"

"If I can download an updated map from a galactic network node for navigation, yes." Doc replied, still slightly inflated.

The old-hand nodded and began to write on the Datapad he had acquired from the bottom of the mechanical room.

Ignorant of everyone else, Doc had begun to lecture about the different types of maps available. "We could make a general subscription, however any information we collect would also become available to others. Now, we could buy a militant grade update, which would let us only download information instead of uploading. It's faster, and far more private. Then there's the smuggler option, which isn't really talked about, but . . ."

Doc continued to ramble on, drawing tables upon his chart. No one bothered to interrupt him but as he talked away, Isa lean-ing closely to Nozomi, before she whispered into the human's ear in a voice that was filled with malice.

"It's your turn to talk."

"About what?" Nozomi asked, unconsciously recoiling from the Selth.

"About your machine and why the Pirates were after it." Isa continued to hiss quietly.

"But how do we know the Pirates were after Nozomi's me-cha specifically?" Telfer asked, his Basic was jarring after his wife's smooth Standard.

"When Pops and I were abandoning the station," Isa's voice had begun to transform into a feral growl. "The Pirates only fired on transport crafts, and they did not advance until our mysteri-ous woman, here, decided to activate her giant . . . thing."

All but the Grondonian waited patiently for Nozomi to speak. She sighed when she realized that she was no longer in a position where she could maintain her secret. Casting her gaze to the floor, Nozomi answered to Isa's interrogation.

"Yes, it's true. The Pirates were most likely after the Nobilis."

Even Doc shut up in order to listen to Nozomi. Moving himself rapidly, the Grondonian took a seat on the floor, entirely enraptured by the words that sprang from the human's mouth.

"My parents were Wing-birds." The human female began a fuller explanation of her events. At that revelation, Kalle snorted out his nose. Wing-birds were Freebies who traveled from place to place, selling 'natural' events, living to 'commune with nature.' They were environmentalists, retros, and they annoyed the hell out of the old-hand.

"I don't see you as that." Kalle explained his reaction.

"I don't know." Isa said calmly. "This is the girl who sold flowers on a space station in order to make a living."

Admitting defeat, Kalle sank lower in his seat and adjusted the chill-pack.

"We were exploring fringe space, looking for a place to settle down." Nozomi continued, becoming more withdrawn. "My brother and I grew up in our parent's long-distance shuttle. My father was a strict traditionalist for a Wing-bird and Mom was a xeno-biologist. They had left Earth when I was young due to lack of work."

"About three years ago, we found a nice lush world where we thought we would not clash with any growing cultures. One day, while wandering in the woods, we stumbled upon a massive mining operation. The Pirates were tearing up an entire mountain.

"Curiosity got the best of us and we began to spy on the Pirates. Then one day they just seemed to leave."

She took a deep breath before continuing. "My parents decided to risk exploring the mine. My brother and I followed them, but . . . but a group of them had stayed behind. They murdered our mother and father. My brother sacrificed himself for me, he was knocked into a coma and for some reason that caused what the Pirates had been excavating, the Nobilis, to rescue us.

"I've been hiding ever since. I didn't think the Pirates would track me down, but they did. I'm sorry."

"If you hadn't shown up, Pops would not have died." Isa's accusation cut through the air.

"I didn't know that they would find me. I hoped they had given up." Nozomi admitted.

"You stole one of the things that they were digging up." The Selth explained furiously. "It's rumored that the Pirates can defy the normal rules of physics, and we know that your . . . Thing in the cargo-bay can do just that. You said that the Pirates seemed bent on collecting that mecha. Maybe they've found a way to turn it into some kind of weapon?"

"Personally, I think it's rather obviously a weapon." Telfer spoke calmly. "But it doesn't sound like the Pirates invented it. Maybe it belongs to an older race?"

"It is an older race." Nozomi admitted, and once more her audience became silent. "She's told me so."

"She?" Doc asked in amazement.

"Yes, she." The human female answered. "The Nobilis is just a child of her race, little more than a teenager. Her peoples are very ancient, and as far as I understand, they explore by sending their infants out into the galaxy. As they grow up, they're drawn to relics where they can learn how to return home, wherever that is."

Feeling the palpable tension in the room, Kalle finally injected his human wisdom by changing the subject entirely. "Well guys, I'm tired and I'm sore, and it's been one hell of a day. I'm going to grab a nap in my room. Doc, what's our ETA to the La-grange point?"

"Eleven hours, give or take a few minutes." The Grondonian answered.

"Great." The old-hand said easily as he stood. "Wake me up in six. Doc, Telfer, Isa, you guys get first shift. Nozomi and I will take the second. If nothing serious occurs, I'd like to be left alone."

Limping through the pain, the ship's owner waddled his way over to his room's airlock. "Let's get those course changes out of the way." He ordered. "Then we can concentrate on other problems. Sound good guys?"

Since they once more had a purpose, the three who were on shift began to apply themselves to whatever tasks that they could. Seeing that all was well, Kalle waved to Nozomi as she disappeared into an airlock. With one last look at the occupied bridge, Kalle entered his own room and retired for some well-needed rest.

Chapter 11

Coffee

Once a Terran specialty, Coffee became humanity's major export and bargaining tool during its first two decades of having joined the Galactic Sphere. The brew was considered delicious and energetic to most species, and although similar drinks existed, it was the multitude of flavors and styles that made Terran coffee such a hot commodity.

Over time, other species spliced the coffee bean with their own plants, eventually creating hybrids that were considered superior to the Terran variety. Even so, there are purists of all species who still consider the Earth Bean the real deal.

Galactic coffee now can be found all over, with the most powerful corporation of brewers being SpaceCash, who along with their multitudes of both blends, and condiments, offer a wide variety of snacks to suit anybody's tastes and budget.

THE HEAT WAS overwhelming, it passed right through his armor and sapped his strength, but Kalle did not stop as *he continued to pull his friends from their deathtrap.*

Beside him, the thing that had split the troop ship in half continued to burn. Its ammunition slowly became hotter, and every second that it had not already exploded was a miraclf. Kalle knew he could have saved himself by opening the area to vacuum and sucking the oxygen from the room but, if he did that his friends would have died.

He was almost done. Only Tw'll was left strapped to his seat. Kalle tried to pull him free but his fellow trooper's restraints were jammed shut from the impact. There was a piece of metal stuck into something beside him, and Kalle pulled it free, and used the sharpened end to saw away at his friend's bonds. They gave, and the heavy body fell into his arms.

Straining his back, his lungs draining from the effort, Kalle began to pull. His eyes never left the hissing, green flames that spewed from the burning weapon. If he could only make it to the blast doors and the safety beyond, then they would both survive.

Kalle never heard the explosion, but he felt it, after it happened, after it rattled his teeth and after his friend became nothing in his arms, after the shaking, and the agonizing pain as the flames washed over him, consuming him alive, and the voice . . . The voice was supposed to be a siren, a warning, but it wasn't saying the usual message. It was calling his name over, and over, and over.

Telfer closed his mouth so quickly his teeth clicked together. Kalle had awoken so violently that he had leapt off the couch and had knocked the husband over in one smooth motion. The old-hand was panting, clutching at the same limb he had grabbed so terribly hard back at the apartment only a few days ago. The arm was seized tightly by spasms, and the hand was little more than a balled fist.

"Are you okay, Kalle?" Telfer asked, but instead of saying

anything, his friend continued to stare at his agonized limb. It took a great amount of concentration, but slowly, one finger moved, then another, and another, until Kalle found he was finally able to flex his hand.

It was only then that the old-hand took the time to realize where he was. He was aboard his personal ship, in his personal quarters.

Telfer was still sitting on the carpet where he had fallen, watching the old-hand and waiting for a sense of recognition. Kalle's sudden relief unnerved his friend. The old-hand offered the same arm he had favored a moment ago and helped Telfer to his feet.

Kalle had changed from his usual spacer clothes, and was dressed in shorts and a tight-fitting undershirt. He had managed to find new bed sheets to cover his couch with. The door to his bedroom was closed so that the four Drudges could get some well needed, uninterrupted, sleep.

"I'm fine Telfer, thanks." He said, stretching as he spoke but this time his actions exposed the full silver tattoo that ran up his right arm and around the back of his neck and the red scar-tissues that covered the inside of his left leg, and accompanied the old various scars that dotted his limbs.

"You were having a nightmare." Telfer reminded Kalle of the very recent history. Still smiling gently, the old-hand walked towards one of his secured closets. It was filled with spacer-gear. Grabbing a fresh pair of clothes he headed for the small, general washroom.

"Is it time for the shift change already?" Kalle asked as he selected a spray of deodorant.

"Not really," Telfer replied. "I was just coming in to crash early. Doc fell asleep on a chair outside, and it's been really quiet since our last course change."

"How early is early?" Kalle poked his body back around the corner. He already had boots and pants on, but his torso was bare. His body was thin and rakish, muscles danced beneath his skin.

Between his heart and his collarbone, an odd tattoo glimmered. It was a design that Telfer did not recognize.

"About four hours." The husband answered.

That was fine with the old-hand. He knew that he would not have slept well anyways once he woke up from that dream. "Did you guys eat at least?" He pulled his shirt over himself.

"Well, neither Isa nor I know the ship, and we didn't really feel all that hungry. We've just been working on the bridge." Telfer explained matter-of-factly. "And, right now, I'm too tired to worry about food. I know Isa doesn't have to eat for a few more hours, so we'll just let you find us some grub when we wake. Does that sound good?"

"I'll have coffee brewed by then." Kalle said lightly before he stepped into the airlock.

When the door opened onto the bridge the old-hand saw that Doc was lying on a row of chairs, but he looked comfortable and the sounds of his heavy breathing indicated that the Grondonian was in a deep state of slumber.

Isa was still in the cockpit. She turned her head to acknowledge her friend, but then she went straight back to pretending to pilot the ship. Since it was in autopilot, the Selth's position was not truly necessary, but Kalle felt safer knowing that the ship was at least being monitored by a reliable pilot, as it was an artificial intelligence that had stranded the *Chrysanthemum* over a century ago.

Passing to the other room that was attached to the bridge, Kalle made his way through the open airlock doors. The executive's room consisted of a meeting table, a small kitchenette, and a washroom. Otherwise there wasn't much aside from old star charts and fiscal reports. None of the outdated information interested him. It was the ability to brew his first cup of coffee since he had left the station that concerned the old-hand.

Filling three cups, Kalle walked back onto the bridge. Isa was busy trying to learn the Terran language that the ship used, and although she was good with alien words, the Selth did not have the natural talent that Kalle did.

<You look like you're having fun.> Kalle said in Isa's native tongue. The Selth rubbed her eyes before she stood from the pilot's seat and took the offered coffee.

<If straining your eyes is something you consider fun? How do you speak that language?> Isa wondered aloud.

"Practice." Kalle chuckled, reverting to Standard.

"It seems, I don't know, like it's a mishmash of dozens of different cultures." Isa admitted. "There are dozens of words that mean the same thing, and the conjugation is odd."

The old-hand laughed before he replied. "Why do you think I prefer to speak in other languages? English belongs to humans, but I don't consider myself Terran."

"Then where are you really from?" The Selth asked, but Kalle's only response was to sip at one of the drinks he held in his hands. Seeing that she wasn't going to get a straight answer Isa turned from the old-hand and pointed up to the Nav-table.

"Doc managed to get his hands on an update contract. He got you a militant subscription, since we're currently carrying some weird things."

The old-hand smiled into his cup. "And I bet Doc was complaining about the age of the system every step of the way."

"And then some." Isa agreed. "Telfer had to put his hardsuit back on just to muffle the noises."

"You should join him. Get some rest, Isa, you deserve it." The old-hand ordered with compassion.

The two friends then stood there until Isa finished her drink. Kalle had completed his first and was well into his second cup. Silently, Isa handed the mug back to the old-hand, before she turned to walk to the quarters. She was almost there, but her hand hesitated over the airlock controls. What had been bothering her finally became too big a burden to bare, and the Selth turned back to confront her companion.

"I don't trust her Kalle, not even as far as I can throw her."

"You can throw Nozomi pretty far, Isa." Kalle had not looked over when the Selth spoke but had kept his gaze fixed upon the bright light outside that illuminated the bridge

"She kept such a secret from all of us." She argued.

"And saved our lives with it." The old-hand rejoined calmly.

"Which wouldn't have needed saving if the thing hadn't been hidden aboard the station!" The Selth practically roared in her anger. Doc snorted through his squashed nostrils before he rolled over, his sleep almost disturbed.

"We don't know that for sure Isa." Kalle finally broke his gaze from the front of the ship to look at his friend in the eyes.

The Selth snorted before she crossed her arms haughtily over her chest. "Yes you do, Kalle. She told you herself. Why do you find it okay that she kept such a big secret from you? Is it a human thing? Or is it because she's a female of your species?"

To Isa's surprise, Kalle slammed the empty cups down upon the headrest of the pilot's chair. His eyes blazed for a moment as the old-hand fought to maintain his emotions. Relaxing the fingers of his suddenly tightened hand, piece by piece, he pried his digits free of the mugs.

"It's not a race or sex thing Isa, and I would appreciate it if you never mentioned such things to me again." Kalle said, his voice betraying the tiniest of trembles. "We all have our secrets, except for your husband. Even you have your mysteries. There are things about you that I don't understand and it's not for want of trying."

"Do you have any secrets, Kalle?" The Selth asked, her voice a little less acidic.

"You're standing in one, Isa." The old-hand replied. Turning his head, he studied the arm that had caused him so much pain. "I probably have the most skeletons in my closet out of anyone here. Nozomi revealed her secret and carried us all to safety when she could have easily left us behind. She's evidently lost much, and that thing—whatever it is—is the only connection she has left with her past. She's an outcast, an orphan, just like you and me."

It was the smallest of revelations but Isa was not ignorant. Kalle had turned back to face the viewport, so he did not see the Selth hang her head in shame. The words that her friend had spoken hurt both of them, but it was a necessary pain. Wordlessly, Isa opened the airlock doors and slipped her way inside the captain's quarters.

Her hair felt like an absolute mess, and the straps of the breathing mask pinched at her skin. She hated wearing the apparatus, but it was necessary in the reduced atmosphere of the hallway. As good at holding her breath as she was, Nozomi knew she wouldn't even have made half the distance to the bridge without trying to breathe, and suffocating slowly was not the way that Nozomi wanted to go.

The airlock opened its first doors and Nozomi stepped inside. She counted the seconds as the doors closed behind her, and waited for the familiar feeling of her ears popping before she removed the O-2 mask.

On the bridge it was quiet, peaceful, and serene. The smallest of buzzing sounds came from the navigator, who slept with a blanket carefully folded around him. Kalle was seated in the pilot's chair. His hands rested against his sides as he stared out into space.

Creeping closer, Nozomi stealthily placed herself directly behind the old-hand.

"Did you sleep well?" He asked.

"I did, and you?" Nozomi replied as she rested herself against the headrest of the pilot's chair.

Kalle scratched one hand up and down the other arm before he answered. "I've had better naps." He admitted. "It's just weird to have people onboard my ship again. I've slept with its ghosts for so long that I had become used to the solitude."

"Are you saying I'm a nuisance?" She giggled.

Kalle, despite his solemn thoughts, chuckled lightly before he looked up into Nozomi's smiling face. "No, I guess that came out wrong." He replied sheepishly "What I was saying, is that I'm not used to it. What I didn't finish with, was that, I wouldn't have chosen anyone else to share it with."

"You're such a sweetheart." Nozomi chided her friend, before she got down to business. "Where's the washroom?"

"There's one in the executive's room. It's clearly marked and fortunately designed for humans." Kalle said happily, pointing out the way.

"You have an amazing home here." Nozomi expressed her thoughts when she returned, unknowingly handing Kalle his third drink so far. Although she had not found her choice of teas she had found a lovely blend of herbal beverages that had been vacuum sealed. Taking the offered liquid, Kalle sipped at it as he pondered his next words.

"It is a nice home, but I wonder for how long?"

"What do you mean by that?" Nozomi enquired.

"Well, it appears we won't all be here for very any significant length of time." Kalle finally found the words he wanted to say. "It's a nice ship, but it needs a crew in order to operate. Let's face it Nozomi, not everyone aboard this ship is free to make their own choices about their lives. Isa might be a Freebie, but Telfer is still under the company's control, the Drudges are probably enslaved for life And Doc? I don't know how long he's going to be with us. It's been nice to have a navigator and a scientist, even if they are both in the same, annoying body.

"And then there's you Nozomi. I don't know what your plans are, and I don't know how I'm going to handle this ship once we get to the station." Kalle explained his predicament.

"I don't know my plans either." Nozomi agreed. "I am a Wing-bird, after all."

Her attempt at humor was not responded to with the exact reaction she was hoping for. Kalle continued to stare straight ahead as he mutely sipped at his drink. Deciding that the joke was just too broad for him, Nozomi hunkered herself down beside her friend, and pulled her shirt over her knees to keep herself warm.

"What I meant to say Kalle, is that, we never know what the future's going to bring, but we can onlyllive for the now, plan for the soon-to-be, and remember our pasts."

"What if we don't want to remember our entire pasts, what then?" The old-hand rejoined.

"That is the kiln that forged us. Even if we would like to forget, we must harness our lessons from our pasts or be doomed to repeat them." Nozomi's words were ones that her father had often spoken, and the gravity had not been missed on her.

<Thanks Socrates.> The English flowed from Kalle's tongue.

<I'll pretend I know who that is.> Nozomi responded. <And I'll take it as a compliment.>

The laugh started lightly, and built, until Kalle was trying not to hurt himself by restraining the urge to guffaw.

Finally, when he had managed to suppress the remaining giggles, the old-hand shook his head, wiped at his eyes, and then said "Thanks."

"You're welcome." Nozomi replied, and the two sat there, watching the emptiness of space pass them by.

Chapter 12

Selthian Dancers:

The elite female wing of the Selthian forces, they have few equals. Selected at birth, the strongest females begin training. Although they attend educational facilities like all other Selths, Dancers spend, on average, 50% of their day training in weapon usage, athletics, endurance, tactics and the Selthian Dancer martial art, which is exclusively taught to Dancers.

When 'Recruited', Selth Dancers are called apprentices and are teamed up with troupes. Each troupe is divided into trios, with one senior dancer hosting two juniors. Upon graduation, Dancers are finally given the official title, as well as custom built suits that assist the dancer in her weakest points, either increasing strength, or agility, or mobility so that all dancers are equal. Lead Dancers, the elite of the elite, are given skin-suits that are more mobile than their counterparts.

Their reputation as some of the deadliest combatants is well earned. In more than one recorded instance, a single dancer has decimated enemy platoons without injury.

Unfortunately for their enemies, there are few surviving re-
cordings available, and only the most elite of militant units
have faced dancers victoriously.

K ALLE'S GRUNTS RESOUNDED through the com-system for
everyone to hear. The old-hand had squeezed himself into a
service hatch that had been recessed into the alleyway's wall and
Telfer had been issued the responsibility of handing tools to his
friend.

The old-hand had awakened everyone two hours before their
estimated time of arrival, and they had all feasted on a meal he
and Nozomi prepared from some of the old rations that had been
stored in the executive room.

Everyone had been issued various tasks to prepare the ship
for landing. Nozomi and the Drudges had been tasked with cov-
ering the Nobilis with old tarps and garbage in an attempt to
hide its identity. Isa had been stuck at the helm, but Kalle had
found a language algorithm that had allowed the Selth to program in Standard so she was able to tune the controls much more
efficiently. Since his job as navigator was currently not needed,
Doc had been asked to assist from the engine room, where he had
stared in horror at the age of the fold drive.

That had led to Telfer being selected as the old-hand's aid,
once again.

//That should do it.// Kalle said as he squeezed himself back
into the hallway. His soft-suit was covered in grease and dust, but
the old-hand wiped his hands clean on his pants with a rather
happy motion.

//I take it that I can throw the breaker?// Doc's voice sang
over the communications system.

//Yeah, but stand ready for an emergency shutdown.// The
old-hand replied.

The airlock door began to glow around its edges, indicating
that power had been restored to the system. Unlike the station,
there was no number pad to touch to gain access, but there was a

magnetic plate that glowed weakly with some kind of backlighting. Reaching into his belt, Kalle removed a small circuit board that he stuck to the access pad. The old-hand fiddled with his Datapad before he pressed it against the wall. The door slid aside and Telfer noticed that it was thicker than any of the others on board the vessel, even though the room they were about to enter was in the bowels of the ship.

//Am I still needed?// Doc asked, but Kalle shook his helmeted head before he realized that the Grondonian could not see him.

//Head back to the bridge.// The old-hand ordered. *//We should be fine from here, but keep your radio on just in case.//*

//Understood.//

Then the radio went silent.

The inner doors began to open and Telfer whistled in amazement. Before the two humans was a very organized row of lockers and crates. One side of the room consisted of another large door, with a heavy blast-shield in front of it. The room was lit in a dark-blue illumination which was comforting to the husband's eyes.

Stretching out his arm, Kalle touched Telfer's shoulder. The moment that the old-hand did so, Telfer's suit reverted to contact communication.

"Safe light." Kalle said in Basic.

"What are you talking about?" Telfer wondered.

"It's light designed so that human's don't have their night vision ruined. I don't think you know where we are, do you?" Kalle asked. Telfer shook his head, feeling his hardsuit's helmet shift slightly.

"This is the ship's armory." The older human lectured as a teacher, instructing his student.

"What's an armory doing aboard this ship?" Telfer said incredulously. "I thought that this was a luxury vessel?"

"It was also a cargo ship." The old-hand corrected his friend. "But what are humans famous for?" Kalle asked, and then he stepped away. Telfer heard the momentary crackle in his headset as his communications system revertek to radio. //*Throughout any species history, there have always been those who prey upon others. The previous owners must have been worried about being attacked by raiders.*//

//*It was a healthy paranoia.*// Isa's voice spoke dryly through the communication system.

//*Healthy for us, anyways,*// The old-hand said lightly. //*Let's see what's in these lockers, shall we?*//

He removed his beloved micro-torch from his tool belt and proceeded to melt away a lock that sealed one of the lockers. With flourish, Kalle pried the hot door open.

//*Wow,*// The married human said in awe. //*That's a lot of spacesuit.*//

The cabinet was filled with one black colored ensemble. It looked like Telfer's hardsuit, but instead of being the sterile white of company class gear, the suit was jet black and the visor was opaque. There were several pieces of equipment that rested around their various portions of the locker. Each one seemed to be a modular component that was dedicated to the collective.

The old-hand reached out, and grabbed Telfer's elbow. "That's an old combat suit. I haven't seen one of those in years." He sounded, reverent. "Modern day military suits have so much more on this baby, but this is a classic."

"Looks like a suit to me." The husband said with a flat tone to his voice.

"Of course it does, you don't havd the training that I do." Kalle closed the locker and in the process broke physical contact. Like a child opening presents, the old-hand burnt off another restraint before he opened a cabinet that was filled with close-range melee weapons.

Lifting what looked like a simple handle, Kalle swung it, and the stick extended into a baton. Telfer had found a sword that was the length of his forearm. The handle was wide enough for both of his hands to close comfortably around it, yet it was also free and light enough for him to wield with one hand.

Telfer brushed shoulders with his friend, while he enquired, "Why are there swords in the lockers?"

Stopped mid-swing, Kalle took a breath before he answered. "Back in the first days of their deeper space-faring, several groups of the human cultures found themselves at war. It started out simple enough; Two ships would come at each other, fire explosives, and both ships would be ruined and the crews would die. Eventually, humans began to invade each other's vessels, but the preferred method of weaponry was firearms. During the fights, the ships were getting more beat up from the inside than they were from without, and so humans began to choose weapons that wouldn't crater the hull if they missed their intended target, hence the sword and baton, and I'm sure if we looked around we'd find more odds and ends like this.

"But that's not what I'm looking for. We're going to be entering a station that doesn't always have the safest of reputations. I'm positive that if we were seen packing swords or heavy rifles we'd be noticed by security. I'm looking for small, personal firearms, things that I can hide about myself."

Kalle walked to the heavy blast door and removed a fine putty, which he began to work between the fingers of his gloved hands. //*The problem with those firearms is that they were still needed, but were only to be brought out in situations of extreme urgency.*// Slapping the explosives against the heavy door, Kalle stepped aside. He had left the tiniest of detonators ticking within the munitions. // *Unfortunately, I haven't figured out the right key to get me in here. Avert your eyes.*//

Telfer felt the reverberations as the floor shook beneath his feet.

Due to the lack of atmosphere, there was no loud bang.

There was a definite and succinct crash though, when Telfer dropped the heavy bag onto the bridge's floor.

"Wow," Isa said dryly as she surveyed the sack of armaments and materials. "You guys really know how to travel light."

The sack was loaded with weapons of all types. There were firearms, needlers, laz-shots, sap gloves, disruptors, hammersticks, swords, knives and batons. They sat in no particular order and had the look of having been haphazardly tossed into the bag, which was strained to its limit. Telfer and Kalle had carried the container together from the weapons' lockup. For safety reasons, the old-hand had ensured that the Drudges were not on the bridge where their natural curiosity could have caused them trouble.

Selecting one of the knives, Isa tested the weight of the blade. She made a small grunt of disapproval before she flipped it through her fingers, effortlessly twirling the knife in a display of skill.

Kalle, meanwhile, had found something else he had missed while the two men had been loading the bag earlier. Raising the item, Kalle began to work a dial on the device's side. Doc, who had distanced himself from the blade-wielding Selth, looked curiously at what the old-hand tendered to with such excitement.

"That looks, interesting." The Grondonian exclaimed.

"Security grade bio-electrical disturbance tool." Kalle smiled mirthlessly out of the corner of his mouth as he brought the dial all the way down to its minimum setting. "Also known as a Grunter. It was originally developed as a non-lethal stun device. It is powered by a generator activated by the opening of its trigger. On its weakest setting it can cause severe pain or numbing of a limb, allowing for relatively safe take-downs." Extending his thumb, Kalle flicked a switch that rested at the top of the handle. The Grunterpopened and hummed with a distinct high-pitched whine. "On its highest setting, it destroys every synapse in a full sized Kackle's body, dropping them like a stone."

"I'll take your word for it." The Grondonian said, as he shuffled to a safer distance.

A subtle hiss caused the bridge crew to stop their inspections and scrambld to close the bag and hide their various weapons. Nozomi and the Drudges stepped onto the bridge. Every member of the troupe was covered in grease and oils. Nozomi had found a pair of coveralls that had fit her, but the results of her efforts had covered her in viscous fluids from head-to-toe. Hiding his face, Telfer tried not to reveal the fact that he was laughing.

"Doc, what's our ETA?" Nozomi asked with a harshness to her voice.

The Grondonian hurried to respond. "About twelve units."

"Good. I'll talk, after my shower." Grabbing the hands of the four children, Nozomi dragged the kids back into Kalle's quarters.

When the doors closed behind them, the adults looked at the bag of weapons that lay upon the floor. "Judging by the sound of her voice," The old-hand spoke quietly. "I think we should lock those things up, ASAP."

Chapter 13

Slave Collars:

Also called Restraining Collars, Slave Collars use both mild waveform disruption and electrical stimulation, with some models even using narcotics, to put the wearer into a state of mind that leaves them both open to suggestions, while the subject remains capable of completing most tasks.

First used as a way to control livestock, collars were adapted by militant units as a way of suppressing captured populations, and as a non-violent restraint of prisoners of war. Slavers adapted the collars for their own needs, using them to hold any Dreg or Skag that they captured without the use of restraints or illegal drugs.

Almost anyone and anything has been found to be susceptible to a collar's control. The only ones of any species that are immune are the 'unbound': those who have had Collar-Counter-Measures, or CCM, installed into their bodies. Since CCM is so expensive, and the installation, very invasive, only the most important personnel are considered worthy of such fittings.

◆　◆　◆

THE NOBILIS WAS INVISIBLE under a pile of tarps, taking up an entire corner of the bay. As Kalle watched, a single washer broke free from the top of the mess and clanged its way down over empty crates, discarded scrap, and finally, landed on the floor with a ping.

It looked as if the pile were ready to collapse at any moment. All that could be seen poking out from the coverings were busted and loose parts, so that the mess resembled a regular junk pile, concealed so that no one would have to stand the shame of witnessing the shattered dreams that lay beneath.

It was perfect.

Tearing his eyes away from the completed disguise, Kalle looked at the three companions who stood beside him. Nozomi was back into the clothes she had worn during the escape from the station. Although Kalle had offered her a weapon, she had declined.

Doc stood beside her. Like Nozomi, he too had refused any armaments. Unlike Nozomi, Doc had not taken the time to shower. He had instead taken a small pill that had left his skin slightly acidic. He smelled zesty and flowery and, it was not unpleasant to the human nose.

The two of them had the duty of gathering supplies in the upper markets, where they would be safe from the dangers of the station's seedy underbelly.

Isa was armed. She had selected several knives and a pair of gloves that discharged energy when they hit something. She wore most of her battle suit and Kalle doubted anyone would have messed with her. She emanated viciousness.

The old-hand was dressed in armor taken from one of the lockers. The vest was tight fitting and his pants were the thickest and heaviest of his spacer-pants. The suit's pockets were heavily laden with ammo for the old-hand's pistol that he wore in a concealed holster, opposite his body from the Grunter that he still carried.

The Chrysanthemum had come out of fold shortly after

Nozomi had stepped back onto the bridge. Various ships of all makes and models had floated about, somehow they managed to avoid colliding with each other.

Although the Chrysanthemum was more than small enough to fit into a dry-dock, Kalle had requested a mooring position. There was less chance of a break-in if there were fewer ways to get inside the ship, and it was far easier to escape if the Pirates came knocking.

With a rumble, the main cargo doors opened. As the light from the station began to pour into the ship, all four of the adults removed their oxygen masks.

Doc wrinkled his face as the smells of the multitudes blasted past him. The Chrysanthemum had just begun an Atmos-dump. In a very short time, masks would no longer needed in the main halls or the cargo area.

As the four stepped through the doors, they looked about the loading area. The bustle of activity was enormous. Doc stepped aside as a many-legged Trundle tromped on by. Many heavy bags weighed it down but the thing moved without protest.

"Isa and I are going to head to an old friend of mine. You two remember what it is that I want you to purchase?" Kalle asked.

Raising one many-digited hand, Doc began to tick off items on his fingers. "Algae, scrubbers, filters, a large assortment of standard fuses, hydronic lighting, several hundred feet of piping, electrical and liquid, and an assortment of spare parts."

"Good." Kalle spoke, as he tapped the Grondonian on the shoulder in a sign of approval. "And don't be afraid to make it all via delivery, but if you do, pay the finder's fee."

Nozomi nodded, but Doc seemed somewhat distracted by a small parcel that he was holding in his hand. Realizing that at least Nozomi had heard the cautions, Kalle sighed before he looked back at Isa.

"Well, we might as well get going." He said, before he turned and wandered off into the crowd.

♦ ♦ ♦

Seedy would not have begun to have described the area that Isa and Kalle found themselves in. The only reason that the Selth felt the least bit comfortable was that she was confident that she could have beaten anyone there to a pulp. Kalle on the other hand, seemed relaxed, almost happy to be among the Dregs, the Scags, and the outcasts of society.

<Just where are we going, anyways?> Isa asked in her native tongue.

The old-hand stepped back half of a pace so that he was beside his friend, before he answered. <It's just an old acquaintance who deals in rare and used ship parts.>

<Well, let's hope the parts aren't as used as this place.> She said quietly.

The human replied with a lighthearted tone in Standard. "Don't worry, your highness, think of this as merely a prelude."

"You really know how to invite confidence, don't you Kalle?" The Selth's voice was very acidic and the old-hand chuckled before he realized that the Urchien that he had requested as their guide had finally stopped walking. They were in front of some old rusted doors. Leaning down, Kalle mumbled to the Urchien, and the thing babbled back madly for a moment before the old-hand doled out a tip.

As their guide disappeared into the masses, Isa's friend adjusted his armor once more, just for safekeeping. The door opened without warning and an old, tall, crooked Valador female stood in the finery that was her privilege.

"Kalle Aaron, how nice to finally see you again." The Valador's Standard was flawless.

Bowing down to one knee, Kalle replied. "Likewise to you Hteathas, I apologize for the unannounced visit, and I see you've expanded operations again."

The Valador shrugged her narrow shoulders, before she stretched her long neck so that her purple eyes were perfectly level with Isa's. The great orbs blinked once, before the neck retracted and Hteathas bowed.

"Selthian royalty, what a pleasant surprise. It is good to see Kalle, that you are keeping company that's more acceptable for you. Come, let us talk business." The Valador turned, and walked deeper into the chamber.

Isa hung back for a moment. Kalle waited patiently.

"How did she know?" Isa finally asked.

Shrugging, Kalle stepped into the room. "I don't know, Isa. It's just one of Hteathas's charms."

"You have really strange friends." Isa sighed before she followed. "And I should know, I'm one of them."

The door closed behind the Selth, once more appearing like an old hunk of metal against the wall.

Across the station, Doc spun about in a circle.

"Just admit it, you got us lost." Nozomi sighed.

"We're not lost. We're *somewhere* on a station." The scientist argued, but a moment later he finally stopped trying to align himself. "It's just where on the station, I'm not so sure."

"I told you we should have stuck to the main hallways. You had to go chasing down that special parts dealer. Well, are you happy now?" Nozomi's voice let her frustrations show. She had spent time on stations before, with her family, but had never gotten so badly lost before in her life.

"Why don't we just call the others and tell them the truth?" She groaned.

Doc slipped to his knees as he spoke back. "That won't be necessary. I just need a few minutes, now that I've purchased what I needed, and we'll be guided back to the ship."

A very impolite snort emanated from Nozomi's nose as she tried to think of something to say that wasn't entirely insulting. She failed, and since the human didn't have anything really nice to utter, she moved away from the Grondonian.

They had already purchased the supplies Kalle had entrusted them with, but then Doc had gone off in search of some rare electronic parts that the more upscale area of the stations didn't sell. The two of them had wandered the halls for almost twenty minutes before Doc had found a supplier who had carried what he wanted, but he had forgot to ask which way to return to the docking bay, and *then* he had tried to discover a shortcut.

And that was how the two of them had ended up mislaid.

Nozomi wanted to leave her companion's company, but she also did not want to be separated from the only familiar face she knew, even if it did belong to *him*.

The Grondonian had ignored her sounds of disgust. His head was bent downwards as he manipulated several small tools into the parcel that he carried with him. The human felt a flush of anger ride from her head to her toes. Turning away from the Grondonian, she stomped deeper into the catacombs of the station. She didn't want to travel too far, all she wanted was a little distance between her and Doc.

A nearby Dreg began to shuffle rapidly towards a dark corner of the hall. Confused by his actions, Nozomi watched him as he disappeared. Suddenly, she realized every Skag and Dreg had vanished from the area, and for one frightening moment the human understood that something bad was about to happen.

Nozomi's scream was cut short. The sound almost caused Doc to accidently jam his screwdriver into the delicate electronics which he had just finished assembling.

It was not difficulty for the scientist to suddenly leap up to his feet. He was nimble and fast, which was not something that a casual observation would have pointed out.

The gravity was high enough on the station to allow the Grondonian sufficient traction to take the corner at a full out run, but low enough that he still moved without fatigue.

The blast of compressed air and water dissipated when it hit the wall beside the Grondonian's head, with a force sufficient enough to pit the metallic material. Cursing, Doc flattened himself against the floor, touched off of the far wall, and rolled back behind the corner.

Slavers had collared Nozomi.

The collars were evil devices: They snapped around the neck of the captive and once in place, they emitted electronic waves that made almost any species susceptible to suggestion. Doc had seen that Nozomi had adapted the dreaded slave-stare, as four Slavers busily tried to guide the captive human away.

"She's a Freebie, you dolts!" Doc screamed out loud, but the Slavers ignored galactic law as a trio of air-blasts tore up the corner of the wall closest to the Grondonian's head.

Reaching into one of his pockets Doc fished hungrily for the device that he hoped would save his fellow crew-mate.

"I had no idea that Valador's were like that." Isa commented, smacking her tongue against the roof of her mouth. "Their pilots always seemed so withdrawn."

Kalle and Isa had found themselves at the mercy of Hteathas' hospitality. While the old-hand and the Valador had discussed politics and prices, hersguests had been offered strong brew, and a weird type of sweet bread. The old-hand had warned the Selth that to refuse the food was a grave insult, and so the two guests had eaten. It had not been hard to do.

While they had socialized, Kalle had purchased a new recycler and a military class power core from his friend. Both had been experiments that militant companies had rejected due to the initial overhead cost. The old-hand had been assured that the initial high price was more than offset by the almost infinite durability of both.

//MAYDAY!//

The cry from both of their communicators stopped the two in their tracks. Kalle had instinctively flattened himself against a wall. The look of irritation that crossed his face would have been comical if it weren't followed by a sneer that said something about possibly skinning a certain Grondonian alive.

Raising his Datapad to his face, Kalle found himself interrupted by Telfer's voice, which crackled over the communications system.

//This had better be important, Doc.//

Even the husband sounded irritated.

The *Chrysanthemum*'s navigator groaned in his mind. He would have slapped that human, if the Grondonian wasn't commonly abhorred to violence.

Another air-blast chiseled a door beside him, and Doc rolled to safety. His hand that clutched the radio almost smacked him in the face, but he brought his flailing limb under control long enough to speak.

"Listen, you arrogant human. You and your ilk have only been rude to me and when I try to save your skin you get all huffy, yipe!" There was a sudden pain in one of Doc's legs, and he tucked himself into a ball. The round only bruised the Grondonian's flesh, but it had been powerful enough to knock him over.

//If it's urgent, spit it out already.//

"I'm being shot at by the Slavers who've captured Nozomi!" Doc screamed as he scampered for what limited cover that there was.

//Doc, what's your location?//

The new voice over the radio was the one that the scientist had been hoping would have answered.

"I'm somewhere on the station, Mr. Aaron, is that good enough?" The Grondonian's voice was rather testy.

"That'll have to do Doc. Just keep talking." Kalle responded even though he was already in a flat out run. Isa was not less than a pace behind him. An odd shaped knife had appeared in her hand and those who saw the two moved aside.

//And what do you want me to talk about, how nice the air is here?// The snippety voice shot back, but the next moment Kalle's Datapad began to hum with something that sounded suspiciously like Doc was singing a naughty song. A locator beacon had become visible on the old-hand's Datapad, although distance

and location of the scientist's signal wasn't a promising sight.

Turning about, the human ran several paces backwards as he attempted to talk to his Selthian comrade. "Isa," Kalle panted the words out between evenly measured breaths. "Head back, to the ship, and get it ready, to launch."

It looked like Isa was about to protest, but her jaw snapped closed and the muscles around her face tightened. Without another comment, the Selth turned a corner and split away from the old-hand.

"Will you please hurry, I only know two more verses." Doc huffed. He poked his head through the doorway he had been using as cover, but no one shot at him. Concerned that it was too quiet, the Grondonian leapt through the open door and realized that the Slavers had used an ascending service elevator. Fortunately, another elevator that had already taken its counterpart's place.

Sighing to himself, Doc once more continue his song.

Isa exploded into the cargo-bay. Telfer, who had been guiding several plates of cargo lifts about, was pulled off his feet as his wife grabbed him.

"As soon as you get this cargo loaded, I want you to be prepared to fly. I'm heading to the bridge." Then her powerful arms pulled her husband into an embrace, and their lips found each other's. When the Selth broke the kiss, she took one more breath. "That's because I'm glad you're safe." She declared, and then vanished into the bowels of the ship.

One hand graced the part of his lips that were still wet from his wife's touch. Casting his eyes to the workers who were loading the ship, Telfer shrugged.

"You heard her, boys. Sorry to rush you. Here, let me help with that."

Doc apparently had a vast repertoire of songs with obscene lyrics stored in his mind. His singing voice was pleasant and easy to listen to, and if only the Grondonian had first introduced himself with a song, he might have come off as less intolerable.

Kalle silenced his Datapad. There was no mistaking the look of the glaze-eyed Nozomi and her accompanied Slavers. Their captive marched along without looking left or right, betraying the truth about the collar, it was a militant design.

The Grunter began its high-pitched hum, and Kalle felt the weapon that he had concealed in his hand warm as it gathered energy. His other hand gripped his slugger-pistol.

The Slavers had not taken notice of the old-hand. They were more interested in clearing a path for themselves through the crowded marketplace. Taking advantage of the throng of peoples about them, Kalle matched pace with the rear guards, and waited until one of the Slavers noticed him.

The smile that creased Kalle's face was full of malcontent, and it was the last thing that the Slaver saw before he felt a cold touch of a Grunter against his ribs. Then the human pulled the trigger.

The discharge was so great it snapped all of the nerves inside the Slaver's body, tightened every single muscle, and flung the new corpse several feet to smash against the wall of the hallway. At the same time, the old-hand raised his other arm, and fired his pistol point-blank into another of Nozomi's escorts, who toppled over as if they were a marionette whose strings had been cut.

Tracking his weapons about, the old-hand targeted the other escorts, but they had been so nervous that their weapons were already raised. One escort's weapon's blast hit Kalle dead-center in the chest. The old-hand's outer layer of armor did its duty as the gel that it was composed of hardened instantly, saving his life, but the pain that fired throughout his body was so intense it threw off his returned shot and the slug ricocheted off the hallway's ceiling.

Four more guards appeared from around a bend in the hallway and began firing into the crowd indiscriminately. Two more rounds caught Kalle in his torso, and a third nailed his leg just above the knee. Dropping backwards, the old-hand forced himself into a role that took him behind a scrap-dealer's booth. He tried once more to aim at the retreating targets, but another round smacked into Kalle's shoulder.

That hit spun him about, but the old-hand managed to steady himself against the wall as the various items in the booth cracked and dinged as they were assaulted by the weapons' blasts.

Then there was only the sound of the wounded crying out in agony.

The Slavers had vanished around the corridor.

As the ringing began in his ears, the old-hand hurriedly re-loaded his pistol and jabbed one of the nanite-brew needles he carried with him into his neck in order to control the swelling.

Doc's voice crackled through Kalle's Datapad. The Grondonian's words were fast and upset.

//*Oh sure, the one time I take a shortcut, you show up and start shooting. They're running now and I am staying in pursuit.*//

"Good job Doc. Keep on them. I'm going to try to head them off." As Kalle spoke the words, he tested his muscles and joints.

Doc's radio signal indicated where the Grondonian was, and the direction that he seemed to be taking was not promising. The Slavers were heading to the exterior of the station, most likely, towards their ship.

Beginning to run again, Kalle spoke through his Datapad

//*Get my ship into space, NOW!*//

Isa did not have to be told twice. She had vaulted into the pilot's seat the moment she had entered the bridge. Although Telfer and the Drudges had worked furiously to unload the supplies they had abandoned the rest and it would just have to be held on-station until the *Chrysanthemum* returned.

"Did you hear that, guys?" Isa asked into her headset. She was already running her hands over the controls: starting engines, warming fuel cells, engaging pumps,gtorqueing up the dampener system.

A signal appeared on one of the screens. It was an indication that the cargo-bay doors were being closed.

//*Loud and clear, dear. We're ready when you are.*// Telfer's acknowledgement was loud in her ear as she waited for the mooring clamps to release.

The Slavers had occupied one of the statio's dry-docks, but instead of the one big ship that Kalle expected to find, he found himself surrounded by short-range tender shuttles, and their very aggravated crews.

A gyro-slug bounced off the floor between the old-hand's legs as he ran towards Nozomi and her captors. The human ducked behind a small bin. It wasn't the best cover, but it did absorb two more rounds instead of letting Kalle's armor, or flesh, attempt to stop the damage.

Catching his breath, the old-hand escaped from the limited security he had been hiding behind, and hurried for a cargo hauler that had been abandoned. Its driver had turned hard before leaving the vehicle. As he fled, his lack of weight on the seat triggered the safety mechanism and the hauler had come to a stop.

The avenging human continued to pull on his pistol's trigger. One of his slugs caught an opponent in the shoulder, and the Slaver screamed as she fell behind cover.

Doc arrived through a different entrance than the old-hand. From his position he saw the shot Slaver fall to the ground. She was wounded, but still in the fight. The Grondonian watched, hesitantly, as she pulled a tiny cylinder out of her vest's pocket, but as she pulled the pin on the micro-grenade, he found the courage to act.

Screaming at the top of his lungs, Doc charged out from his cover and ran towards the woman. She looked on in horror as the Grondonian leapt into the air and landed with his full weight upon the Slaver. The impact bowled her over and Doc found himself unable to regain his footing. He rolled, feeling something catch under his back. As he came to his feet Doc reached around and discovered that he was holding the grenade.

With superb reflexes, the Grondonian snapped his arm and shoved the explosive back towards its original owner. She saw the grenade as it flew straight and true towards her, and in reaction she scrambled to her feet as she prepared to run.

Kalle's slug caught her in the head, and she collapsed limply on top of the grenade as it rolled under her feet.

Exposed to everyone else's fire, Doc scampered for cover as the grenade detonated behind him. The two found themselves side-by-side as they hid behind the cargo hauler together, and theo tried to catch their breaths.

"What's up, Doc?" Kalle asked, offering an appropriated weapon to his companion, but Doc shook his head in rejection. Desperate to keep an eye on Nozomi, the scientist poked his head out from behind cover. He flattened himself immediately afterwards, and the crate that protected the Grondonian shuddered as it was hit multiple times.

"We can't wait." Doc urged his companion to greater action. He had seen that Nozomi was being loaded onto one of the remaining shuttles.

Kalle wanted to storm ahead, but the fire against him had become too intense. Beneath their feet, the deck vibrated as the Slaver's tenders began to move through the docking airlock.

Frustration boiled through the Grondonian's body. He had been, at least partially, responsible for the Nozomi being kidnapped. Even if his opinions of the woman were not of stellar quality, the guilt he felt at her capture was too much to bare.

"Whatever you do, don't move too far from this station. I'll get word to you as soon as I can." Doc yelled above the din of the firefight. "Cover me!"

"What? Hey wait, DOC!" Kalle failed to grab a hold upon the Grondonian as Doc leapt over the containers and began a mad sprint for Nozomi's shuttle, and its closing doors. Battle instincts took over and Kalle attempted to suppress the opposition with his slug-thrower.

Weaving back and forth, Doc dodged bullets, avoided impacts, and somehow made it through the screen of enemies who were all firing at the old-hand. Clutching his parcel as tightly to his chest as he could, the Grondonian sprinted to the closing ramp of the shuttle, and with one last burst of energy, he flung himself inside the ship, barely avoiding losing a foot as the ramp sealed closed.

Raising his head, Doc surveyed just what kind of situation he had gotten himself into. There were a dozen enslaved passengers, who sat calmly in their assigned seats, and they were accompanied by half that many, but no less intimidating, guards.

Doc swallowed nervously as one of the Slavers bent down to look at whoever had the audacity to climb aboard. The Slaver studied Doc intensely for a moment and then he laughed.

"Treasure trove boy, the boss is going to love us for this one, a real, male Grondonian."

With a grim feeling, Doc shuddered where he lay, paralyzed to the floor.

With his companions' retreat, the Ulnor Slaver was left abandoned on the station, but he did not mind. There was one shuttle left behind, its pilot had fallen on a grenade, so he still had his chance to join the others if his plan all went well.

He had circled around the fighting and had approached the human, who had attacked them, from behind. In his hands, the Ulnor carried an open slave collar. If he managed to capture the attacker, than by Slaver law, the Ulnor would be granted the tithes of his felled companions, and a four part bonus was just too much for the him to give up.

When the human's Grondonian companion left the attacker's side, the human had become engrossed in assuring his partner's safety, and had left his flank unguarded and exposed.

It was his chance.

With the quick pace his people were famous for, the Ulnor

dashed forward and snapped the collar closed around the human's neck. Filling his lungs, the Slaver roared out in his thickly accented Basic as he raised his head, and held his hands aloft in triumph, "Victory is mine!"

Something hard and unyielding pressed against his ribs, and the elation he had felt diminished as his gaze lowered to reveal the Grunter, and the very conscious human who held it against the Slaver. As the Ulnor watched, the collar beeped twice, and then its indicator lights flashed brightly and smoke escaped from the seals of the collar. Dead and useless, the restraint unlatched itself and fell to the deck. There was only one thing possible that could have stopped the collar from performing, the Ulnor had inspected the restraint just a few short hours ago, so that meant that the human had to be, "Unbou-!"

The Grunter's discharge cut-off the Slaver's voice mid-word. As if swatted by an invisible giant's hand, the Ulnor was flung several feet. Its nervous system, overloaded by the current that traveled through it in that instant, released control to the powerful forces that destroyed it. The heart of the Slaver stopped as the charge that was delivered burned it to death and cardiac arrest set in. The brain inside the Ulnor's head rose several hundred degrees under the powerful blast, and the protective fluid became steam as the skull, once the cavity of protection for the brain, became little more than a pot for the Slaver's thought-center to cook within.

When the Slaver landed, it was already a corpse. The old-hand gave it no more thought as he turned back to watch the fleeing shuttles leaving the bay. Frustration laded his tone as Kalle yelled directly into his Datapad.

//*Their shuttles are launching!*//

Isa had already seen all of the tenders as they disgorged themselves from the station. As soon as they were free from the launching pad, the small ships broke formation and scattered, but they all began to fly to one destination.

The mothership was ominous and intimidating. The bulbous hull of the large cargo-hauler dwarfed the *Chrysanthemum* in size, and visible weapon ports blistered the flat hull. The rear port had opened as if it was a gaping maw, ready to consume unwary vessels that flew too close. As if they were a swarm grateful to be sacrificed, the Slaver's tenders flew into the opening as the mothership's engines began to burn.

//Cut them off, catch them with a tether, ram them if you have to, but stop their ships from leaving.// The old-hand continued his order.

"Telfer," Isa asked as she slid to the side, avoiding a medium freighter as she attempted to close the distance between Kalle's ship and their target. "Are you armed yet?"

As soon as the cargo doors had closed, Telfer had taken Joshua with him to the armory, where the young Drudge had identified the single anti-ship weapon that the *Chrysanthemum* carried. Isa's husband had hurriedly dressed himself in the combat suit and the two of them had tried to make it to one of the exterior hatches so that Telfer could attempt to do something.

//I'm heading to the hatch now, but it's hard with the ship rocking so much.// Isa's husband answered as the Selth rolled around a cabin cruiser. *//I just need another minute.//*

He had tried so hard that Isa did not have the heart to tell him that it would be too late. The superior engines of the mothership began to tell as the distance between the two vessels widened. The last shuttle launched its own tow cable onto its capital vessel's hull in desperation.

Then it was gone, vanished, only to appear for a brief moment many lengths away before vanishing entirely from site.

With regret, the Selth turned the old-hand's ship about, and began to bleed the velocity that the vessel had acquired. There was no way to pursue their target without a good navigator, and not without leaving their captain behind.

The pursuit was over, for now.

Chapter 14

Celestial Algae

During the early days of their space explorations, Terran spaceships carried their own atmosphere with them in storage. They used scrubbers in order to reduce the amount of exhaled gasses that the crew had to face, prolonging the time that they could stay aboard ship or station without resupply. Several attempts were madr to bring along plant life that could help convert the exhaled gasses back into important, life-giving air, but none were proven acceptable for their species until the Terrans crossbred a brand of their green algae with the native wild weed called Cicliostrontantemum, which is available as a food source from the ocean covered planet, Naquatica.

Celestial Algae is made available in a variety of forms. Its hardiness, and fast growth, as well as the ease of adjusting it to produce various gasses, makes Celestial Algae popular as a form of scrubber system and air purifier. Algae rooms are generally built with hanging racks of pads, where algae is worked into them and they are kept constantly moist from water directly piped from the recycler. As the algae grows, it can be easily trimmed and either converted into food or fuel.

Almost all ships utilize algae rooms, due to their low cost for both installation and maintenance, although, from time to time, it is a good practice to clean out pads that have become too overgrown and risk clogging the ventilation systems.

As HE STOOD AMONGST THE captured idle, Doc exhaled in a futile attempt to relieve the stress that caused his hands to shake and his knees to weaken. He had one advantage above all of those who stared ahead in numb expressions: he had not been collared. It was almost insulting to him that the Slavers had treated him so callously, but then, he *had* voluntarily run into their departing shuttle.

Maybe it was because of how he had entered the shuttle, or maybe it was because of his physical stature, but either way, his hosts had ignored him for the most part, and had failed to search him. That was why Doc still had his tools, and the mysterious parcel that had started the latest chain of events.

Once they had left the station, his 'hosts' had urged Doc, rather strongly, to seek a chair. He had taken his place beside his captured crew-mate and waited to see if the *Chrysanthemum* would somehow rescue them, but when Kalle's ship had failed to stop them, Doc had not been surprised.

Alf the slaves had been unloaded into a common area inside the mothership. There they had joined a plethora of previously enslaved individuals from other stations, systems and planets.

Nozomi stood in front of him with an unchanging and blank expression on her face. The only actions that indicated that she was alive were the motions of her breathing and her occasional blinking.

Shaking his hands in order to calm himself, Doc worked up the nerve to pop open the tiny service compartment on his companion's collar. As he studied the mass of circuits the Grondonian whispered to himself, "Well Nozomi, if this works, you'll be free. If not, you'll be brain dead. How am I going to know the difference?"

Taking two of his small screwdrivers, Doc touched each one to either end of the power supply, and then, closing his eyes, he brought the metal shafts together and shorted out the battery. There was a small zap that sounded from inside Nozomi's neck-piece, and suddenly she straightened out in instant panic as her cognitive abilities returned.

Clapping one of his hands over her mouth, Doc leaned forward and spoke in rapid Standard. "Play along, you've been slave-collared. I think I burnt out the main emitter so it gives the impression that you're still enslaved. Do you understand?"

Instead of trying to speak, Nozomi adapted the same glassy stare as all of those around them, but her vocal chords sounded in one short gasp. Taking that as a good sign, Doc released his hand from her mouth and then proceeded to stuff his beloved parcel into one of the human's hands.

"Good." The Grondonian continued. "Keep this safe until the ship has stopped its fold. If you have the opportunity, launch this device into space when we are in layover."

"What is it?" Nozomi asked quietly, barely moving her mouth at all as her body remained immobile.

Even considering the situation, Doc managed to work irritation into his voice as he hurried to explain. "I call it my jump-communicator." He took a breath before he continued. "When we stop, find a way to get it off the ship. It will automatically return to the *Chrysanthemum*, by folding space around itself. The others will be able to find us from that, at least, I hope so."

Nozomi tucked the device into her clothes and arranged her fabrics around herself, hiding the fact that she had such a thing on her person. "Why give this to me? Why not keep it? You're not collared."

It seemed impossible, but even more irritation ladled Doc's voice when he spoke again. "There are several things riding against said idea, my dear." His voice was eternally patronizing. "The moment I got myself captured the crew began sharing accolades about how they had managed to get their hands upon a genuine male of my species. They wish to give me to their captain as a ... gift." The scientist shuddered before he continued.

"Now, it would have been foolish of me to expect you to understand why this is an issue, so allow me to explain. The females of my species are not the suave, sophisticated members of society like I am, they are our brutes and warriors. A single female Grondonian can make an entire platoon of Kackles tremble in their boots.

"I had managed to avoid contact with said women by working abroad from my home world, but alas, now that we are captured, I find myself in a severe quandary. I hold no illusions on where I stand in the strong or weak side of the universe. My intellect is golden and I am physically spry, but I don't have even an ounce of hope in countering, ... lady's strength.

"The other problem is, among my species, I am actually considered very attractive and physically desirable."

Nozomi had to fight back the urge to laugh in Doc's face, especially when she realized that he was serious.

"No matter how hard I try, I am afraid that she will find me ... enticing, and I will not survive a night of ... passion." Doc shivered again. "Copulation for us males is a one-time deal. You see, um, certain parts of our anatomy disengage from ourselves during the act of passion and while our, vital organs continue to constantly impregnate our partners, the loss of such a member of our bodies leads to severe hemorrhaging, hypovolemic shock and eventual cardiac-arrest and permanent death."

"Is there any other type of death?" Nozomi interrupted, both amused and horrified at the same time.

"The only males of our species that survive are those who can seek immediate medical attention of the highest quality, and judging by the state of this vessel, I am fairly certain I will bleed out far faster than I will receive the required medical aid." He spoke with resignation.

"That being said, I may have a small chance, but I fear what brings me hope, dooms you in my stead. The ship is full to capacity, which means our next stop is most likely where the majority of the slaves are to be purchased. I hope that the captain is too busy at the moment to deal with me, but if that's the case than that means that you are to be sold very, very soon.

"Regardless, for both our sakes, you must get the probe into space as soon as we stop, or else neither of us will make it out of our present predicament."

"Oh, come on, Doc." Nozomi whispered, but the message of hope that she wanted to share died in her throat as Slavers appeared outside the common cell. Doc swallowed nervously as, without any ado, alf the Slavers made a beeline for the Grondonian, who tried to shrink and hide himself behind Nozomi.

It was futile and the scientist found himself surrounded by his captors.

"Grondonian," The biggest of the Slavers spoke in a near deafening bass. Doc pointed a finger at himself and looked about quizzically, hoping someone else would step forward. Finally, he spoke in the smallest of voices.

"Me?"

"Yes, you!" The hulking thing replied. "Our boss is very interested in you. Come with us, now."

Slumped and defeated by the sheer numbers, Doc followed his captors out from the common cell. Nozomi turned her body just enough so that she could watch her companion's departure out of the corner of her eye. She waited, not moving, not making a sound, until all of the guards, and their toy, had departed.

Seeing that she was lost among the crowd, Nozomi removed the package from her clothing. The device was no bigger than her fist. It was smooth, metallic, long, and shaped like a bullet. The flat side had a small hole in it, and the long part of the cylinder was composed of a smooth material, with tiny, pin-headed sized pockets scattered throughout.

"Well, Doc." Nozomi said after she figured any more time not spent staring numbly ahead would arouse the suspicion of the local guards. "I hope it works."

They had been efficient, and that was something that Doc admired, even though he felt uncomfortably vulnerable. The Slavers had stripped him down to his traditional undergarments, prepared him with a quick and professional cleansingy had led him through the cramped hallways of the vessel, and had more or less thrown him into the most luxuriant quarters of the ship.

It was almost opulent. A wide bed, reinforced to take the undoubtable mass of the captain, lay against the far wall. Rustic, but well-polished, night cabinets were secured on either side of the sleeping space. A small, but tidy washroom was available near the door. It was almost a pleasant place, but it was not where Doc wanted to die.

At least he would meet his end meticulously dressed. During his cleansing, he had been measured, and when he was delivered to the room, he arrived at the same time as a rack of clothes in various species' styles.

He had chosen something that was hopefully tastefuls a mix of Grondonian traditional wear and what was apparently an ancient human fashion known as a topcoat.

The cold air of the ship still penetrated his clothes, but that was not what caused him to shiver. He was anxious about his future fate, and at the same time he was hopeful still that he could find a way to escape his present predicament.

His optimism died when he heard the main door open. Slowly, with great agonizing forbearance, Doc moved his gaze to study the bulky mass that was standing in the doorway. He was very tempted to scream. From her long, thick arms, to her short but intensely powerful legs, the female Grondonian was one large corded mass of muscles. Her prominent jaw seemed to twitch with every breath, and her neck was sinuously taught. The four breasts of the woman heaved with barely subdued passion.

She was in heat; desperate heat.

<Hello sweetie!> Her voice was so low and hoarse from the hormones that coursed through her body that the walls seemed to shudder, along with Doc's entire body. <Let me slip into something more comfortable.>

Without further introduction, she stepped inside and slammed the door shut behind her. It didn't matter that the door was supposed to slide closed on its own power, she wrenched it sealed with one arm, snapping several of the tiny motors that usually propelled the door.

As she passed Doc by, on the way to the washroom, the captain ripped her clothes off so fast that she tore right through materials that were supposed to resist the terrible forces of vacuum. Her top didn't last a second, and she still wore one ripped sleeve even as she grabbed at her pants. They disappeared in one great tug, and fabric floated around for a moment before the dampening system caught the material and pulled it towards the floor.

<Meep!> Doc said meekly, as he cringed. He was grateful that he was left alone again, and he held one hand over his chest, where his anxiety over his fate played the worst at his body.

What he wasn't expecting was what stepped forth from the room. She was not the same woman who had just wrenched the door closed, but instead, she was decked in traditional male Grondonian garb, the simple white cloak, with a green under suit, but she had decked her clothes with jewels and fine metals, and, somehow she had managed to apply a thin layer of Verte Green across her features, highlighting her eyes in a most brilliant display.

The illusion was shattered though, when she once more ripped the door wide. On the other side was a collection of more collared workers, and carts loaded with foods and delicacies. They poured into the room, hurriedly set the table and bench that had been hidden within the wall with all the trimmings, and removed themselves so suddenly Doc blinked, and swore that he had imagined it.

At least, he would have believed that, if the captain didn't once more wrench the door shut, and this time a small puff of smoke came from the ruined electronics.

<Well,> She said, clapping her massive hands together, the sinews and tendons danced across her arms under the impact, and the sound echoed off the metal walls. <Now that we're ready, please, take a seat.>

Nervous, but unwilling to find himself on his host's bad side, Doc slid onto one bench, leaving more than half the sear remaining, she into the other, filling it in its entirety.

Between them, the table was set with things that Doc hadn't realized he had missed. The room darkened as the captain played with her Datapad, and the only light that presented itself was from the two glowstones that rested on either end of their shared furniture. They were native stones, phosphorescen, relaxing.

Raising her hands, the captain opened them before putting them to the sides of her head. Her giant muzzle trembled and quivered, and her nostrils twitched as she breathed. Every motion of hers was an effort of subdued savagery, every moment, somewhere, something in her twitched as violent strength was subdued in her attempt at the greeting of peace.

Imitating her, Doc placed his own fingers to his temples.

She exhaled, he inhaled.

He exhaled, she inhaled.

They shared their air.

In that moment, they were one. Their minds both traveled back to their home world, both journeyed thousands of light-years, both danced amid the swamps and rainforests, both shivered at the poles, buried themselves in the sands of their deserts, and then they returned.

Removing her hands, the captain placed them down upon the table, palms upwards, waiting.

< Call me as I am, Rrlra of Vestnmum and Chstks. >

Placing his hands atop of hers, his palms also towards the sky, Doc responded.

< I call you as Rrlra, call me as I am, Grr'Kory of Roatsa and

Blthor. >

< I call you as Grr'Kory then. > Rrlra said, and closed their hands together.

With the formal greeting completed, the captain released Doc's hands, and leaned back in her seat. Resting her elbows on the little remaining space, Rrlra rested her rather prominent chin on loosely laced fingers.

< How long, for you? >

< Five Galactic Standard Years, you? > Doc replied automatically, his worries having been subdued somewhat by the formality.

< I haven't been home in nine. > The Captain replied, sighing in their species way, her shoulders slumping as she exhaled, but while she was trying to be gentle, the gust of air that escaped her was more than felt by her companion.

Lifting a glass each, they toasted to their home world. When the liquid touched his tongue, Doc almost gagged. It was Grondonian Draught, a drink that was strong enough to make a male immune to pain. It was a traditional pre-mating drink, a last request for numb flesh before the execution. If it was a hint of what was to follow, then he knew his time was short indeed. Against his better judgement, he drained it quickly, trying not to cough.

To his surprise, Rrlra was consuming her second. That was not common among their peoples.

< Forgive me, but regular ales are nothing to me. > The Captain said, sheepishly, when she realized that Doc had frozen up, the empty glass still in his hand. < I am not implying anything. >

Reaching forward, she plucked the vessel from Doc's fingers and set it upon the table, before she poured herself a third and drank it, in full view of her still-nervous companion. < But after the stress of the day, I need to unwind. I hope you understand. >

Doc tried to appear nonchalant, but he was still confused.

< It's been so long since I've had any companionship. > Rrlra spoke next, quietly, as if she was ashamed. < The last contact I had with another of our kind, a sister, she berated me for not

having already bred an army of my own. She didn't understand that I have a career, responsibilities. Not to mention, we are few and far between out here. >

Beginning to relax, Doc allowed the captain to fill their glasses, and they toasted together.

<To the swamps and trees. > Doc whispered.

<To our sun and our moons. > Rrlra agreed, then offered a selection of dried slugs, recently moistened in broth. Unable to refuse, Doc tore one in half, and while he placed his portion on his tongue, she did the same with her own side. It was their way, the recognition of the need for both male and female, the understanding of strength and mind.

The beginning of a union feast. It brought hope to Doc.

Despite the fact that he was more than likely doomed, it meant that he was, at least, probably spared for a few hours. The union feast was a method where the female learned as much as she could about her potential children's sire. It was an extended event that lasted several weeks. It was where each side came to an understanding, where each partner made their decision if they wanted to be united with the other. Although Doc viewed death as rather conclusive, there was a belief that he would survive and live on through his children.

It was a small measure of grace, but he was willing to believe in any thread of hope, no matter how tenuous.

< So tell me,> She smiled softly. <What's a handsome man like you doing out here anyways? >

Time no longer held the same understanding that it once did. Since her only activities had consisted of either standing, staring at a wall, or sitting, Nozomi had lost track of how long she had kept up her ruse. She had been forced to use the common commode once, but the press of enslaved bodies had kept her captors from being able to see her.

She had gotten some sleep. At one point, there had been a small buzz that had emanated from the cell's speakers. All of the collared ones had partnered up, turned their backs against each other, and slipped to the floor where they remained in a sitting position. Nozomi had found herself partnered with a Wealot. Her companion was huge compared to her, but its warmth and gentle fur had been a small comfort.

When the buzzing stoppedf the slaves closed their eyes and fell into slumber. As nervous as she was, Nozomi had forced herself to lie still. She didn't know how much time had passed, but she was awoken when her partner had begun to stand.

To stop herself from going insane, Nozomi had rehearsed songs and poems in her head, done complex mathematics, and had even begun to compose a play. By the time she was well into the fourth act of her play, on its third mental rewrite, an event happened to break the monotony.

She had begun to lean against her companior to alleviate the pains in her legs and feet. Although the Wealot had suffered at first without protest, it soon began to move and twitch. Suddenly, it snorted and shoved her away with its back. Nozomi took a single step forward and stood still, uncertain of what was going on, and just as uncertain as to what she should do.

With a yell that was loud and powerful, the Wealot ripped the smoking collar off from around itself. Her partner was shaped like a stout, tall oak, its neck was so long the collar had only burned it at the shoulders.

The equine-like head shook as the alien's brain cleared itself of the fuzziness that had once occupied it.

Alarms began to go off all around the cell. Nozomi was so concerned about the Wealot that she almost didn't notice all of the other slaves backing away from her former companion. The sirens must have had a subliminal command to make room, and since she was still attempting to continue the ruse, Nozomi stepped away from the Wealot, and she did so just in time.

Dozens of Slavers ran into the cell. Upon seeing itsscaptors, the Wealot growled out in Standard, "I'm a Freebie! This is illegal! Stop!"

When not one of the Slavers listened, it confirmed Nozomi's fears that she had not been captured accidently. Her captors had willingly broken galactic law.

The Wealot had come to the same conclusion. Lowering his head to his shoulders, it began to snort and foam at the mouth as it worked itself towards a berserker rage. Something kept the Wealot in check though, as it became obvious that it did not want to fight, but it would kill if it were cornered.

It got its chance. A stun-line shot out, its tips crackling with dangerous electricity, but the Wealot was ready and he leapt the attack. When it hit the ground, the Freebie was on all fours. His charge was sudden, violent, and the Slaver who had fired the gun was flung through the air to land limply at Nozomi's feet. She used all of her willpower to stay idle. The guard was not moving or breathing, and his chest was indented from the force of the Wealot's impact.

Continuing its rampage, the Wealot flung another guard into the air, and another Slaver skidded into a crowd of its companions. Nozomi wanted to run to the Wealot's aid but there were too many guards, and she doubted the frenzied alien would recognize her efforts as help.

The chaos stopped with the odd, deep sound of an EBD gun discharging. The Electro-Biological-Disturbance had instantaneous results, and the Wealot stumbled as the rage left its body. It sagged and then fell forward. After a pause, the Wealot took a deep breath and released its air with a hearty snore.

Without any more worry, one of the Slavers walked over and slapped a new collar around the sleeping captive. The results were instantaneous, and Nozomi hid a shiver as the Wealot instantly snapped to attention, even in its sleep.

Another guard walked over to the dead Slaver that lay at Nozomi's feet. Raising one hand, the Slaver pointed at Nozomi and some other slaves. "You four!" The Slaver demanded in Basic. "Pick Orgo up and take him to the recycler."

Faking the slow, careful pace of the collared, Nozomi bent

and took one of the dead guard's arms. She waited until the other three indicated slaves had each grabbed a limb, and then she straightened up and began to follow the guard who had given the order.

The limb was still pliable, a reminder that she was carrying someone who had, until moments ago, been alive. Despite her loathing of the Slaver's profession, she felt partly to blame for Orgo's death. Though, at the same time, she wondered and feared if she was going to be called out, if she were so transparent that it would become vague, waver, and disappear, exposing her and ending her ruse.

It was hard work. The dead guard was heavy but none of the other slaves complained so Nozomi kept her mouth quiet and her complaints silent. Although it wasn't the opportunity that she needed, it was a change from staring at the wall.

Doc woke up to the feel of warm drool dripping down his shoulder, pausing at his chest, before running down his stomach and pool beneath him. His side felt suddenly cold and chilled, and the change in temperature brought him to alert status.

It was something he instantly regretted. The problem with Grondonian Draught, was that it numbed you for certain events, but the hangover, if one survived, was often so brutal that those who endured it sometimes wished for death instead.

Opening one eye, Doc tried not to scream at the splitting headache that raced through his brain with such ferocity he feared his head would combust.

The reason for the temperature change was because Rrlra had sat up and positioned herself at the edge of the mattress. Her powerful hands gently held her own aching head as she waited for the combination of drugs and alcohol to leave her system.

For the smallest of moments, Doc felt something akin to pity for her, but then he remembered that his life was on the line. More than one of his race's women had been known to start wars because of hangovers.

A loud call-signal rang throughout the room. Unable to help himself, Doc groaned and tried to smother out the sonic punishment with the help of his hands. It was useless, and his companion's course language and spiked volume indicated that the captain shared his misery.

As the alert died away, an annoyingly high-pitched voice came over the com system, its Basic was rough and accented.

//Captain, we've come out of jump and have arrived at our destination.//

"Good." The captain replied, her voice gravelly and rough. "Now leave me in peace before I find you, rip your skull out, and beat you to death with it."

//My, my, you seem cheery this morning.// At the announcer's comment, Rrlra straightened up and pulled one giant fist back in preparation for a brutal and sudden redecoration of her quarters, but before she could unleash her vengeance the voice continued. //There's also been an incident. Orgo's dead. Do you wish his belongings?//

A feral snarl emitted from the captain's lips as she screamed, "I'm the captain and I always get the belongings. Always!"

//Well, you better come claim them soon. He's on his way to the recycler.//

"Then tell them to wait!" And with honest enthusiasm, the captain of the Slavers buried her fist into the audio pickup. Having recovered her composure, she stood and walked with very slow and cautious movements to her washroom. She didn't bother to close the door as she changed out of the clothes she had worn to bed and readied herself to face her crew.

They had drained an entire bottle together, had enjoyed foods from across the galaxy, and had warmed up rather nicely, but all the while, Doc had been unable to shake the feeling that the meal was going to be his last supper.

He had told her about his capture, about Nozomi, about their escape from the Pirates, and she had listened. She had asked about their escape, about how they had survived, and Doc had made mention of their freedoms, had asked that it be returned.

She had turned him down, and in time, he understood why.

She had a duty, and had set her and her crew down a vicious course. It was illegal, brutal, and the action would bring her the respect of her mother, her aunts, her sisters and cousins and nieces.

It would bring her respect among the other Grondonian woman, and despite how Doc felt, he also respected her for it.

It was the nature of their kind.

So, he had decided to try a different tactic. They had stumbled their way to her bed, where he had tried to convince her to free Nozomi as a gift to him, but thanks to the debilitating effects of the alcohol, he had been inarticulate and unable to think straight, until eventually, they passed out together, she on his shoulder, he sitting up. Both still fully clothed, but they had drawn a little closer together.

Returning from her morning rituals, the captain bent down and lifted Doc up by his shoulders. As their faces drew level with each other, she leaned forward and planted a tender kiss upon his lips. It caught Doc by surprise as there was honest passion behind her action. Breaking away, the captain stared into her captive's eyes with longing and regret before she shoved him onto the mattress and pulled both of his arms above his head. There was a click as she closed a set of restraints about Doc's wrists, securing the male Grondonian to the headboard. He was too stunned to say anything, so he did nothing.

<I'm sorry. > She said, softly. <But you cannot leave. I'd lock the doors, but . . .> She motioned to the motors she had destroyed . . . <Our union feast is not complete.>

With one more gentle kiss, the captain turned her back on him, and ripped the front door open.

Doc's groan of anxiety when she pulled the door shut was heard by his ears alone.

Her shoulders burned and her back began to twitch, her palms had begun sweating and her grip had begun to loosen. She was in danger of dropping the limb of the corpse that she held, but she struggled forward.

When the call to halt rang out, Nozomi almost sighed in relief. The corpse the four slaves carried was dropped unceremoniously to the decking. Hurrying to keep her ruse, she tried to adapt the same position as her coworkers. It was tough to do; all that she wanted to do was run and dump the probe outside.

Why they had stopped became obvious as a deep voice almost rattled Nozomi's teeth. The speaker was terrifying. She was a giant, even compared to a Wealot. The smallest part of the female Grondonian's wrist was still thicker around than the widest part of Nozomi's legs. Her shoulders were as wide as Nozomi was tall. When the captain took a step, Nozomi expected the decking to buckle and protest loudly, but instead, the giantess walked quietly and gracefully, even as she clutched one hand to her head in a sign of severe pain.

"Captain." The Slaver who had been guiding Nozomi and the troop spoke. "You look absolutely miserable."

"I feel absolutely miserable." The captain agreed with a bass rumble to her tone. "And that stupid man you found me is going to really suffer tonight!"

"He's still alive? He must be tougher than I thought." The guard responded to his captain's comment.

"No, he isn't tougher." In an unusual display of behavior, the Captain's eyes grew distant and she sighed happily to herself, stunning her companion before her face hardened again.

"We were just beginning to enjoy each other's company, we shared a drink, were on the bed together, talking, and the next thing I know I'm waking up with one nasty hangover, and I'm being told that Orgo met his death."

"Ho, that's why you're cranky." The Slaver began to laugh. "You didn't get any action last ni-UMPH!" his comment was cut short as his captain turned and laid a punch into his chest. The blow knocked the Slaver flat, and the female Grondonian paid the gasping Slaver no more heed as she began to systematically remove gear and clothing from Orgo's corpse.

Slowly, and in intense pain, the Slaver guard pulled himself off the ground. One of his arms refused to move, and it wasn't until he ordered Nozomi over to help him that he managed to get to his feet.

By the time Nozomi was done, so was the captain. Her arms were full of whatever she had removed from the dead Slaver. With menace clear in her steps, the female Grondonian walked until she was a hair's breadth away from Nozomi's guard, and Nozomi herself.

"Understand this." The captain snarled. "I am already upset, so you will keep your mouth closed or I will personally snap every bone in your body. Do you understand?"

The look of fear on the guard's face was genuine, but he managed to somehow snap to attention before he offered the words, "Yes Captain!"

"Good." The captain snapped. "I have to get ready. Our contacts are almost due to arrive and I want those slaves cleaned and prepped. I'll see you back at the cell in one deca."

The guard nodded, and the captain walked off. Once she was out of sight the Slaver doubled over, and moaned his next order. "Pick him up, and let's go."

Still feigning the stupidity of the collar, Nozomi bent and looked at the stripped Orgo. The dead Slaver was practically naked. The captain had taken everything, right down to the corpse's socks.

Moaning at the pain in his chest, the living guard looked away to be sick, and that was all the time that Nozomi needed. She reached into the folds of her clothing, palmed the probe, and crammed it into Orgo's mouth. The smooth device slid perfectly down the corpse's neck and Nozomi still had enough time to grab her assigned limb before the guard turned back to face his team.

"Alright, let's get this stiff to the recycler already." The guard ordered, and Nozomi and her fellow slaves moved to comply.

Chapter 15

The GSSE:

For the most part, planets, species, and corporations police themselves, or hire out to militant companies to provide enforcement of their local laws and customs. That being said, since the Sphere consists of multitudes, each with their own rules, a council was created in order to help maintain a universal set of standards.

The Galactic Sphere of Standards and Enforcement (GSSE) is a council of 27 of the most powerful organizations the operated out of the V'sigar system. Together they are responsible for creating laws, and punishing those that refuse to abide by them.

For example, Freebies are not allowed to be captured as Slaves, as they have purchased a pass for their freedom. If a Slave is found to be a captured freebie by a GSSE officia,, the Slavers and the purchasers, run the risk of having their rights to collections and ownership revoked. A second offense could lead the guilty into being sold as Slaves themselves, and their equipment auctioned ofr to pay their fines.

The Confederates currently hold the majority of the

*enforcement arm contract, and have, at any given time,
the availability to launch 3 destroyers immediately from
the GSSE primary station, with the promise of additional
reinforcements if required.*

THE TOOL'S HANDLE PRESSED into her palm and Isa closed her fingers over the screwdriver that Sudhir had handed to her. Twisting her arm back and around, the Selth brought the tool close to her face, so she could see what she was doing.

Somehow, Isa had managed to worm her way under the cockpit. Her feet were above her, on the bridge's decking. The Drudge that helped her had been her assistant for the better part of several hours, and although he did not know what the name of a single tool that he had been handing to her was, Sudhir had been able to get what she needed thanks to his telepathy.

As she tried to guide the wires into the terminal block, Isa's vision doubled and blurred. Blinking her eyes didn't work, so after a few more attempts, the Selth rubbed the back of her hand across her face, and that helped enough so that she was able to finish her latest task.

Everyone was tired. No one had managed to rest since Nozomi and Doc had disappeared. The Drudges had grabbed fitful naps here and there but the adults had operated constantly on a combination of adrenaline, sense of duty, and strong black coffee.

When the Slavers ship had left, Isa had tried to return to the station, but security had banned her. Apparently, the station's owners had been upset that there had been a running firefight through their halls, and that the *Chrysanthemum* and her crew had been involved. It had not looked good for the ship, until Kalle had spoken to the authorities. Isa had not been invited to the conversation, but whatever Kalle had said had been convincing and short. In less than five minutes the *Chrysanthemum* was 'invited' to a dry-dock.

Isa had been expecting to be met with intimidation upon landing, but Kalle had been waiting at the landing point, along with all the materials that the crew had been unable to load before their rapid and unexpected earlier departure.

No sooner had the human stepped aboard then he had distributed tasks to everyone. Joshua had been ordered to learn the ins and outs of the cargo bay, its operation, and the use of a ramp that only the old-hand had known about. It was amazingly large and spanned the width of the cargo-bay. The ramp was hidden inside its own secret compartment underneath the bay's primary decking.

Once Joshua had mastered the controls, Kalle had over-pressurized the interior of the ship and had set the Drudge to wander the ship from top to bottom and find any leaks in the hull, no matter how small.

Adorinda and Fallon had worked in the algae room. It was one that Kalle had installed when he had first purchased the *Chrysanthemum*, and it had been partly responsible for the moldy smell that had been in the air when the refugees had first boarded the vessel. It was undersized though, and Kalle had made himself and Telfer expand the room to twice its size while the two young girls had smeared algae into all of pads before they were placed.

With the use of a crane, the old-hand had the mechanical room's hatches removed. They were the giant recessed domes that were both on the top and bottom of the hull. Once the great hatches were moved aside, Hteathes' crew had delivered the large components of the new recycler an, a new water reservoir and dual pump system.

As the new parts were being lifted, Kalle had cut out the old equipment as best as he could, and had used the crane to help remove the defunct apparatuses.

Isa had thought that there might have been some rest after that, but she was wrong. Kalle had sealed the ship up tight before he, Telfer, Sudhir and Isa had hurried to install all of the new equipment.

Together the four of them had pulled though. Pausing only long enough to eat a quick meal, the old-hand had dragged Telfer around the hull and had sealed up all the minor hull breaches. New circuits and computers had arrived for the bridge, and Isa and Sudhir had drawn the straws to improve the equipment in order to bring the bridge up to modern standards.

Throughout the time they had all labored, everyone had been cut or hurt, especially Telfer, and Isa had been responsible for patching up the various injuries.

They had launched after that, but had done nothing but float in a holding pattern as Kalle and Telfer performed tests on their equipment, close enough to the station that if they needed help, it was readily available. The three other Drudges had busied themselves cleaning up the mess left over from the installations.

Isa had hoped that some of the surviving Slavers who had been captured would have revealed where the mothership had gone, but the few who were questioned had been unable to reveal anything useful.

Satisfied that the new circuit board was installed properly, Isa squeezed her way out from under the cockpit. Finally free from the painful position, the Selth lay upon the decking and closed her eyes for a moment as she fought back the urge to stay where she was and just let sleep claim her.

There was no chance of that. One of the panels in the science station began beeping loudly enough to get Isa's attention. She pulled her tired body to her feet but she was still behind Sudhir, who was already at the panel.

They were being hailed by an encrypted burst package. The monitor flashed as the computer system translated the data into Standard.

CHRYSANTHEMUM, PICK ME UP.

The signal was coming from the tiniest of probes. It was only visible on the sensor because it transmitted a transponder code. Tapping away on the monitor, Isa aimed a tether line at the device. The combat computer that was finally online, thanks to Isa's trials and tribulations, calculated the exact angle and power needed.

Outside of the ship, a small charge fired and a tiny claw shot into space. When it got close enough the claw closed over the metallic object, and slowly began to retract, pulling the claw and its captured target back towards the *Chrysanthemum.*

Everyone waited by the airlock door as Kalle stepped through the outer hatch. Behind him, the door closed, and sealed the interior space from the cold void of vacuum outside. As the atmosphere inside the tiny chamber equalized to the rest of the ship, the old-hand held the small probe and studied it intensely.

When the inner doors opened, Kalle removed his helmet. His face was stern and severe, but also quizzical and curious.

Adorinda fought back against a yawn but she ultimately lost. Reaching out with her two small hands, she rubbed at her eyes, smearing more of the blue/green algae across her already coated face. Fallon, who was just as dirty, tried to help her sister, but it wasn't until Isa stepped in to help that the little child was finally able to see again.

When the youngest Drudge looked back up, she noticed that everyone was unchanged, stuck in an eerie tableau of fatigue, shock and confusion.

Telfer's voice, spoken in the hushed tones of the exhausted, broke the spell and almost caused the little girl to jump.

"That, was flying through space?" He asked.

"Apparently." Isa answered slowly. "Although I don't know how."

Kalle shrugged his shoulders, and was about to pass the inanimate device to Telfer for further examination when a beep sounded from the old-hand's Datapad. Turning his arm around, he studied the writing that flowed across his device's screen.

WHAT WILL MAKE A VERY FINE SHIP ONE DAY?

Kalle paused briefly, though soon recalled his first conversation with his verbose friend and knew the answer could be only one thing. He confidently spoke the word, "Bottle."

The text on the Datapad was replaced with a visage of Doc's

face, and the sound of the Grondonian's voice filled the air.

"Kalle Aaron, I'm glad you had the intelligence to decipher the code. Don't turn me off. This is very important. That device that you are no doubt hovering around is my jump-communicator. I had only just finished completion of the device before Nozomi and I were kidnapped. If you can drag my device to the Nav-table, it will download the information of our location to you. Hurry, as I don't know when I managed to get this thing into space so I don't know how much time we have before we are forced to move again."

The Datapad reverted to its usual displays. They all stood in silence for a moment as they absorbed what they had heard. Finally, the captain of the *Chrysanthemum* sighed in relief and began to walk towards the bridge.

Only a few, scant minutes later, the old-hand's ship pointed its nose in the direction the Slavers' vessel had travelled. It hung there, quietly, serenely, and in the blink of an eye it vanished into space.

The single bright light that came in through the viewport was both calming to him, and at the same time, a reminder that they would soon be forced to engage the Slavers once again.

He stared at the illumination as his mind whirled in confusion caused by both fatigue and tactics drawn up from years past. It was a horrible feeling. His nerves were tight, and his stomach ached with anxiety and excitement. Raising the cup of water to his lips, Kalle tried to wash down the pill that he held between his teeth. His throat was dry, and he only managed to get the pill down as the glass ran empty.

Closing his eyes, the old-hand waited, counting the seconds quietly in his head. He knew from experience that he did not have long to wait.

When the rush hit him, his eyes snapped back open and his breath changed from the relaxed pace of the near asleep, to the rapid and shallow breath of the drugged energetic.

He was alone on the bridge. No sooner had the *Chrysanthemum* entered fold space tean its captain had declared that all crew was to rest. Together, the Drudges had taken his bed, and Isa and Telfer had found respite on his couch. The old-hand though, had not taken his own advice. He had needed to plan and strategize, and he doubted that he could have done so while in the land of the dreamers.

Sighing to himself, Kalle stretched out his twitching muscles and placed his glass down upon the floor. The sound of one of the airlocks opening stopped him in the middle of his actions, and he tilted his head backwards to see who was stepping back onto the bridge.

Two suited figures stood at the entrance to the old-hand's private quarters. Telfer seemed small as his tired features were partially obscured by the appropriated hardsuit he had taken from the armory. Isa looked positively vicious in her combat armor. It did nothing to ease the menace she portrayed as her face wore the look of someone who had been interrupted from a lovely dream. She did not speak as she marched towards the executive office. Her husband made his way to one of the observation chairs, where he collapsed into the seat with an audible grunt of relief.

Smiling at the artificial energy that still sang throughout his veins, Kalle asked Telfer in a light and cheery voice, "Did you two sleep well?"

The husband's first response was non-verbal as he fumbled his fingers into some semblance of an obscene gesture. Then, despite his own fatigue, he smiled as he spoke to his friend. "So well, that we didn't want to ever wake up."

"I've known the feeling." The other human said quietly before the two sat in contemplative silence.

Isa returned from the executive office. She balanced three large mugs of coffee in her arms. Grateful, Kalle took the one that was offered to him and sipped. He hadn't even taken two sips before he felt his blood pounding between his ears. The old-hand blinked in shock. Isa had included stimulants into the drink, unknowingly adding to Kalle's already drug-ravaged system. Once all the medication left his body, he was going to come down hard.

Tipping the mug upside down, Kalle drained it in one go, swallowing madly to keep up with the hot liquid. He didn't feel it as the brew burned his tongue and mouth, his extremities were starting to numb.

Setting the mug beside his empty glass, the old-hand stood quietly and walked to his room's airlock, leaving the suited couple to tend to the bridge.

Telfer watched Kalle disappear. Unsure of how to handle his friend's change of mind, the husband turned to his wife as he indicated the closed door with his thumb. "What is with him?" He asked.

Isa sighed as she squeezed herself into the pilot's seat. "I don't know." She admitted. "I've known him ever since he arrived on the station, but the last few days have only revealed that I didn't know him at all. He's dropped hints to me that he came from a hard life and I can tell that he's been trained in mechanics, electrics and combat, but other than that . . ." And as she trailed off, Isa shrugged her shoulders. It was a motion that she had learned from her husband.

"Well," Telfer said with a smile on his face. "I didn't realize that he could be such a slave-driver, but I now know that at least you two share something in common."

His attempt at humor worked, and he dodged the playful swat of his wife's arm.

"But honestly," He continued. "Don't you find it odd that he's been able to afford so much, and that he owns his own ship?"

"I've been asking myself those questions over and over." Isa admitted. "But I think, when Kalle is ready, he will let us know." The Selth's words were clear to her husband. There was no point in asking questions, because there were no readily available answers.

Removing his helmet, Telfer stood from his seat and retrieved the empty glass and mugs. Hesitating for a moment the human bent over and kissed his wife softly on the lips.

"I'm envious of you, you know." Telfer spoke softly.

"Why, because I have such a good husband?" Isa asked lightly.

"Well, that too." Telfer said, looking upwards, but then he let his eyes settle back upon his wife's. "I'm envious that you seem to be so calm. I've never been off the station, let alone chased after slavers in an antique and unarmed vessel before. I'm so nervous that I'm shaking inside this suit and yet, here you are, calm as ice."

Isa continued to smile, but her voice was very gentle and soothing. "I'm not calm at all, Telfer. Inside, I'm a nervous wreck, but Selthian nobility does not show fear. I'm envious that you've always been able to wear your heart on your sleeve."

"Tit for tat then. Aren't we in a messed-up situation?" Despite his words, the human was laughing as he disappeared into the executive office. Isa just shook her head.

Telfer had barely disappeared through the doorway when Kalle's room began to open. Isa paid it no mind as she read the layouts in front of her, assuring herself that the ship was still functioning well. She only looked up when she heard her husband's exclamation of surprise.

The suited figure was intimidating. The dark armor caught the light, absorbing it. The thick boots and pants were patterned with rails that ran down the length of the legs. Metal tubing glinted in the light. The chest was heavily armored. Medals were burnt onto the breastplate, indicating the past of the wearer. A gold lanyard was welded onto one shoulder. Up one arm, two silver lines ran from wrist to neck, imitating a tattoo that Isa had seen very recently on the wearer. The silver bands were only broken once, by a rank insignia of a diamond, crossed by two rifles that rested on the shoulder.

Even Telfer, who had been born and raised under the company's controlled conditions, recognized what the figure's armor meant.

Kalle Aaron was a Confederate Veteran.

♦ ♦ ♦

His nerves had not settled in the slightest, and each measured step rang throughout the abandoned hallway. The sound reverberated against the metallic decking, ringing out each pace as he approached his destination. It was the beat of his own clock of fate.

> *Kalle paced across the bridge. His movements were deliberate. Every joint of his suit had small generators attached to them, and every lift of a leg, every bend of an arm, every flex of the fingers, charged the battery which had laid idle for so long.*
>
> *Telfer had not stopped staring at the other human. The shock and disbelief on his face was plain and evident.*
>
> *Isa though, was calmer as she spoke dryly, "How long?"*
>
> *The old-hand halted his walk only long enough to make a glance that asked its own question to the Selth before he took his walking back up.*
>
> *"How long did you serve?" She asked again.*
>
> *The only answer Kalle gave was to point to the two silver bands that mimicked his tattoo. Telfer understood his friend's actions as he translated the motions into speech. "Two full terms." He said in awe.*
>
> *"Five years." Kalle finally agreed. "During which I fought for them, bled for them and earned my freedom with them."*

He began his final inspection. The gauntlets were closed tightly. The chest plate was secured. The compressor on his back had stopped its constant humming, signaling that his oxygen tanks were full of frozen-solid air, giving him hours of freedom should he be forced into vacuum.

> *"They molded me, trained me and taught me to never abandon your friends as long as there is hope." Kalle continued*

*as he checked his Datapad that he had stuck to his arm. It
gave a status report on the condition of his suit.*

*"I don't know if you would really consider Doc a friend."
Telfer said from his seat.*

*"He's a member of this crew." The old-hand's statement
was fact. "He is one of us, and he needs our help."*

*"You're sounding really noble." The other human said,
with a hint of admiration in his voice.*

Grabbing the edge of his Datapad, Kalle removed it from its
place on his left arm, and slapped it onto his right thigh. Pausing
his pace, the old-hand lifted his helmet and began to attach the
life ribbon from the back of his suite to the port on the back of
the last piece of armor he had to don.

*Kalle rested in the captain's chair. He did not look up from
his task as he carefully packed a bag full of mining-explosives.*

*"We are not ready for war." He expressed his thoughts
aloud for the other two adults to hear. "We have no real
offensive capabilities, short of one, untested variable that
might even the odds."*

*Telfer looked at his friend curiously but Isa got the pic-
ture immediately.*

"Nozomi's mecha." She said.

*"The Nobilis moved faster than what I've understood
to be physically possible, and the way that Nozomi pretended to pilot it made it seem to me like her machine had its
own sentience." The old-hand paced his words carefully as
he spoke. "Maybe, I can appeal to it for help."*

*"Well, I've heard of worse plans, but not many." Isa
said. "But I don't see any other choice."*

"Thanks for the vote of confidence." Kalle chuckled.

His arm began to burn and itch under his flight suit. Kalle
thought about scratching it, but decided to ignore it instead. An

old song began to ring through his mind. It was a tune sung in gallows' humor.

Humming the jingle to himself, the old-hand lifted his helmet over his head. As it sealed itself and began its own tests, he breathed in the familiar smell of burnt metal and seared meat. The memories came rushing back: memories of battles fought, memories of chaos, memories of fear and excitement and, the memory of his flesh burning and the pain and agony left behind on both body and mind.

It took him a moment to recover from the shock. He fought with it and barely bit back the urge to scream and tear the helmet from his head. He wanted nothing more at that moment than to flee, to turn his ship about and abandon all of the tasks he had set out for himself.

Then his training took over. His emotions became a dull sensation in the back of his mind, the knots in his stomach loosened and his pulse steadied out. He was once more Kalle Aaron, soldier, warrior, and leader.

Reaching out his hand, he opened the door to the cargo bay and stepped inside.

The Nobilis was no longer under the tarp. The great white form sat upright, its legs were crossed and its hands rested against the floor. It faced the giant doors of the bay so that its back was to the old-hand.

Without a sound, the flesh in the center of its back, below where another creature may have had shoulder blades, opened. One hand moved of its own accord and rested, as if it were waiting.

Stepping onto the offered palm, Kalle was lifted to the opening. When he stepped inside, the flesh closed behind him, plunging him into darkness until his Datapad lit up with information. The air around him was safe to breath and so the old-hand allowed his suit to vent.

As he looked back up from his electronic screen, Kalle realized that the walls were changing. They grew bright as shapes scrolled about. What began as amorphous blobs took form and became letters that the old-hand understood. Scrawled out before him in Basic and Standard was the sentence:

WELCOME, KALLE AARON, WE HAVE BEEN EX-PECTING YOU.

Chapter 16

Rights of Freedom:

A Freebie is someone who has purchased a Right of Freedom certificate number from an organization. While it is common and good practice to purchase a certificate from at least three organizations, even having just one protects the Freebie from being unjustly collare.,Ccaptured, or enslaved.

If a Freebie is threatened with improper restraint, they can file a complaint with the GSSE; however, since it is known that the GSSE is a bureaucracy and must first begin a lengthy legal investigation, most Freebie licenses come with a Right to Protection clause written in, which allows limited resistance without repercussion

The most famous of these protection clauses belongs to the Confederates. All Citizens, not Civilians, are automatically registered as Freebies by all of the organizations of the GSSE, and they have the right to defend their freedom if it is unlawfully restricted, using whatever means necessary, and may call on the nearest Confederate forces in order to help reinforce their positions.

*This clause it written into every Confederate con-
tract and agreement, forcing anyone who wishes to work
with the Confederacy to follow along with their rules and
protections.*

WE?" KALLE ASKED AS HE SAT into a chair that had mysteri-
ously formed behind him.

YES, WE.

The writing scrolled about him.

NOZOMI HAS NOT TOLD YOU EVERYTHING
YOU NEED TO KNOW, AND FOR THAT I AM SORRY.

Kalle had thousands of questions, but he forced himself to
ask one at a time.

"We, do you mean Nozomi and you?"

YES, AND HER BROTHER.

"Well this day is just full of surprises." The old-hand whispered sarcastically to himself. Allowing himself to relax, he sank
into the living seat. When the chair warmed itself, the human
had to fight the urge to jump back to his feet, but it was just the
Nobilis, making itself even more comfortable for its pilot. The
heat was soothing, and it worked its way throughout the cockpit.

YOU CAN REMOVE YOUR ARMOR FOR NOW. IT
WILL STILL BE A WHILE BEFORE WE ARRIVE.

His ears stopped ringing. It came as a surprise; Kalle was certain that the amount of drugs in his system should have kept his
blood pressure at dangerously high levels.

Chuckling, the old-hand adjusted his position, but kept his
gear intact. "Thanks," He said, shocked at the sudden slurring in
his words. "But it takes a long time to extract myself from this,
and I don't want to undergo the effort right now. Considering
the fact that you're drugging me, I'd like to stay ready enough in
event of an emergency."

I AM NOT DRUGGING YOU, KALLE AARON. I CAN
SEE THAT YOUR BODY IS BREAKING DOWN. YOUR
HEART IS SCARRED, AND YOUR BLOOD PRESSURE

HAS INCREASED WELL PAST SAFE LIMITS. WHAT YOU ARE CURRENTLY FEELING IS THE EUPHORIA OF A DAMAGED RETICULAR ACTIVATING SYSTEM. I CAN HELP YOU, BUT I WILL NOT DO SO WITHOUT YOUR PERMISSION.

"I, don't feel, that bad at, all." It was hard for Kalle to form the words in his mind, and it took tremendous effort to speak them out loud.

YOU SHOULD HAVE NO FEELING IN YOUR EX-TREMITIES. THE DRUGS IN YOUR SYSTEM HAVE DISTORTED YOUR SENSES. I HAVE CHANGED MY MIND. I WILL LET YOU UNDERSTAND.

His pained arm began to burn. The limb's agony was beyond what he had ever suffered before. It hurt so much that the anguish paralyzed him. All of the muscles locked, all of the joints stiffened, and Kalle discovered he couldn't even scream. His lungs refused to work, his chest seized and burned with the fury of a thousand suns. His other arm became a useless weight. In the distance, far away, he heard his Datapad began to scream out in warning as his vitals fluctuated rapidly.

As his vision blurred, the old-hand managed to read the next text that scrolled across his sight.

YOUR BODY IS REBELLING AGAINST YOU. YOU ARE DYING.

He wanted to reply with a snide comment, but it was impossible for him tn manage even a simple breath. His suit reacted, and it closed off the helmet's vents before it pressurized around his mouth, forcing air into his mouth and nose. The chest plate pulled away from his skin, and created a negative zone, sucking on Kalle's torso and it forced his lungs to inhale.

IF YOU WANT TO SURVIVE, YOU MUST STOP THE DRUGS FROM RUNNING THEIR COURSE. I CAN HELP YOU, BUT YOU MUST LET ME HELP YOU.

The old-hand moved his dead-like limbs to the collar of his suit. His fingers fumbled as his vision began to fill with redness.

Another breath was forced onto him by his gear but it did not mitigate the pain. His right arm fell, dead to his side. His left trembled, and the biceps failed. The limb fell, but his hand landed upon his Datapad. With the last ounce of his abilities, the old-hand punched in an emergency code and his suit shut down and ruptured its own seals.

The smell of the air changed and despite everything, the old-hand felt his eyes grow heavy and his head rocked forward against his chest before the deep, blessed darkness overtook him.

"Are you getting up, sleepyhead?"

The voice was very familiar. It was a little lighter in tone than what he was used to hearing, but there was no doubt about who was speaking.

Kalle opened his eyes. Nozomi was leaning over him. Her eyes twinkled in the dim glow that was thrown from the overhead lights. She was different. Her skin was darker than ever, and her build was altered. She was still slight, but she was more muscled. She was dressed in rough and ready explorer clothes. Her pants were lined with pockets, her shirt was fitting, but loose enough to allow circulation, and her vest seemed to have been thrown together from various materials.

As Kalle wondered what had happened to him, he felt himself speak, and the voice that rang through his ears was not his own.

"Yeah, yeah, Sis, hang on a moment."

As his legs swung over the edge of the bed, Kalle realized what was going on and why he wasn't in control of his body . . . His conscious had somehow been transported into that of someone else.

"C'mon Aiji," Nozomi urged. "Let's get going. Mom and dad are almost to the caves by now."

The young body felt wiry and strong; it was the gift of a life lived with fresh air and healthy eating. As he bent down to tie on his boots, Kalle felt a pang of envy for the young man who was uncaring about both the present and the future.

As soon as the boots were on, Aiji grabbed an old beat up jacket. The weight was comforting, and various devices clicked against Aiji's chest. He was not wearing a shirt.

Brother and sister leapt out of the small ship that they called home. Together, the two of them ran into the jungle. The air was humid and sticky, but Aiji felt no discomfort.

They moved like deer, leaping and jumping over some obstacles, crouching and rolling under others. Even though they wore thick boots, the two moved almost silently. It was the run of those who lived in the wild, who had embraced nature rather than having tried to dominate it. The pace the two set would have exhausted Kalle in the first few minutes.

Beside the two youths, a small, six-legged animal leapt along with them for a moment, before veering off to crash through the woods. Although Aiji noticed it, he said nothing. Life was meant to be lived, and it was that simple.

When they stepped out from the trees, they happened upon a giant mountain that was pitted with hundreds of holes. There were metal platforms all over the hill, but it was silent, and inactive.

"They are really gone, aren't they?" Aiji said.

Beside him, his sister nodded. "Yeah, they stopped mining overnight, and there hasn't been any motion since."

"What, did they just give up?" The brother asked, but Nozomi shrugged, and then smiled.

"Who knows and who cares. Mom and dad are already inside." Aiji reached into a pocket on his jacket, and pulled out a tracking device. The information that scrolled across it was in a writing that Kalle was not familiar with, but he knew that Aiji understood it. He must have snuck tracking tags into their parents' garment at some point.

Reaching out, Nozomi grabbed her brother's hand and began to run towards the closest of the openings. The two sprinted, racing each other in an attempt to be first.

The inside of the cave was dark, but there was still enough illumination to see with. There were dim lights everywhere. They cast a pale shadow, but neither Aiji nor Nozomi slowed their pace. The coolness of the air was a welcome relief to them after the humidity of the jungle.

The two siblings finally decelerated to a careful crawl. "Mom and dad are only a few feet above us." The brother whispered. "We have to be really quiet."

Understanding their predicament, Nozomi nodded, and laid one finger across her closed lips. The two crouched and darted from cover to cover. Both of them seemed to have an instinctual knowledge of what would hide them.

When the two finally entered the chamber, Kalle felt the air leave his chest. There was a giant hole in the middle of the mountain, some of it was natural, but some of the hole was carved. It was wide enough to easily fit the Chrysanthemum in twice, from end-to-end. The walls were covered with walkways but no one was anywhere to be seen, not at first. Craning his neck upwards, Aiji caught the sight of a pair of traveler's boots above him, and he ducked back under cover.

The voices of the sibling's parents were loud in the empty space.

"They really did a number on this, didn't they?" The mother said in awe.

"Yes, but I can't help but wonder what they were doing here? What were they mining?" The father asked.

"Ore?"

"Well, whatever they were mining for, they probably found it. After all, they're gone now."

They paused their conversation for only a moment.

"What's that?" The father asked. Aiji looked down

to the bottom of the pit. There was something giant that was lying still, unmoving. Reaching into one of his many pockets, the youth removed a pair of electro-binoculars. He raised them to his eyes. There was the half-buried body of the alien that Nozomi would later come to call the Nobilis.

The parents had thrown caution to the wind as they hurried down a flight of stairs. Nozomi hissed quietly, and the two siblings hid as their parents rushed by the mouth of the siblings' cave.

His sister made a motion with her hand, and Aiji nodded in understanding. They began to slowly move down a sub-tunnel. It was a tight fit, but neither of them seemed perturbed by narrow spaces. They slowly tired under the effort however, when the two made it two floors above the base of the excavation, the rush of adrenaline came back.

"This thing is almost alive." The father spoke in his native tongue.

The mother was bent over as she poked the Nobilis in the chest. "It's at least a bioroid. Look at this thing's flesh. It's pliable, and shows clear signs of circulation beneath it." The mother replied.

"So, is this what the Pirates were after? Why would they just abandon it?" The father asked.

Quietly, the mother stood and shook her head. "I don't know, there are just too many questions." She shivered. "Let's get out of here before they come back. They might have just left to acquire more gear, or a VIP."

The father reached for his wife's hand and together the couple moved towards the catwalk. They were still many feet below the siblings. Sparing a moment, Aiji looked over at his sister and jerked his head once as a symbol, a communication to follow their parents' example.

They turned to head out of the caves, when suddenly Aiji twisted back around. At the bottom of the cave floor, lay the fresh corpse of their mother. Smoke rose from the hole that had been made through her chest. *The wound was cauterized, but the lack of bleeding did her no favors.*

Beside their mother, their father calmly and quietly faced the masked figures. There was no mistaking them. They were the dreaded people who had haunted children's' stories, who were talked about in quiet, backwater pubs: Pirates.

They had appeared in an almost ethereal fashion. Like ghosts and phantoms, they filled the room. Their footfalls were quiet, despite their armor, betraying the advancements of their gear. It was then that Aiji noticed something else: a ringing in his head. They must have been using a sonic suppression technology.

Aiji turned back to his Dad; he never spoke, never said a word. He stood protectively over his wife, the mother of his children. The only thing that indicated the man felt any emotion at all was that his eyes blazed with the full force of his rage and anger.

Without sentiment, or ceremony, the Pirates advanced, and as one they jabbed their sticks into the father's chest. The smell of burnt flesh instantly filled the air. The father never screamed, he just fell, collapsed, and lay still.

Nozomi stifled a cry and hid her face. Grabbing his younger sister by her shoulders, Aiji turned to run, to hide, to escape, but it was already too late. Behind them an entire force of Pirates had arrived from nowhere. They were just staring at the brother and sister, unmoving, uncaring.

"RUN!" Aiji screamed, but there was nowhere to go, no place to hide. They were captured, and were more than likely about to face the same ends as their parents. Everywhere they looked, they only saw more Pirates.

Together, the people who had killed Aiji's parents raised their sticks and advanced.

Although Aiji knew he was outnumbered, he refused to go down without a fight. He crouched. The Pirates charged *them and with nowhere else to go, Aiji grabbed his sister, and threw the two of them off the catwalk. His feet slipped, and he rolled in the air.*

When he hit the chest of the large machine, Aiji felt his bones snap. His head crashed and he felt his skull shift. Something in his neck popped and then the young man felt nothing below his shoulders. His lungs stopped working, pierced by his shattered ribs.

Nozomi's weight, as she landed on top of him, pressed the damaged bones into vital organs.

As his life fled from his body, Aiji heard his sister cry. Over the singing in his ears, he heard her horrified scream as she, still beside him, begged for him not to die.

All he wanted to do was tell her it would be okay, that everything would be fine, but he felt himself sinking, felt himself vanishing. It felt like one giant blanket being wrapped around him. His vision blurred, as if obscured by something. It was over. He was gone, sucked into the ground itself.

Almost simultaneously, every organ in Aiji's body quit, and the young man passed into the realm of the dead.

Kalle awoke with a start.

Moving his left hand, the old-hand was surprised that he felt no pain in his limb, or anywhere for that matter. He checked his Datapad and saw that he had been trapped in the vision of Aiji's past a while. It was almost time for the Chrysanthemum to come out of fold.

Things had changed while Kalle had dreamed. The inside of the Nobilis was clear, transparent. Kalle was floating in a sea of liquid, except he wasn't. He could still feel the form of the biological seat around him and he could still taste the soothing air.

"Nobilis, what is going on?" Kalle asked into the air.

YOU HAVE JUST AWOKEN FROM AN IN-DUCED REST. I HAD TO SLOW YOUR BIOLOGICAL

FUNCTIONS TO A NEAR HALT. IN THE PROCESS, I
ALLOWED YOU TO WITNESS HOW I MET NOZOMI'S
BROTHER. NOW, LOOK DOWN.

There, stored within the liquid that was the Nobilis' blood,
was Aiji. He still wore the same beaten clothes from the vision,
but his flesh was cleansed, and his ribs looked more intact than
Kalle had felt they should have been.

THIS IS WHERE HE NOW LIES. I ABSORBED HIM
IN ORDER TO SAVE HIM. HE WAS SOMEONE WHO
HAD NOT ATTEMPTED TO HURT ME. THE OTH-
ERS, THE ONES YOU CALL THE PIRATES, HAD DONE
HORRIBLE THINGS TO ME.

The walls of flesh changed form as the Nobilis revealed the
moment that it became aware.

The Pirates were everywhere. Their lethal sticks were pointed
at Nozomi, but she had become ignorant to the horror of her
own imminent death; her mind had been made distant by the
death of all those she held dear. Tears streamed down her face,
her hair fell about her as she screamed her agony into the air, her
mind having snapped under the sight of her family's murder,

The Nobilis moved. One giant hand shot out and crushed
a Pirate between its massive fingers. One other Pirate leapt forward and buried its stick into the Nobilis' side. It did not hurt
the grand alien. The arm rocked back down, and crushed that
Pirate flat.

The giant hand that had not killed, covered the weeping girl
and saved her from death as dozens of lasers collided again the
shielding fingers.

Heaving itself upright, the beast took its revenge out on the
ones who had been trying to enslave it. The massive feet crashed
down, over and over again, crushing dozens of Pirates with each
step. The free arm waved about and released energy that liquefied
and disintegrated all that it touched.

There was only one place to store the crying girl, and Nobilis pressed its precious cargo against the back of itself. For one

frightening moment, Kalle thought that the flesh wall would open, and a ghostly illusion of Nozomi would enter, but that was not the case.

Bending its legs, the mecha gathered its strength, and leapt into the sky. The mountain gave a moment later as the sheer force of the machine destroyed the rock. There was no safe place on the planet. Space was the retreat that they needed.

Unfortunately, there was a very large capital ship in their way. Kalle tensed as he saw multiple gun blisters aim themselves at the Nobilis, but the mecha was unafraid. The ship continued to grow in Kalle's vision until it was all encompassing, until it was the only thing that Kalle could see.

When the Nobilis crashed into the hull, the metal tore like wet paper.

Decks flew by, Pirates died by the hundreds, and the main reactor became visible. Without pause, Nozomi's mecha crashed through that too. Energy crackled all around them but the beast that was the Nobilis kept on going until it was past the other side of the hull, and into deep space.

Behind them, the capital ship listed, and, caught by the gravity of the planet, began the inexorable fall towards the surface. The Pirate's large ship crackled, and flamed through the atmosphere Its reactor gave and exploded before it ever hit the surface of the planet. A moment later, the atmosphere of the world combusted, ignited, and turned the once-living planet into a living star.

The walls once more became black.

"So, that's how it began?" Kalle said to himself.

YES. I AM LIKE THEM, ALONE.

"What I want to know," Kalle asked, flexing his hand, which felt amazingly sensitive compared to how it had been only a short while ago. "Is why you hadn't fought back against the pirates before Aiji merged with you."

I DID NOT UNDERSTAND THAT I COULD. MY PEOPLE SEED THEMSELVES ABOUT THE UNIVERSE, BUT I MUST HAVE BEEN LEFT IN A DAMAGED STATE.

I GREW ALONE, BARELY ALIVE, BARELY COMPRE-
HENDING MY OWN EXISTENCE BEFORE I MERGED
WITH MY COMPANION'S MIND. WE SAVED EACH
OTHER.

I OWE HIM, AND THOSE WHO WERE SACRI-
FICED FOR MY FREEDOM. THAT IS ONLY ONE REA-
SON WHY I WILL HELP YOU RESCUE NOZOMI. SHE
IS, IN A WAY, PART OF MY BLOODLINE NOW.

"Then you know that Nozomi's in trouble, and that I need
your help?"

YES.

"Are you willing to fight with me?"

FOR NOZOMI, FOR AIJI, I WOULD GIVE MY LIFE,
AND SO WOULD YOU.

Kalle laughed, bitterly, and then he became serious. Removing his gloves, the old-hand placed his naked hands upon the two
sides of the living chair that he sat within.

"Show me, Nobilis." He said with his voice calm but his tone
cold. "Show me what I can do."

Chapter 17

We hope that you are enjoying your subscription to Gorda Gionni's Ever Expanding Encyclopedia of our Galactic Sphere. Thanks to your purchase, we can continue to provide updates and information to you and our clientele in a timely and proficient manner.

Your comments are important to us because they help us provide the best service in the industry. So please, if you have not already, take a moment to fill out the attached survey so that we may continue to serve you best.

As always, if you have any questions concerning our product, please contact our customer service department for free by using our app near any bright-star communication router.

TIME HAD PASSED SINCE Nozomi had dropped the body of Orgo into the recycler. All the collared slaves had been organized into ranks, and had been ordered to stand at attention. Frozen in that tableau for the last few hours, the only action that any of the slaves had done was blink, sneeze, of cough.

The cell doors opened, and Nozomi had to refuse the urge to

turn her head and study who was walking the length of the hall. She discovered the answer when the captain appeared in her vision again. She was still intimidating, and her gaze was positively toxic as the Grondonian studied each and every slave. Nozomi felt the gaze touch her, and pass over her. Behind the captain came an entourage of other Slavers. They stopped at certain individuals and straightened clothing here, touched up hair there.

One Slaver stopped in front of Nozomi, and launched a wad of spit at her face. Despite the fact that every nerve in her body wanted her to duck, Nozomi took the blast full on before a towel was rubbed over her cheeks and forehead, and the Slaver who was guilty of such deeds grumbled under its breath. Nozomi didn't recognize the species, or its language, but she finally understood what was going on; she was being cleaned up for the sale.

As the towel was removed Nozomi's mind began to work madly on a solution that could still get her free. All she had to do was alert the buyers that their purchase was illegal, however long that would take.

Once more, Nozomi focused on a distant spot on the wall, and pretended to be useless.

Doc shivered. He had tried crossing and uncrossing his legs, but that had stopped working a long time ago. He had to use the washroom, badly, but since he was chained to the bed the chances of making it to the toilet before an accident were growing slimmer.

Something chimed against the wall, and it interrupted Doc's agony briefly.

//To all crew, purchase ship has arrived, prepare all stations. I say again, purchase ship has arrived, prepare all stations.//

As the signal disappeared from the air, Doc winced. Then, screwing his eyes shut, the Grondonian offered a silent prayer and concluded it with the spoken words. "Please Nozomi; I hope you've gotten the communicator away by now, because if you haven't, it's too late for the both of us."

◆ ◆ ◆

As the announcement faded from the air the Slavers stepped up the pace of their preparations. Clapping her hands for attention, the captain screamed at the top of her lungs. "Honor guard, assemble!"

Several Slavers who had been lurking around the captain snapped to attention and immediately formed about their leader. It was a protective circle, a formation that declared, 'if you want to kill my captain, you have to go through me first.'

From behind the female Grondonian, a tiny alien ran forward, knelt at the captain's feet, and began to polish her boots. Pulling one leg back, the captain kicked the tiny slave out of the way. Crying out in pain, the little alien disappeared. Nozomi fantasized extending her foot, just far enough to trip the pompous bitch the next time she passed, but she refrained from doing so. Nozomi's plan demanded perfect timing and patience, but that was something that Nozomi was rapidly losing. Still, she gathered herself, and waited as the party of Slavers got to the end of the cell.

The captain spun, and her voice ordered out a command. "Slave unit, face me!"

Although she struggled to turn like all the other collared ones, Nozomi did so, somehow maintaining the facade.

"Slave unit, quick march!"

It was more like a shuffle, but Nozomi still attempted to sustain the pace that the others used. The slave unit moved in perfect cadence directly behind the captain and her honor guard.

As a Wing-bird, Nozomi had never belonged to a militant unit. It felt like she was behind everyone else, whether it was not swinging the arms high enough, or not keeping in exact pace. It was as if Nozomi could feel the scrutinizing gaze of each of the Slaver guards.

They cleared the length of the deck before they were given the order to "Mark, Time!" The entire group of slaves, bar none, stopped in place and began to lift first one leg, then the other.

Even the four, six, or many legged aliens managed a method. Nozomi tried, but two years on the station had not been good for her physical strength.

A new shuttle became visible. It landed in the docking area of the Slaver's mother ship. Whoever had arrived in the shuttle must have been ultra-important, as every Slaver took one more moment to check that they, and their closest associates, were presentable.

The sounds of the shuttle setting into its landing spot was muted, because there was still vacuum out on the pad. All that Nozomi heard was the minor rumble of the pad vibrating and then the landing area retracting into a massive airlock. The shuttle was pulled forward until it finally came to rest in front of the marching slaves and their guards.

A door opened from the back of the shuttle, and Nozomi set her eyes on a different company's representative. The new representative had a very high air of nobility about it. It was a member of the Ziz race. They were so androgynous that it generally took complex DNA testing for outsiders to tell their three different genders apart.

The Ziz strode down the bridge, and as the company representative was still making its way down the ramp, the Slaver's captain turned to her crowd and roared out another order. "Slave unit, HALT!"

As one, the entire unit stopped its marching so uniformly that Nozomi felt alone. She had stopped too soon. She did not dare to look around to see if any of the Slavers had noticed her tiny faux pas.

By the time Nozomi brought her pulse back to a standard beat, the Ziz and the captain were in conversation as they, and the entire honor guard, funneled towards the ranks of slaves.

"As you can see, we have brought only the best material for you." The female Grondonian spoke her Standard proudly. The Ziz stopped and admired one of the first slaves in rank. Reaching forward, the Ziz used one hand to pull the lips of the Wealot away from its teeth. Humming, the Ziz let the lips slap back into place.

"You have always provided us with exceptionally wonderful physical specimens before, but they always seem to have some issues with their mental capacities. I hope you have rectified that error." The Ziz spoke in a calm and soothing voice. It sounded like it was talking in lullabies.

"It will be rectified before pickup." The captain replied. The two began to walk closer to Nozomi's position.

"The problem with Skags and Dregs is that they are already of poor cerebral capacity." The captain continued.

The Ziz nodded in understanding. "Yes, I know, but they are still more cognitive than what you've given us recently."

They were almost beside Nozomi.

"Yes well, I got these at prime breeding." The captain boasted.

Nozomi decided to make her move. She filled her lungs, opened her mouth, stepped forward, and suddenly experienced the feeling of what an EBD gun did to a human body.

The words she planned to say froze in her throat. Her eyes became heavy, and she sagged, limply, unable to help passing into the electronically induced rest. As she lay on the cold deck, as her consciousness faded, she felt the old collar being removed, a new one being slapped into place, and a voice, speaking out of nowhere said, "These damn collars keep malfunctioning. Good thing I realized hers was out of alignment."

"Yes, good thing indeed." The captain's voice said, and those were the last words Nozomi heard before she passed into darkness.

Telfer Laughlin stared at the monitor, not understanding anything that flashed by across it, but the point was moot. He did not sit in the captain's seat because he was going to give orders, but because he was going to observe.

Beside him sat three of the Drudges, Sudhir on his left, Fallon and Adorinda on his right. In the pilot's seat, Isa waited as her hands tested the controls. Everyone paused, patiently, knowing that, very shortly, they would be at the destination whether they were ready or not.

With one more check of her equipment, Isa braced herself. The engines' termination was loud. The sounds and vibrations shuddered throughout the *Chrysanthemum* as it came out of fold, right on schedule. Out of the main viewport the stars became divided from each other and their objective became visible.

For a moment Telfer thought something had gone wrong with his body. He had heard rumors that some people went crazy during the transition from fold to normal flight.

Ahead of them, a giant moon spun on its axis. Between the moon and the *Chrysanthemum* were two vessels. One was the Slaver's mother ship, but the other vessel wore a specific crest on its side. Touching his thumb to the captain's control console, Telfer spoke out his warning.

//Kalle, they've already made contact with a company purchaser.//

The walls of flesh closed behind the old-hand as he adjusted the gear that Joshua had just handed to him. Behind him, the young technician scampered up the stairs to the compartment that held the cargo-bay controls.

Now that the time had finally arrived, Kalle felt the old calm wash over him. Muting his communication system, he spoke to the only being that could hear him.

"Are you ready?"

THEY ARE NO THREAT TO ME, AND THEREFORE, NO THREAT TO YOU.

A breath was taken. Possibly the last one that he would ever have aboard the ship, but Kalle had faith in the strange alien that contained the body, and somehow parts of the spirit, of Nozomi's brother. It was time for war, time for battle. The old-hand engaged his pickup so that the entire crew could hear his words.

"Two ships are nothing. Stay back, we'll handle this alone."

//We?//

But Nobilis' pilot did not respond to Telfer's question. Within his compartment, Joshua opened the cargo-bay. Kalle felt Nobilis lean forward, and then the pressure of the mecha's movements shoved the old-hand deep into the seat.

Even though his spacesuit compensated quickly, it still felt like something huge had just punched him in the chest. The acceleration was far steeper than what Nobilis had subjected him to before.

The company purchaser released a small squad of fighter craft. They had been on standby which was a good omen for the old-hand. It was typical company policy to have fighters waiting while the negotiations were taking place. It was far easier to bargain advantageously when one had the capability to destroy the group on the other end of the transaction if something went sour.

No matter what good news the fighters provided, they also provided another problem; Kalle did not want to gain the wrath of someone who might prove valuable as an ally. It took all of the old-hand's effort to speak because the Nobilis was still accelerating towards its target.

"Just . . . cripple . . . the fighters."

UNDERSTOOD.

Out in front, the lead company fighter shot at the white being, but the rounds were easily avoided. Spinning about, the Nobilis cruised to within striking distance. Inside the white mecha, Kalle felt like his eyes were going to sink through the back of his skull. The force of the maneuver pooled his blood into his extremities and his suit compensated. Needles pressed through flesh and small pumps hurried to transport his life fluids back to vital, life-sustaining organs. Air pressures were adjusted, making it marginally easier for him to breath under the stresses that were placed upon him.

One arm of the white mecha snapped out, and ripped the drive engine from the lead company fighter. Without its propulsion the ship was unable to alter its heading or velocity. It continued to float away, slowly disappearing into space.

At the sight of their leader being so easily thwarted, all of the company vessels opened fire, including the capital ship.

Bolts of condensed energy were flung at the Nobilis, but it did not mind. The giant's hands reached out, grabbed another fighter, and used it to shield its pearlescent flesh. The ensnared combatant grew red with the intense buildup of heat under the various impacts of the space faring weapons. Fearing for his life, the pilot of the fighter ejected from its doomed craft.

Discarding the useless shell Nobilis continued on its warpath.

Snapping out one foot, the white mecha destroyed another ship's maneuvering jets. Yet another vessel found itself at the mercy of its own weapon. Curling into a ball the Nobilis deflected the gauss round directly into the one who had fired it.

Then they were through the first wave. The ships that had survived the Nobilis' wrath hurried to turn about, but they did not have the raw power of the white machine, and the Nobilis widened the gap between fighters and itself, as the expanse between the white mecha and the company purchaser closed faster and faster.

The old-hand recovered consciousness just in time to realize that the Nobilis was about to hit the company vessel, but the white mecha spun around the capital ship. The movements caused such exertions to the old-hand that he felt his vision become touched with crimson before he blacked out for a second time.

It was a pity, because Kalle missed quite a show. Somehow, the white mecha seemed to cling to the hull of to the capital vessel as it spun about, two, three times, and then immediately shot away from the company purchaser, directly for the Slaver's mother ship.

The company purchaser had been holding back compared to the amount of weaponry that the Slaver vessel tried to destroy the Nobilis with:Mmissiles, torpedoes, invisible beams of death, kinetic mass weapons, all were fired. Some rounds exploded when in close proximity to the white mecha while others passed on by and turned about in an attempt to seek and destroy the Nobilis.

It was all for naught. As if completely arrogant, the white me-cha stopped and let all the weapons head towards it.

Back inside Nozomi's mecha, Kalle felt his breathing resume normalcy. His body ached and screamed in pain, but he was alive and so he fought his way back to alertness. He shouldn't have bothered. He had never ever seen so many weapons inbound for him alone before. Since there was nothing to do, Kalle gripped the walls of living flesh tightly.

When Nobilis finally moved the pressure once more snapped Kalle into blackness. The white machine shot upwards so fast that it became a literal blur. All the projectiles, even some that were no longer a danger to the white mecha, were sucked into the space where the Nobilis had once been. The explosion was rather spectacular.

For a moment there was tranquility, then the Slaver's mother ship rocked and spun. The white giant had collided with the hull and clung to the vessel.

From his seat in the cockpit, Kalle felt a very strong urge to vomit into his helmet. His body felt weak, and his bones ached. Muscles trembled with fatigue, and his head throbbed angrily at him. He knew he was in no real condition to fight, but then he had survived worse in his life. Training took over where will-power failed.

The package Joshua had handed the old-hand was opened. One hand gripped the needler that had been taken from the *Chrysanthemum's* armory, the other hand held onto the firing trigger for the satchel charge that he wore across his back. One push of the button and the mining explosives would detonate, at least damaging the Slaver's vessel, if not cratering the hull.

Peering out the clear flesh that composed his ride, Kalle wit-nessed the hand of the mecha smash through the hull and peel back some of the metal as if the armor was little more substantial than tinfoil.

I HAVE NOT OPENED THE SLAVES OR ANYONE

ELSE TO VACUUM. I AM PROTECTING THEM. YOU
MAY EXIT.

The Nobilis openep its cockpit and Kalle Aaron pulled himself onto the mecha's back. The giant's arm was still inside the
Slaver vessel. The large limb was bent, allowing Kalle to step onto
the open palm. It was a far easier method of descent than leaping
to the floor.

The Nobilis set Kalle gently upon the cargo-bay's floor. The
old-hand faced the hordes that surrounded him. A grim sense
of reality overcame the old-hand. There were more than enough
Slavers to easily kill him.

Rather than wait for someone to become bold, Kalle triggered the external speakers on his suit, and his voice was broadcast throughout the cargo-bay.

"Under galactic code, I, captain of the *Chrysanthemum*, demand the freedom of my illegally captured crew."

More than one Slaver winced. It was a good sign, and the
old-hand finally stepped off of the Nobilis's palm. No one dared
to face him, except for one female Grondonian, who strutted forward until she was almost toe to toe with the old-hand. She was
easily half again as tall as Kalle but the human did not quiver, or
back away.

"What are you talking about? Look at the damage you've
done to my ship." She roared.

"I can easily do far more to this ship if you talk to me like
that." The old-hand replied, icy calm inside his suit. He had no
doubt that the Grondonian female would kill him if a fight en-
sued, but then, she did not have one very particular ally. "Or if I
am harmed, or my rights are not respected. I will have my companion rip this ship to pieces."

It was a promise, not a threat, and suddenly the Slaver understood that she and her cohorts did not overpower the lone
human, but instead, their fate rested in the mercy of the lone man
and his giant alien.

A hand clapped against its mate, and attention suddenly

focused onto the uniformed Ziz. The significance of what he had done did not pass Kalle by; he had risked the life of the one thing that could make the freeing of his friends easy, or very difficult.

<Honored representative.> Kalle spoke in the Ziz's native tongue. As he bowed, the human opened his hand and dropped the trigger for the bomb. It was a sign of compliance. "I apologize for this intrusion, but I have reason to believe you were about to make a poor choice of purchases." He revertek to Standard.

With a motion that was between a curtsey and a bow, the Ziz made known that it had found favor with the greeting. "Traveler, you do me honor with my people's greeting. I must admit though, your entrance was far coarser than it needed to be."

"I apologize honored representative, but I am missing two of my ship's crew. They disappeared many units ago, but one managed to get word to us that they had been captured by Slavers."

"And was it these Slavers in particular?" The Ziz asked, without any apparent emotion to its voice.

"This was the Slaver's main vessel." The old-hand agreed. "And both of my crew were recognized Freebies."

"That's a lie!" The female Grondonian spewed the words from her lips. Already feeling sore from the flight in, Kalle's temper snapped and he spun so that the needler was once more aimed at the female Slaver.

The Ziz continued. "These are grave accusations that you make, captain. Do you have proof?"

"Proof enough, if all slaves are assembled. Allow me to walk the ranks." The human spoke quietly, but his suit amplified his voice. The female Grondonian seemed about to protest when the Nobilis shifted, reminding all of its very real and dangerous presence.

"Let us walk then, captains." The Ziz said. "If one is found at fault, let them pay for the damages caused." Without anything more to say the Ziz began to walk the lengths of the ranks. The two captains fell in beside.

Together the odd trio walked up one rank and down the

next, but neither Doc nor Nozomi became visible. Kalle began to feel nervous, not out of embarrassment, but out of concern. Had he arrived too late? Had he been unable to help his friends?

The last slave was like the others, a stranger to the old-hand. The female Grondonian waited impatiently. Her body's position hinted at her expectations; The Ziz would allow her vengeance, it was only proper after such slights.

Instead of reacting in fear or concern, Kalle moved his gun once more so that it pointed at the female Grondonian's head. His icy demeanor remained as Kalle tightened down the trigger.

"Where is Nozomi?" He growled.

"I don't know who you're talking about?" The Slaver replied, grinning. She advanced, and all around Kalle the other Slavers readied their weapons.

The Ziz spoke again. "Was it human?"

Everyone stopped.

"Yes." Kalle answered. "She is human."

"About this tall?" The Ziz continued, motioning with one hand. Kalle shook his head. The representative had indicated an incorrect height. He knew what the Ziz was doing; it was checking for honesty. If Kalle had agreed, the Ziz would have had reason to suspect that the old-hand was lying.

"No, honored representative. My crew member stood yay high." Kalle motioned with his free hand. "She has long hair and skin that is darker than mine."

"Just like the girl whose slave collar failed then?" The Ziz spoke out, not to Kalle, but to the Grondonian. The large female swallowed nervously.

Kalle pressed for information as the Ziz's bodyguards brought their weapons to bear upon the Slavers.

"Where is she?" The old-hand demanded.

Nozomi slowly became aware of her surroundings. She was in a cell, lying down on a cot. Her body felt weak and her muscles refused to respond. She was still suffering the effects of the EBD blast.

Her eyes fought to focus on a shifting, changing shape that hovered above her. Whoever it was, they were dressed in intimidating armor that Nozomi did not recognize.

"What is your name?" A voice asked, not from the suit. Nozomi let her head turn, and she realized it was the Ziz representative that had spoken.

"I am Nozomi Makino. I am a Freebie. My identity code is one niner eight fife alpha gamma six three two. I am registered with the department of the following companies-"

The Ziz shook its head calmly. "You need not continue. I can tell that you are honest. Tell me, are there any other Freebies who were captured?"

"Doc, my companion." The words rushed from her mouth. "He's a Grondonian, and I know that one of the Wealots was too."

The Slaver's captain, who Nozomi realized was standing beside the Ziz, suddenly became very nervous. Calm as ever, the Ziz removed something from its company clothing, and it pointed the deadly gun at the female Grondonian's body.

"Release the prisoners, now. All of them." The Ziz ordered.

Everyone hurried to obey, except the Ziz and the darkly suited figure. Once the room emptied, the intimidating one bent, and lifted Nozomi gently into its arms.

She smiled and let her full weight sink into her rescuer. After everything that had happened it seemed too good to be true, but Nozomi was going to continue to survive as a Freebie.

"Thank you." Nozomi sighed.

"Don't sweat it, Nozomi. Aiji wouldn't have liked it if I had left you to rot in a collar."

The voice from the suited figure caused the human female to feel renewed with energy and she flung her arms around the old-hand's neck. The sudden shift of weight caused both humans to fall, but Nozomi landed on top of Kalle, so she was somewhat cushioned although his armor was rather hard.

"Doc's invention worked?" She asked, and then something clicked in her mind. Nozomi stopped and looked at the shielded visor of her friend.

"Wait, Aiji? Nobilis helped you!" Realization brought a softer smile to her face. "Is he okay?"

"He's probably better off than you are right now." Kalle explained. "But Nobilis is waiting for us. C'mon, let me help you to your feet, we need to find Doc."

Even with his armor, Kalle easily stood, and pulled the far lighter weight of Nozomi up until she could lean against him.

His bladders felt like they were about to explode.

There was a chance that, if he let them, he would not have to suffer the excruciating night that awaited him. Death by toxin was horrible, but at the same time it was probably better than being turned into a pretzel before dying of trauma.

Doc swallowed nervously. It sounded like the Slavers were celebrating which meant that Nozomi had probably failed. She was most likely sold, and that meant that Doc was going to be subject to an overenthusiastic female's whims.

The main door was pried open. Screwing his eyes closed, the Grondonian waited for the horrible news.

"Well, that's a sight."

The voice spoke in Standard, and its tone and accent were familiar and very welcome. Opening his eyes, Doc saw the sight of a fully dressed Confederate pilot, and the human woman who leaned against him.

"Hey Doc." Kalle spoke again, a mix of amusement and confusion on his face. "How are you doing? Anything I can do for you?"

"Yes!" The Grondonian screamed. "Undo these restraints. I have to use the washroom, NOW!"

Chapter 18

CAPTAIN KALLE AARON LISTENED to the sounds of his ship as it floated away from the Malore station for the third time. He and his crew had returned all of the freed slaves who had wanted to journey with them. The Ziz had been willing to let the old-hand and his ship do the work, but not without its reward. Since the *Chrysanthemum*, Nobilis, and their crews had stopped the company from purchasing illegal goods, the company had not pressed charges for the crippling of the few fighters, and had even given the crew of the *Chrysanthemum* a company credit, redeemable at any store that their Ziz comrade owned.

All the way back to port, Kalle had taken the rest that he so badly needed. When they finally made it to the station the crew had found themselves assaulted by the families of the freed slaves, and had been saturated with rewards and gratuities. The cargo-bay had been loaded with knick-knacks, food, and various other things. One family had paid for the refueling, another for water, another for an atmo-dump, and another had paid the mooring fees.

Kalle had been only too happy to spend a few more days working on the *Chrysanthemum*. The new recycler had been calibrated, the Algae room was growing at a healthy rate, the engine converter was unpacked, although not installed, and the cargo-bay had been completely retrofitted. It could partition itself into quarters.

Excusing himself, the old-hand stood from the captain's seat.

Telfer Laughlin was sitting beside his wife. He had squatted on the ground beside the pilot's area and he and Isa were laughing at the antics of the Drudges as they took turns at a game that was as timeless as the galaxies: charades.

Above the bridge rested the large observation deck. Attached to it the room was a library. While docked, a large shipment of soft-books had arrived in the cargo-bay. Only a short time later, they had vanished. There was only one crew member who would so desire such knowledge.

It wasn't too long a walk but Kalle was still tired by the time he got to the library. The pain of the previous days seemed to weigh him down. Ignoring his weakened state, the old-hand opened the door. Doc was there, dressed in loose garments resemblind what he had been forced to wear back with the Slaver's captain. He was sitting, staring at the box of books. He had not opened it.

The Grondonian looked up, but he did not speak nor blink his multi-faceted eyes as Kalle selected a chair and dragged it over to sit across the box from Doc.

"When do you want me off of your ship?" Were the words that came from the Grondonian's mouth. He was curled in on himself, and had wrapped his long arms about his legs. He rocked slightly on his back, awaiting the captain's words with dread.

"That depends, Doc." Kalle replied. "If you do something stupid, or endanger the lives of any of my crew, or if you get us into trouble, I might just flay that earthy skin from your body, but if you're not rushing, I would like to extend an invitation to you. You've proven to be the noblest one aboard this ship, and your intelligence is nothing to sneeze at. I need a navigator Doc, one who's made fold transportation his lifelong work. I can't think of anyone better suited for that role."

The disbelief that wormed its way across the Grondonian's face was astounding. "You're inviting me to stay with you?"

Kalle stood and did not bother to push his chair back.

"Yeah, Doc." Kalle opened the door. "That's an invitation. If you don't have any other work lined up. Get some rest, because you're mapping our next jump in a few hours. I want your mind fresh."

Puffing his chest out, the Grondonian smiled. "I always do my best."

"Just keep proving that, Doc." Kalle laughed as he walked away.

The old-hand breathed the fresh air as he began the long walk to the aft of the vessel. It was a luxury that he had never thought he would have had until he was retired. He did not hurry. He knew that rushing would not change things.

When Kalle opened the door to the cargo-bay, he caught Nozomi staring at what had continued to save her life, and that hosted the only other surviving member of her family. She did not turn to see who had joined her right away, and when she did her eyes were hooded with shame.

"You still thinking about leaving?" Kalle asked, instinctively understanding his friend's glance.

Nozomi nodded in confirmation. The old-hand placed both of his arms on his hips.

"May I at least know, why?" Kalle spoke kindly.

"I don't want to endanger anyone anymore." Nozomi answered. "Because of me, a station has died, and I've put all of my friends' lives at risk."

"Welcome to my world." The old-hand said slowly.

Taking a deep breath Kalle held it and forced his body to relax before he spoke. "Look, Nozomi, I know you might not feel that great right now, but consider this; You could run and risk your life day in and day out, hopping from one lie to the next, or you could stay here, with your friends, who already know enough about you, and we accept you. Besides, even with Pirates hunting us, we could use you and Nobilis. And, I like to know that my friend is alright."

The smile that creased Nozomi's face also brought her eyes out from their darkness. "Did you just say you want me to hang around?"

"Yeah, I did." Kalle explained. "We might not be much, but we're all a part of this crew. You, Nobilis, and your brother are all welcome to stay on my ship. If you're willing to pull your weight now and then, I could use another crew member."

"And what about payment?" Nozomi asked, but her question was only partially serious.

"You don't have to pay. You're my friend."

"Not that, silly." Nozomi giggled. "How am I supposed to make a living?"

"We'll talk about that later, when we see if we can even make money." Despite the almost seriousness of the conversation, both humans were laughing. Then, once it was all said, Kalle became solemn. "But you don't have to stay if you don't want to, Nozomi. If you ever want to leave, I won't get in your way except for this once."

Walking over to the old-hand, Nozomi threw her arms around her friend. She squeezed him tightly, and for a moment, she felt okay with herself. When she let go of him, she wiped a little moisture away from the corner of her eye.

"Thanks, Kalle." Nozomi smiled softly. "I hope you know what that means to me."

"I have an idea." He chuckled. "Get some rest. We've all been through a lot."

They embraced once more, before the captain took his leave and began the long walk back to his quarters. After the events of the last few days, he felt more than confident that those on the bridge could more than handle any emergency that might come up.

Telfer Laughlin was squatting on the ground beside the pilot's seat, where his wife continued to pretend to pilot the *Chrysanthemum* while it drifted ahead to its next destination. He and Isa were laughing at the antics of the Drudges, and the couple laughed freely until Telfer was wiping tears from his face.

Smiling, Joshua raised his hands in his peoples' sign of victory. Thanks to his antics, Fallon had guessed her brother's charade before Sudhir had plucked the idea from Joshua's mind. With a squeal of eagerness, Adorinda jumped to her feet and hurried to take her turn.

With a smile that was so wide and genuine he worried it would split his face, Kalle looked back at those he was beginning to consider his crew—perhaps more than just a crew—and laughed before stepping into the airlock.

It was time for him to get some rest. After all, the *Chrysanthemum's* crew could handle the ship for a few hours by themselves.

Fin